THE GENTLE ART
OF MURDER

The Dorothy Martin Mysteries from Jeanne M. Dams

* *available from Severn House*

THE GENTLE ART OF MURDER

A Dorothy Martin Mystery

Jeanne M. Dams

This first world edition published 2015
in Great Britain and the USA by
SEVERN HOUSE PUBLISHERS LTD of
19 Cedar Road, Sutton, Surrey, England, SM2 5DA.
Trade paperback edition first published
in Great Britain and the USA 2015 by
SEVERN HOUSE PUBLISHERS LTD.

British Library Cataloguing in Publication Data

Dams, Jeanne M. author.
  The Gentle Art of Murder. – (A Dorothy Martin mystery)
  1. Martin, Dorothy (Fictitious character)–Fiction.
  2. Murder–Investigation–Fiction. 3. Women private
  investigators–England–Fiction. 4. Americans–England–
  Fiction. 5. Detective and mystery stories.
  I. Title II. Series
  813.5'4-dc23

ISBN-13: 978-07278-8481-7 (cased)
ISBN-13: 978-1-84751-585-8 (trade paper)
ISBN-13: 978-1-78010-634-2 (e-book)

Except where actual historical events and characters are being
described for the storyline of this novel, all situations in this
publication are fictitious and any resemblance to living persons
is purely coincidental.

All Severn House titles are printed on acid-free paper.

Severn House Publishers support the Forest Stewardship Council™ [FSC™],
the leading international forest certification organisation. All our titles that
are printed on FSC certified paper carry the FSC logo.

Typeset by Palimpsest Book Production Ltd.,
Falkirk, Stirlingshire, Scotland.
Printed and bound in Great Britain by
TJ International, Padstow, Cornwall.

ACKNOWLEDGEMENTS

Among the many to whom I owe thanks for help with this book are sculptors Tuck Langland and Derek Sellars, who gave me a great deal of advice about sculpture and art in general, and art schools in England and America. There are also many other artists I met years ago when I worked at a local university, who remain in fond memory and helped me with characterizations, though they don't know it! And as always I owe much to my friends Christine Seitz and Jaime Owen, who read the manuscript and showed me where I screwed up. Any remaining errors are certainly my fault, not theirs.

ONE

'Very well, gentlemen, let's begin. I presume that our missing colleague will appear in due time, but I do not propose to wait for him. We have important matters to discuss, and I for one am eager to be off on my holiday to Greece.'

'And who's keeping us all here, I'd like to know?' said Dennis under his breath.

'With any luck he'll get caught in a political riot,' replied Matt, frowning and sinking lower into his chair.

John Chandler, the department head, was droning on, apparently oblivious to the murmurings of his subordinates. 'Of course I've often visited Greece before, but what architect can resist the pull of the pure classical influence that pervades that country? Not only the Acropolis with its unparalleled structures, but the small, lesser-known gems that await one around every corner . . .'

'Another "Survey of Art History" lecture,' murmured Will. 'Somebody wake me when he's finished.'

The door opened, interrupting Chandler. 'Ah, Mr Andrews, so good of you to find time to join us. I'm sure your latest opus needed a great deal of arduous planning and attention. Mind you don't slip on that dusty patch. Clay or something of the sort, I assume. We really must ask the students to keep the studio a bit tidier, eh, Mr Singleton?' He directed a humourless smile at Dennis, whose sculpture students worked tirelessly to keep the studio as clean as was consistent with their work.

'We could do,' said Dennis, 'if the cleaner would honour us with her presence a bit more often than once a term.'

'Budget constraints, my dear man, budget constraints! Which brings me to the principal reason for this meeting. I'll not keep you long, but I thought you'd want to know well in advance that we'll all have to tighten our belts next term. I want you to look at your materials requests and cut them at least in half.'

There was an immediate uproar of anger and disbelief. 'We've cut to the bone already,' roared Sam Andrews. 'I spent the morning trying to work out how my students can learn without film, chemicals, paper and proper darkroom equipment!'

'Perhaps,' said Chandler sweetly, 'you've heard of digital photography? The latest thing, or so I'm told. I believe it requires neither film, nor darkroom, nor chemicals, only a camera and a computer.' Before the infuriated photographer could reply, Chandler turned to Matt. 'And the same applies to your students, Mr Thomas. Prints have been made for thousands of years by the ancient techniques you so admirably try to teach your students, but we live in the twenty-first century. The giclée print can be beautiful if properly done. I recommend it to you.'

'Even for that, the students need a proper colour printer,' said Matt. 'I've asked every term I've been here, but we still have only a cheap office—'

'I'm sure your innovative and *devoted* young students can solve the problem, Mr Thomas.'

A quick intake of breath, sounding like a hiss, came from nearly everyone in the room. Matt's sexual preferences were well-known, but only the head ever made snide – and untrue – suggestions that he numbered his male students among his amours. Matt's dark eyes flashed and his cheeks turned a mottled red, but he shut his mouth firmly.

'I believe that leaves only sculpture to deal with. Your expenses, Mr Singleton, have been extremely heavy for the past several terms.'

'The increased need for copper in the developing countries has driven the cost of bronze through the roof,' said Dennis. 'Clay isn't cheap, either. Nor are wood and stone. What do you suggest I do about it?'

'I'm so glad you ask. I *suggest*, Mr Singleton, that you, like the rest of my staff, are mired in the backwater of outmoded methods of artistic expression. I say again, we are in the twenty-first century. Far more interesting, far more relevant sculpture is being produced nowadays using – I believe the term is "found materials". You will no doubt correct me if I am wrong. Not only do these materials avoid the clichés so often found in works of bronze and marble and wood and so on, they also have the very great advantage of being free.'

He raised his hand against further comment. 'Thank you, gentlemen. I expect your revised budgets to be on my desk by the end of the day today. That's all, and I hope you enjoy your holidays.'

'What about the budget for painting, then?' shouted Matt over the general angry buzz, but he was ignored as Chandler left the room, neatly avoiding the small smear of dry clay near the door.

Dennis was right behind him. 'John, one moment, please.'

Chandler turned, grimacing. 'What is it, Singleton? I'm really *very* busy, and I warn you, I can come up with no more money for sculpture.'

'What's being done about my application?'

Chandler's grimace turned to a frosty smile. 'Nothing. It was plainly not worth troubling the committee with it. You simply haven't the qualifications for a principal lecturer. You'll excuse me.' He turned and went into his office, closing the door behind him. There was a soft 'snick' as the lock was engaged.

Dennis considered smashing the glass panel on the door, then looked at his hands. His sculptor's hands. However satisfying it might be, it wasn't worth it.

On the way back to his studio he encountered Sam, who was scowling, an expression like the one he felt on his own face.

'Off to clean up your studio, Dennis?' said Sam.

'Off to clean up your darkroom, Sam? Or clean it out?'

'Damn little to clean out. I'm down to nothing in the way of chemicals.'

'Then let's go imbibe some chemicals ourselves. Kill the taste of that meeting. The first round's on me.'

'Then you'd better have plenty of money with you, because mine's going to be a barrel of the best. It'll take at least that much to drown my sorrows.'

Gillian watched them as they walked out of the building in the direction of the nearest pub. She shrugged, then went inside to find the departmental office. As a new graduate assistant, she hadn't been invited to the end-of-term meeting. She thought maybe she was just as glad. Her boss and his colleague hadn't looked happy.

Gillian had been in the building, her new workplace, only twice before: once for her interview, once to see over the sculpture studios and be taken on a quick tour of the Fine Arts building. It was an odd-looking structure, basically a cube, but with bits stuck on or cantilevered out here and there to accommodate the needs of the varying departments. Sculpture, with its heavy raw materials and sometimes massive finished products, was housed on the ground floor. Painting was on the third floor, the top of the building, for the light. The other departments had been sandwiched in between, with darkrooms, print rooms, storage cupboards, supply cupboards all ready to hand for the teachers' and students' needs.

But it was getting old. Built in the late sixties, not one of the best periods of English architecture, it was showing its age. Bits of the concrete façade had peeled off, giving the exterior a leprous look. Windows no longer fitted properly, the flat roof leaked here and there, and worst of all, as the focus of the arts changed to include design and various media concerns, the carefully planned interior just didn't work anymore. Rooms intended for one purpose were being used for another, so offices sat cheek-by-jowl with studios, darkrooms had windows (carefully but not always effectively covered). The erstwhile staff room had become a storage room, the student lounge was a lecture room, and the floor plan was wretchedly confusing.

Gillian wandered up one corridor and down another, peeking into studios and lecture rooms and once a capacious broom closet, before she finally found the office. She knew that they were temporarily without a secretary, but Mr Singleton had promised to leave a copy of her teaching schedule for the coming term in her mailbox.

Her mailbox! She felt a little flutter when she thought about it. She was actually a teacher in an art school! All right, a graduate teaching assistant. Never mind that the pay was almost non-existent and the recognition absolutely non-existent. She had a teaching job! She could properly call herself an artist, a real-life sculptor.

She opened the office door and stopped just inside. Somewhere in an inner office two men were talking, and it was plainly a private conversation.

Not that they were taking the trouble to keep their voices down. Probably they thought they were alone in the building.

Gillian hesitated, undecided whether to leave or stay. The door's hinges hadn't been oiled recently; they shrieked like a soul in torment. Lucky they hadn't heard her come in; they were probably talking too loud. But if she opened it to leave, and they heard . . . Better stay and hope they didn't come out this way. What a good thing she hadn't turned the light on!

Cowering like a frightened mouse in the darkest corner, all her new-found confidence gone, she tried not to listen, but she couldn't help hearing. 'You'll just have to find a way then, won't you?' said one of the men in the raspy voice of a chain-smoker, and indeed Gillian caught a whiff of cigarette smoke drifting in from the other room.

'Damn it, I don't have the money! And put that damn thing out. You know there's no smoking in the building.'

'Right. So sack me.'

'I've half a mind to do just that, and to hell with it all.'

'But we don't think you will, do we? After all, I get more attention for your precious department than anyone else in the whole pathetic institution. You can't afford to lose that, can you? *Or anything else?*'

The last words were spoken in a way that Gillian didn't understand at all. They sounded almost like a threat. She swallowed, wishing desperately that she could get away.

'Somebody's going to murder you one day, you bloody—'

'Now, now! Language! I'll leave you before you get too tempted, my hot-headed friend. But I'll expect to see the usual at the end of the month. Enjoy your holiday!'

Gillian tensed, but the corridor door to the inner office opened and closed and she breathed again. But had both men left, or just the one?

Just the one. Gillian heard a loud thump, as of a fist striking a hard surface, and then a long string of profanity. Drawers were opened and slammed shut. At last, at last, a chair squeaked as it was relieved of weight. The corridor door opened and shut. Silence.

Whew! Gillian allowed herself a long sigh and moved from her corner. Now to get away with no one seeing her. She wasn't sure what the shindy had been about, but she was quite sure the two men hadn't meant it for public consumption.

She opened the office door just far enough to let her head stick out. No one in sight, and there was a door out of the building at the end of the corridor. She slipped out the door and closed it with great care.

It squeaked loudly. She froze, but no one came to investigate. She tiptoed down the hall and left the building with all the exhausted relief of an escaped prisoner.

She had forgotten all about her schedule.

TWO

I was sitting in my garden half asleep when Nigel walked up the path. It was a drowsy sort of afternoon. The summer had been unusually kind to my garden, with just the right mix of sun and rain. The flowers in my border were blooming with such energy I thought they might burst from the effort, and the bees taking advantage of this bounty made a constant, soporific humming. The bells of the Cathedral, calling the faithful to Evensong, floated over the peaceful scene like a benison, and the roses, off in a bed of their own in lordly eminence, spread their perfume over my whole garden.

I say 'my garden'. In truth, though the plot of ground belongs to me and my husband, Alan, the garden is all Bob Finch's doing. The dear man has a drinking problem, but his energetic mother, who also cleans our house, keeps him sober much of the time. In those lucid periods, he's the best gardener any fortunate home-owner ever had. In England, a well-kept garden is not only a thing of beauty and a joy forever, but also an important factor in one's reputation with the neighbours. I might be an American expat and a renowned snoop, but as long as my garden kept up the best English traditions, I was accepted as almost one of the natives. Of course my husband, who had lived in Sherebury all his life and was a perfect dear, didn't hurt, either. I counted myself a lucky woman to have met him after my beloved Frank died and I moved to England.

Watson raised his head from his paws, and then dropped it again, not even bothering to wag his tail. Samantha and Esmeralda, the two cats, never twitched a whisker. I waved a languid hand. 'Come and sit down, Nigel. I'm too lazy to get up. Have some lemonade.' I waved at the pitcher on the table.

Nigel Evans sat, poured himself a glass of lemonade, loosened his tie, and mopped his brow. 'I can't remember a summer this hot,' he said with a sigh.

'But of course you're far too young to remember very many summers, aren't you? Anyway, what are you doing all dressed up on a day like this? Shorts and a tee would be more in order, I'd think.'

'Meeting. Term's going to start next week and we needed to get organized. We're getting a few new computers in, so there's installation to worry about, and then training. And then next term it'll be all to do over again.'

'On a Sunday? And for that you needed a tie?' Nigel worked with the computer systems at Sherebury University, and the dress code in that department was casual in the extreme.

Nigel was still young enough to blush. 'Well, you see, I've been moved up a notch or two. The thought was to impress the peons.'

'Nigel! You got a promotion and you never told us!'

'Yes, well . . .' He sipped his lemonade, his face still flushed.

'And what did you mean about doing it all over again next term?'

'It's the budget, you see. It's tight all over the uni, so we have to do everything piecemeal.'

'Even in IT? But you're right at the heart of all the university operations. Surely you need the proper equipment to function.'

'We do. But the powers that be don't seem to see it that way, so we use the chewing gum and baling wire approach. That's one reason I dressed up today. The Head of Finance was to be at the meeting, and I hoped to convince him that the dear old uni was being penny wise and pound foolish.'

'But you didn't manage it?'

'He never showed up. Sent a message about an important obligation elsewhere. I tell you, Dorothy, there's not a whole lot more important to the functioning of the whole university than the computer system. It goes down, everything grinds to a halt.'

'Well . . . surely the teaching . . .'

'Classroom assignments are made by computer. Students' and teachers' schedules are done by computer. Textbooks and other materials are ordered by computer. An awful lot of the lectures use PowerPoint presentations. Hundreds of classes are taught online.'

He was ready to go on, but I held up a hand in surrender.

'Okay, okay, I get the point. Actually, I had a thought a while back when I was reading a suspense novel. The villains were making plans to destroy some government or other, and I thought that all they really needed to do was disable all the computers. That would bring the world to its knees. But I'm sorry you're having such a lot of grief. Let's change the subject. How are Inga and small Nigel Peter?'

I was keenly interested in the Evans family. I had played a small part in assuring their marriage, some time ago, and Alan and I were godparents to the baby. Well, hardly a baby anymore. 'Nearly four, isn't he now?'

'Nearly four in years, and a hundred in devilment.' Nigel reached into his pocket for his phone and handed it to me. 'This is what he looked like last week when we had all that rain. He's discovered the great joy of muddy puddles.'

The little boy in the picture was wearing a yellow mac and rain hat, yellow wellies like Paddington Bear's, and a broad grin. All were splashed with thick brown mud. 'A little darker mud,' I said, laughing, 'and he'd look like the Tar Baby.' I'd been reading him some of the Joel Chandler Harris stories.

'I think that's what he had in mind. Inga says, next time could you read him a story about a clean child?'

'A clean four-year-old boy is a contradiction in terms. He'll outgrow it.'

'Soon, we hope. Because, as a matter of fact . . .'

'Nigel! Are you going to tell me he's going to have a baby brother or sister? What a good thing you got that promotion!'

'The extra money will come in handy,' he said, 'because Inga's going to have to give up her work at the pub soon. She tires easily, and the Nipper's a handful. She won't be able to manage him and a new baby and still work. But we'll work it all out.'

'Well, you both know we're eager babysitters when necessary. When's the new addition due?'

'End of March. We're hoping around Easter, and we hope you'll both stand godparents again. But that's not really why I dropped by.' He leaned forward in his chair. 'I'm issuing an invitation to you both. One of Inga's old friends, Gillian Roberts, is starting her first term teaching at the uni, or really in the art school. It's a more or less separate entity, you know?'

'No. Explain.'

'Oh, dear, I'd have to go into a lot of the history of Sherebury University, and I'd bore you rigid. The gist of it is, the Wolfson College of Art has been here a long time, back when the university was little more than a glorified training institute. Then it became the Wolfson College of Art and Design and joined forces with the university. Now art students can be awarded degrees, not just diplomas, but the *entente* is sometimes not all that *cordiale*, and the art school tends to elevate its nose and move its skirts aside from university matters. That said, they do manage to jog along fairly comfortably together. Most of the time. Anyway, the art school is having a sort of reception for new teachers next Wednesday, just before the term officially begins. Inga and I are going, more or less to support Gillian, and we wondered if you and Alan would like to join us.'

'Indifferent wine, peculiar snacks, and a lot of noise?'

Nigel grinned. 'You've got it. And a tour of the facilities, with student work on display. Oh, and a string quartet that you won't be able to hear over the talking.'

'The mixture as before, in short. We'd love to. Just let us know the time.'

Wednesday, September 3

I was glad we had decided to go. Only a few brave souls had shown up, and Gillian was looking rather bereft when the four of us walked into the vast sculpture studio.

I knew the bereft one must be Gillian because she was the only woman in the room, and the only person who'd made any attempt to dress up. She wore a colourful, loose shirt over black leggings and her honey-coloured hair was drawn up into an elegant French twist. No one would have called her beautiful, but her face would be pleasant when it wasn't looking anxious, and what I could see of her figure was slender and well-proportioned.

She was talking to a short, stocky, balding man clad in chinos and a T-shirt, both streaked with some grey substance. A few other men, just as casually clad, stood around talking, with very little animation. Altogether, the party could not be said to be going with a swing. There wasn't nearly the noise level I'd expected. I could actually hear the string quartet, though they were playing something modern and atonal, and I'd have been just as happy had they been drowned out.

Nigel and Inga took us over to Gillian and introduced us. She gave us a radiant smile and said, 'I'm *so* glad you came,' and no one could doubt her sincerity. 'I'd like you to meet my boss, the sculpture professor, Mr Singleton.'

'Dennis,' said the man in chinos, putting out a hand. It was hard and dry. 'Forgive the way I look, won't you? I've been working.' He pointed to a large shape on a pedestal in the corner, shrouded in a damp cloth. 'It's shaping well, and I didn't want to stop, but I had to make sure Gillian's party came off.'

'Not just mine,' she said. 'There are the other new teachers as well.'

'Painters!' said Dennis. He made it sound like a four-letter word. 'Will Braithwaite gets four new grad teaching assistants, and I get one. Will gets all the materials he wants, and I'm to make do with beer cans and driftwood.'

Gillian opened her mouth, took a good look at her boss's face, and shut it again.

'But you're not interested in departmental politics. Get yourself something to eat and drink, and then let Gillian take you on a tour of the place. Antiquated though it is. There's some work on display in the gallery that you may enjoy.'

With that he went back to his work. As he pulled the cloth off, I saw that it was a tall mass of clay in a swirly sort of spiral. I couldn't have said why it looked angry, but there was an energy about it that made me uneasy. I looked away and walked over to the table where refreshments had been set out.

One sip confirmed that the wine was every bit as bad as I had feared. I could feel a headache coming on at the very smell of the stuff. The nibbles provided worked out to a small bowl of peanuts, about three per customer, and some tiny sandwiches filled, apparently, with brown glue. Nigel and Inga drifted off to talk to people they knew. I looked at Alan. He smiled at Gillian and said, 'I, for one, would very much like to see over the school.'

'It's quite a hodgepodge, as Dennis said. Only about fifty years old, but it reminds me of an old country house that's been done up over the centuries. Corridors going nowhere, two steps up and three down, rooms cut up into smaller rooms, or walls pulled down to make rooms bigger. It was planned sensibly to begin with, but . . . .' She shrugged. 'Well. This is the sculpture studio, or one of them. At least they had the sense to put it on the ground floor. Heavy pieces would never fit into our lift. It's a bit wonky as well. It was out of service all summer, being repaired, I hope, and they've only just taken the sign off today. I'd suggest we walk up, if you don't mind.'

'I'll give it a try,' I said. 'I'm not a great fan of elevators, especially wonky ones. Lead the way.'

Inga and Nigel had seen it all before, and Inga could claim her pregnancy as an excuse not to see it again. They had driven their own car, so they wished Gillian well and waved goodbye, and Gillian began her tour. She showed us the rest of the ground floor of that wing, the other sculpture studio designed for wood carving, with a wooden floor. 'So if a piece of wood is dropped, it won't come to much harm, as it might on concrete.'

We saw the small gallery where staff and student art work was displayed. 'This is what's left of the end-of-term exhibition.'

I couldn't make much sense of it. 'Does no one do representational art anymore?' I asked timidly.

'Not much. It's viewed as passé, and our head doesn't care for it. The students are taught the basics, of course, but then most of them go on to conceptual work.' She lowered her voice, though no one else was around. 'To tell you the truth, I love figurative sculpture. I work in bronze, and a lovely little nude . . . ah, well. *Autres temps, autres moeurs.*' She said it with such an air of world-weariness, her twenty-some years sitting heavy on her shoulders, that I had to hide a chuckle.

'Where is the great man today?' I asked idly. 'I'd have thought he'd be here to welcome new people.'

She frowned. 'I don't know. I haven't seen him since the end of last term. Of course no one much has been here since then, actually, and the head was going on holiday to Greece, so . . .' She shrugged. 'The stairs are this way.'

We were shown, in various wings and up various stairs, the print rooms and the photo studios. 'Darkrooms still?' Alan commented. 'I thought it was all digital these days.'

'Again, to give the students a thorough grounding. For black-

and-white work, many photographers insist that the continuous-tone print is far superior. But of course you're right. Who knows how long we'll even be able to get the chemicals?'

By the time we arrived at the painting studios on the third floor (fourth, to my American mind), I was beginning to flag. I made what admiring noises I could, but Alan could see I'd about had it. 'I think this is about as much as we can take in, my dear,' he said gently to Gillian. 'We need some time to process it all. But I'm afraid I'm a bit lost. If you could show us the way out?'

'Well, the stairs for this wing are all the way on the other side,' she said apologetically.

'Going down stairs is always harder for me than going up,' I said. 'I have titanium knees, and they don't work quite as well lowering my weight as raising it, for some reason. And three flights . . . maybe we could try the elevator?'

'It's just around the corner.' Gillian led us to it and pushed the call button. 'It's awfully slow . . . oh! It was already here.'

The doors opened slowly. We entered and Gillian pushed the button for the ground floor.

It was a slow, creaky elevator. I didn't care for it much. It even smelled old and musty, with some unpleasant overtones of something I assumed to be art materials of some sort.

I tried to concentrate on what Gillian was saying. 'I'm so grateful to both of you for coming today. Almost everyone else was a painter or the guest of a painter, and they're always so superior. At Hallam, where I took my degree, it was always that way, even among the students. Those painters think they own the art world. And it's even worse here, because they seem to get the lion's share of the budget, and paint and canvas don't cost nearly as much as bronze. It's just not— Oh, drat!'

The elevator had stopped between floors. I felt a flood of panic out of all proportion to the situation. 'Alan?' I said in what was almost a whimper. He took my hand in a firm grip.

'Hang in there, darling,' he said in the voice he used to his grandchildren when they needed to be calmed. 'Gillian, could you try again?'

'I've tried to take us up to the next floor, since it won't go farther down, but it just isn't responding. I thought they were meant to have repaired it over the break. I'm so sorry!'

'Not your fault. It's all right, Dorothy. We're perfectly safe.'

'I know . . . but . . .'

'My wife suffers from claustrophobia, Gillian. Perhaps you'd best sound the alarm, so someone can work out how to get us out of here.'

I was beginning to find it difficult to breathe. The more I told myself I was being foolish, the worse it got. I was holding Alan's hand so tightly I wonder I didn't break his fingers.

The shrill cry of the alarm rang out, nearly deafening me. I wondered if anyone else was in this wing. I wondered if anyone would hear. I wondered if I would die of asphyxia before someone came.

But then the alarm shut off and I could hear voices calling to us. 'Everyone all right in there?'

'No,' said Alan. 'No physical injuries, but we have a claustrophobic lady who needs to be rescued at once.'

That made me feel like a fool and a major nuisance, which helped a bit. I thought I could breathe for a little while longer.

'Right you are. The fire service is on the way. We'll get you through the trap door if we can't get the lift to move. Meanwhile, you might open the trap if you think that'll help the lady breathe a bit easier.'

'What do you think, love?'

'Worth a try,' I said in a shaky whisper I couldn't recognize as my own voice.

'I can reach it,' said Gillian eagerly, 'if you'll give me a back.'

Alan obligingly bent over, keeping his tight hold of my hand, but before Gillian could scramble up, the elevator started to move upward, very slowly.

'Thank God!' I said fervently.

'The doors won't open automatically,' said the voice from above. Almost, I thought, from Above. 'As soon as the lift's reached the first floor, we'll force them, and you'll be right as rain.'

I didn't know I was biting my lip until I tasted blood.

It was only a few more minutes, though it seemed like hours, before we saw the crowbar between the doors. I nearly fell into the arms of the fireman who had freed us. 'Oh, I'm so sorry, so sorry to cause such a lot of trouble, so stupid of me. Thank you, thank you!'

'Not stupid at all, madam. Claustrophobia's a nasty thing, and I know right enough there's nothing much to be done about it. Here, sit down and have a glass of water, for I'll be bound your mouth's dry as straw.'

It was, indeed, and the water tasted like heaven. When I had regained something resembling my right mind, I looked around for Alan. He was talking in a low voice to one of the firemen. I stood, only a little tottery now, and went over to him.

They stopped talking.

There was something odd about their silence. I looked from one to the other. 'What? What's going on?'

Alan took my hand. 'Are you feeling better?'

I nodded. 'Much. What's going on?' I repeated.

'If you're sure you're all right again,' he said doubtfully.

'Alan, tell me!'

'It's only that they've discovered why the lift wouldn't go down to the ground floor.'

'Why?' I asked, knowing from his tone of voice that I wasn't going to like the answer.

He took my other hand. 'Someone's caught on the springs near the bottom of the shaft.'

I drew in my breath. 'Oh, dear God! Alive?'

'No.'

THREE

I was very glad Alan had taken my hands. I gulped. 'Then we . . . the elevator . . . Alan, are you telling me we killed someone?'

'They don't know how the man died. They don't know anything, really, not even who he is. No one saw the body until they brought the lift up to this floor and stopped it, and someone started down to check the machinery.'

'What do you mean, started down? The blasted thing wouldn't *go* down.'

'Sorry, climbed down, I mean. There is machinery at both the top and bottom of the shaft, and ladders so it can be serviced.'

'But isn't that horribly dangerous? If the cage started to move while someone . . . oh! Is that what happened?'

'We don't know, love. Try not to think about it.'

That's like being told *not*, under any circumstances, to think about a pink and green elephant. I gave Alan a look he knows well.

'All right. Why not try thinking about Gillian? This is going to be a terrible ordeal for her, poor girl. Just starting off in her first job, and having, one gathers, to deal with a certain amount of departmental infighting, and then a grisly death on the day of her welcoming party. Quite a lot for a child her age to deal with.'

'For anyone, of any age.' I loosed my hands and looked around. 'Where is she?'

We were, I thought, in the photo department. At least photographs adorned the walls, some of them quite lovely in my eyes. Four or five men were standing around in firemen's gear, but no women. No Gillian.

'I expect she's gone down to seek out her department head. Dennis something, was it? He'd seem like a pillar of stability just now, I imagine.'

'Excuse me, Mr Nesbitt, sir. If I might have a word?'

It was one of the firemen, and he drew Alan away, but not so

far that I couldn't hear what he was saying in the stage whisper
that is so much more carrying than a low murmur.

'It's looking as though this is a matter for the police, sir. I
sent one of my men down there to take a look at the chap, and
it may be that the poor soul was dead before he went down the
shaft. You being the chief constable, sir, I thought I'd let you
know.'

'I appreciate that, Griggs,' said Alan, looking at the man's
identity badge, 'but I've been retired for quite some time, you
know.'

'Yes, sir, but we all still know you. And I'd take it very kindly
if you'd just take a glance at the body while we're waiting for
the investigators to come through.'

Well, of course that sent cold shivers running through me.
Alan in that awful shaft, with that awful elevator looming above
him? Alan jeopardizing his life, when he wasn't even officially
a policeman anymore?

My first instinct, when he looked over at me, was to put my
foot down and demand that he not do this insanely foolish thing.
But as I opened my mouth I remembered all the times Alan had
protested vehemently about some risky action I was about to
take, and how much I resented being told what to do. We'd
worked that out, but now the shoe was on the other foot.

I closed my mouth, opened it again, and said mildly, 'Be
careful.'

For the rest of my life I'll remember and treasure the look on
his face, compounded of gratitude, love and understanding.

Even that look did not, however, keep me from lurking, terrified, as near to the elevator shaft as I dared go. I could not look
down and watch Alan's progress down the ladder. I must have
asked six times, of various people, if they were *sure* that the cage
was out of service and wouldn't go grinding down to destroy my
husband.

After an eternity or two, he climbed back up and was helped
out of the shaft by one of those delightful firemen. (I know, I
know, *firefighters*, but as they were all men I couldn't force my
mind to embrace political correctness.)

'All done, then?' I said with a cheery brightness that didn't
deceive Alan for a moment.

'You're a pearl of great price,' he said, with that look again. 'All done, and not a scratch. The SOCOs will take over now that I've made our friend Griggs happy.'

'He was right then?'

'I'm no doctor,' he said very quietly, 'but it doesn't take much medical knowledge to work out that a man might have been dead before he fell, when there's a chisel buried in his back. And that information is in strict confidence.'

I was very glad Gillian wasn't around at the moment. I wouldn't have been able to look her in the face. 'A chisel,' I murmured. 'Such as might be used by a sculptor.'

'I *think* it's a chisel. A bit hard to tell when only the handle is visible. Don't go imagining things, Dorothy. Ah, here come the chaps. I'd best go and tell them what I did in the shaft.'

I was delighted to see that our old friend, Detective Chief Inspector Derek Morrison, was heading the team. Derek is everything a policeman should be, the sort Americans picture when they think of 'the wonderful English police'. Courteous, intelligent, and very, very thorough, he helped Alan solve many a crime way back when, and had co-opted both of us unofficially several times since Alan's retirement.

Alan walked over to have a word with him, and I went back to my chair and pondered.

Plainly the man had been murdered. One doesn't get a chisel in one's back accidentally, and it would be an impossible way for anyone but a contortionist to commit suicide. But why, then, if the man was already dead, why tumble him down the elevator shaft?

Maybe he wasn't dead. Maybe the murderer wanted to make assurance doubly sure. I shuddered at the thought.

No, the more likely reason was to hide the body, at least for a while. A body is actually a very awkward thing to dispose of, especially from the top story of a building. There aren't too many options. Get him up to the roof (with difficulty, given the stairs involved) and throw him off? Then he'd be discovered almost instantly.

All right, take him down in the elevator and out of the building and into a vehicle and across town to the river and throw him in. But the chance of being seen during one of these operations was frightful. The nearest place to the Fine Arts building where one might legally park a car was much too far away to drag a body, no matter what it weighed, and a man can be pretty hefty.

Given time and the right chemicals, you could presumably dissolve a body. Would an art school have the sort of acids, and the sort of large tanks, necessary for such an operation? And then I'd read a story once involving an artist who silver-plated his wife, or mistress, or somebody, which involved dumping her in a vat of something rather nasty. But either of these disposal methods seemed pretty far-fetched and expensive and would require a lot of specialized equipment.

There was always refrigeration. A body could be stashed in a large freezer for quite a long time, if the freezer wasn't much used. One could tuck it away until nightfall, at least, when other methods of disposal wouldn't be as noticeable. But why? Why not choose the quickest, easiest method at hand, one that might lead the police to conclude the death was accidental?

With a chisel protruding from the victim's back?

I shook away the fantasy ideas. No, whoever disposed of this body must have needed to do it in a hurry, and so chose the most expeditious method that came to hand. The chisel was perhaps forgotten in the stress of the moment, and once the murderer remembered, he could hardly go back and remove it.

He, or she. Could a woman have struck that blow? Could she have forced open the elevator doors to expose the shaft, and shoved the body over? I wondered how long ago it had been done. There had been that unpleasant odour in the elevator . . . No. I definitely did not want to think about that.

In fact, I didn't want to think about the murder at all, not by myself. Where was Alan, anyway?

'All right, love?'

It was amazing how often he knew what I was thinking.

'Fine,' I said, and it wasn't a lie, now that he was back at my side. He is a very comforting man. 'Have Derek and co. discovered anything interesting?'

'Nothing startling, except that at a quick glance, there seems to be remarkably little blood, given the man's injuries.' He was still speaking in an undertone, and I followed suit.

'Well, of course. If he was dead when he fell, or rather when he was pushed—'

'But there wasn't even much bleeding from the stab wound, though it was in a position where there should have been a lot. I won't go into detail, but even without the medical examiner's report, it doesn't make a lot of sense.'

'Maybe he died in the fall, after all, and was stabbed – no, that won't work, will it?'

'We'll know more when they get him out of there and on to an autopsy table.'

'Meanwhile, do they even know who he was?'

'Yes, but it doesn't get us much further. One of the teachers had a look at one of the photos the SOCOs took and identified him immediately. He was the head of the art school, and apparently one of the best-hated men in Sherebury.'

I took a deep breath. 'Oh, dear. Poor man. No shortage of possible suspects, then, I take it.'

'Perhaps. But do remember, my darling Miss Marple, that of all the considerations in a murder investigation, motive comes dead last.'

'As often as you've reminded me, I'm not likely to forget. But you might want to rephrase that sentence, dear.'

He grinned and gave me a peck on the cheek as Derek came over.

'Derek, it's always good to see you, though I could wish it were under different circumstances.'

'We do usually seem to meet over a body, don't we? A policeman's lot—'

'—is not an 'appy one,' Alan and I chorused. 'Yes, well, we're going to have to have you and Beth over for dinner sometime and talk about something non-criminal,' I went on. 'But at the moment, I've been trying to work out what all this might mean, and I can't make any sense of it.'

'Nor can we, at the moment,' said Derek. 'We're hoping the autopsy may give us a definitive cause of death, which certainly seems obscure just now.'

'And how about time of death? Any notions about that?'

'For reasons which you'd probably prefer me not to go into, we're certain the man's been dead quite some time. That, of course, makes pinning anything down quite difficult.'

'Anything like who was where at the relevant time. Indeed.'

I exchanged glances with Alan. 'So,' I went on with lamentable smugness, 'with "means" anybody's guess at this point and "opportunity" perhaps forever unknowable, that leaves motive, doesn't it?'

Alan rolled his eyes to the ceiling. 'I should never have let you get involved in murder cases.'

'It's a natural phenomenon,' I said, still smugly. 'Nothing to be done about it.'

'And jolly helpful at times, Dorothy,' said Derek, with a warm smile. 'Your insight into the people involved has often pointed us in the right direction. Admit it, chief.'

Alan held up his hands. 'It's a conspiracy. Very well. But I would remind you that in this particular case, my wife doesn't know any of the people who even might be involved.'

'But,' said Derek with a grin, 'I'll bet you five pounds she will do as soon as she possibly can.'

FOUR

'The thing I can't understand,' I said as we were on the way home, 'is the elevator. Or the chisel. One or the other, but not both.'

'Expound.'

'Someone socks the guy in the jaw, he falls, hits his head, dies. The socker panics. Say he's on the third floor – second, to you. He sends the elevator up to the top floor, forces the doors open on his floor, and tumbles the guy down the shaft so he won't be found for a while and when he is found, it will look like an accident. But then what's with the chisel? Or, alternatively, someone stabs the guy in the back. Why then does he shove him down the shaft, without removing the chisel? Yes, the body will be hidden for a while, especially if it's during the summer break when no one much is here and he's put an "out of order" sign on the elevator, but when it's found the chisel will make it plain at once that it's murder.'

'Except that he doesn't seem to have been murdered by the chisel.'

'Too little blood.' I nodded. 'Then what's the chisel doing there? And you think there's also too little blood for him to have been killed by the fall. So what in the world *did* happen? The man is genuinely dead. Somebody killed him, somehow.'

'Not necessarily. He could have died of natural causes.'

'Of course. But then why all the elaborate obfuscation?'

'Well. I can see you've worked out that the lift shaft is the best way to hide the body for a while.'

'Yes, just about the only way, if he was killed on any except the ground floor. Pardon me, if he *died*. And even if he died on the ground floor, anyone would be taking one unholy risk of being seen if they tried to take the body outside. And why hide the body at all if he died of natural causes?'

Alan took both his hands off the wheel and raised them in the classic gesture of frustration. 'Dorothy, I don't know! I don't know anything until the ME has done his job. We're doing what Sherlock Holmes always warned against.'

'Speculating ahead of our data. I know. I suppose I'll just have to be patient and wait until the reports come in. But it's driving me crazy. And speaking of driving . . .'

Alan grinned and concentrated on steering.

Friday, September 5

The Sherebury constabulary were dealing with no other major cases, so the autopsy was performed promptly. Derek phoned Alan two days after the grisly discovery, and I listened in on the speaker phone.

He sounded depressed. 'No joy. In fact, we're back to somewhere before square one. As we thought, the man died around six weeks ago, with a two-week fudge factor, so far as the forensic evidence is concerned. He was definitely alive at the end of last term – he held a meeting – but no one will admit to having seen him since.'

'Derek, sorry to interrupt, but did anyone tell you he was planning a holiday in Greece? I just remembered Gillian said that.'

'No. That's very useful, Dorothy. We'll look into that. If he did go, we'll need to find out when he came back. If not, then we probably know why, and that gives us a much shorter window for the time of death. It's still going to be the devil's own job to establish anyone's whereabouts, with any accuracy. We'll try, of course, but . . .' I could almost hear the shrug over the phone lines.

'We found nothing of interest in his pockets. The usual money, handkerchief, a couple of flyers for art exhibits, a small picture of a tabby cat. No dabs but his own on anything. As for cause of death, it was neither the stab wound – the instrument *was* a chisel, by the way – nor the fall. We were right about that. He was dead before either injury. The ME is checking for signs of heart attack, stroke, things of that sort. But he's inclined to believe it was some sort of poison.'

'Poison! Good grief, how many times does one need to kill a man?'

'Exactly. And you know as well as I do, after all this time there's precious little chance of detecting the agent. Oh, he'll run all the tests he can think of, and some poisons hang about in the body for quite a time, but so many don't. I tell you, this thing is haunting me. We may just be facing the perfect crime.'

Alan made the appropriate sympathetic noises and hung up, and we settled back to consider the problem.

'Overkill,' I said. 'In the most literal sense of the word.'

'Why?' asked Alan.

'That's the question, isn't it? I had thought maybe the chisel pointed to a sculptor, but if it didn't kill him . . . Why stab a dead man? Unless we're dealing with a maniac who thought the . . . what was the man's title? Dean?'

'Head of the Fine Arts Department.'

'Oh, right. The head, then, was some sort of vampire or zombie or whatever who needed to be killed several times. Good grief, reminds me of Rasputin! How many ways did they try to kill him?'

'I don't recall, but he took a lot of killing, I agree. But I don't agree that we're dealing with a maniac here. I think our murderer is a very cool customer who knew exactly what he was about.'

'He? You think a man did it, for sure?'

Alan shrugged. 'He or she. The language needs a neutral pronoun. As a matter of fact, though, the man – his name was Chandler, John Chandler – was no lightweight. Just getting him to the lift, forcing the doors, and pushing him in would have taken considerable strength. Not to mention the fact that a chisel is a rather unhandy weapon. Blunt, though with rather sharp edges. It wouldn't be easy to force it through skin and muscle, even if one's victim were past resisting. So provisionally, yes, a man.'

'That chisel keeps bothering me. I wonder if they actually use them in the sculpture studios. If most of the sculpture uses odd bits of junk, what would they want with a chisel? Isn't that for sculpting marble?'

'Probably wood, I believe. Perhaps marble. I know very little about it. Gillian did say that the students get a grounding in the traditional methods.'

'Mmm. And there did seem to be a lot of miscellaneous junk

lying around in various studios. But she also said that they had very little budget for materials, which would certainly seem to rule out marble, at least. I think I need to go talk to her about what does go on in the studios there.'

'Perhaps, but do walk warily, my dear. Don't forget that the chisel, whatever role it played in this crime, points directly to a sculptor. And the most prominent one at the school is her boss.'

It wasn't easy to find out when Gillian might be at her job. The departmental phone number was answered by voicemail, and I wasted most of the day waiting for someone to phone back. I finally clipped a leash on our dog, Watson, and together we strolled across the Cathedral Close to the Rose and Crown, the pub and inn owned by Inga's parents, where she still sometimes worked in the bar.

I was in luck. Inga was there, just getting ready to leave for home.

'Hi, Dorothy,' she said with a brilliant smile. 'Hello, Watson.' She fondled his silky ears. 'You'll both excuse me for a moment?'

She headed at almost a run for the loo, and I nodded in understanding. I never had any babies myself, but I remembered the problem from the stories of friends.

She came back looking much refreshed. 'I was just on my way, Dorothy, but can I get you something before I go? A nice G&T sounds good in this weather, doesn't it?'

It was still hot, with a thundery feeling in the air. 'Sounds wonderful, but not just now, thanks, and I don't want to keep you. I'm sure you need to get home and put your feet up. I just stopped by to ask if you had Gillian's phone number or address.'

'Small chance of putting my feet up with the Nipper on the march! Mum's looking after him right now, but she needs to get back here. They've a full house tonight. I do have Gillian's number and address, though.' She pulled out the phone that seemed also to serve as computer, address book, appointment book, picture gallery and probably a hundred other functions I couldn't even imagine. My own cell phone had one function: phone calls. 'Here we are. Want to copy this down?'

She smiled when I took a notebook and pen out of my purse. 'Don't sneer, child. When your battery goes dead or your server

goes down or whatever can happen to that thing, I've still got
my trusty little notebook. Tell me.'

I wrote down the information, gave her a quick hug, and
stepped out into the increasingly muggy afternoon. The sky over
the Cathedral had changed, in the few minutes we'd been inside,
from a deep blue to a slate grey, and the green of grass and trees
had taken on that livid colour that so often presages a storm. As
Watson and I hurried across the close, the faint rumble of thunder
sounded in the distance, and Watson pulled me along at nearly
a run. He doesn't like storms.

There was a flash of lightning as we reached the gate into our
street, and the first big drops of rain splashed down. We got
inside just before the heavens opened and the thunder and lightning began in earnest.

Watson ran to find Alan. The dog loves my company, but in
times of stress, he finds Alan a great comfort. As do I.

'Any luck?' Alan called from his den. He had to raise his voice
over the tumult of the storm, which beat on our slate roof and
against our diamond-paned windows with fury. There would be
water on the floor somewhere, I knew. Our seventeenth-century
home is lovely, but it needs constant repair, and the current
problem was the chinks in the weatherstripping, here and there,
which let in the weather.

I went into the den. Alan sat in his big leather chair, his feet
up on a hassock, with Watson cowering on the floor under his
knees. Both cats, Samantha and Esmeralda, were on his lap,
studiously ignoring Watson and pretending the storm didn't bother
them a bit.

'Did you manage to get the windows closed?'

'Only just. It came up fast, and every window in the house
was open. But . . .' He shrugged, and I nodded.

'I know. We'll have to call Mr Pettifer as soon as the rain
stops, and meanwhile I can mop.'

'Right. As I said, any luck?'

'I just caught Inga, and she gave me a phone number and an
address. I have no desire to go out in this, but I thought I'd call
Gillian. If I can.'

Sherebury, officially a city because it rejoices in both a
Cathedral and a university, is really quite a small town, and our

cell service isn't always reliable. In an electrical storm it can cut out completely, and when I opened my phone, I saw that this was the case. I sighed and plumped down on the other comfortable chair in the room. 'Oh, well. Tomorrow, I guess.'

A brilliant flash of lightning, a peal of thunder like the crack of doom, and the lights went out. Watson yipped, I stifled a scream, and the cats dived under Alan's chair.

'That was awfully close,' I said, sounding as scared as I felt.

'Too close. I'm going to check to see if anything was struck.'

'Not outside!'

'No, indeed. But I'm just going to poke my head out the front and back door, and have a look upstairs.'

He found a flashlight, and I went with him on his little tour of inspection. It was too dark outside, and the rain was coming too hard, to see much, but we could find no damage inside the house, apart from the expected puddles here and there under windows and by both doors. We could see no lights from neighbours' houses, so apparently the power was out there, too.

'One thing,' I said when we had groped our way back to the den. 'It can't keep this up for very long.'

'You're thinking of storms back in Indiana, love. The weather here is different, remember? At this time of year, a storm can last quite a long time.'

I shivered. 'Thanks a lot. And I'm getting cold. I don't suppose we have any wood inside for a fire?'

'I'm afraid not. But the Aga will be warm. Shall we sit in the kitchen?'

The Aga, which came with the house, is gas-fired, and is always on. It heats the water for the whole house and has burners that are always hot or warm. (In the worst heat of summer, I avoid the kitchen.) I've never quite learned the knack of cooking anything more taxing than soup on it, and certainly not baking in an oven with no temperature control, so we also have a small gas stove. But on a day like today, with the sudden drop in temperature, it was a great blessing. We moved to the kitchen, where Alan found candles and set them on the table, and I moved the kettle to the hottest burner for tea.

The animals had crept into the kitchen with us, first Watson, and then, with assumed nonchalance, the cats. The storm was moderating a bit, and since they were in the kitchen, all three of them decided they were hungry. I felt they deserved a treat, so I found some ham in the fridge, which all three devoured as if they were starving. Then the idea of a snack seemed to appeal to us humans, too, so I brought the biscuit tin to the table along with the tea. 'I'm sorry I can't make toast, but I'm no good at toasting it on the Aga or over a gas flame.'

'Not to worry. Chocolate biscuits will always fill the bill.'

We sat by the light of the candles, in the cosy kitchen, and despite the puddles growing by the doors and windows, I thought how lucky and contented I was.

FIVE

Saturday, September 6

The rain continued all night, though the thunder slowly diminished to rumbles far away. In the morning the sun was once again shining brightly, though the air had cooled very considerably.

Alan had been up for a while by the time I got downstairs, and the blessed man had coffee ready for me. I do not consider morning a chatty time, at least not until I have some caffeine in my system, so we sat in companionable silence while Alan read the *Telegraph* and I came to full consciousness.

'Anything interesting?' I asked, nodding at the paper as I poured myself a second cup.

'The storm did a lot of damage over most of the south,' Alan said. 'Trees down all over Sussex and environs.'

'What about here?'

'Shoreham was spared the worst of it. I strolled about a bit earlier. The only damage I could see was that big yew next to the wall in the close. It was struck by lightning.'

'Oh, what a pity! It was a lovely old tree. That must have been what we heard, that awful thunder clap.'

'Yes, the dean will be very upset. He was especially fond of that tree. It's been there for probably a thousand years, at least.'

'I'd heard that, but I always thought it was legend. Do they really live that long?'

'Much longer in some cases. But I fear this one's done for.'

'A shame. But looking on the bright side, it could have been our house.'

'Or Jane's, or the deanery, or any of them nearby. Yes, we were fortunate to be spared. What would you like for breakfast?'

I settled on toast and grapefruit, and while we ate we talked about our plans for the day.

'I'm going to get through to Archibald Pettifer just as soon as I can,' said Alan. 'Those doors and windows have to be made right. He'll probably not be able to get to it for a bit, but I want to get us on his list straightaway.'

'Good. I do get tired of mopping up, though it means the floors stay clean. I'm going to try to find Gillian, either at home or at school.'

'Take the car, then. I'll take Watson for his walk as soon as I've talked to Pettifer.'

Watson, who had been dozing under my chair, was immediately alert at the sound of the magic word. Sam and Emmy woke briefly, observed his doggie enthusiasm with some scorn, and went back to sleep.

I went to phone Gillian.

I had no luck, either at the school or her own number. I decided to go in search of her. If I couldn't find her at either home or school, I'd leave a note. Darn it all, electronics had their place, but good old-fashioned writing could sometimes get the job done quicker.

She wasn't at her flat near the university, which I eventually found after some trouble navigating the maze of streets in the area. I spent too many years in America, where towns were laid out in grids and going around the block meant just that. English towns were laid out, not by surveyors or engineers, but by human feet and donkeys and horses, meandering where they needed to go, and when paved streets came along, they followed the same sometimes maddeningly irrational paths. But after leaving Gillian's flat and making several wrong turns, I found the car park for the Fine Arts building and walked to the rather unsightly pile.

The school term had evidently not yet begun. There didn't seem to be any students around. I entered the building by what I thought was the right door and was immediately lost in the maze of corridors. Surely there would be someone I could ask for directions! They wouldn't leave a building unlocked and unoccupied. Would they? I rather wished I'd brought Watson. This was, I reminded myself, the scene of a particularly odd murder, and there was great likelihood that the murderer was around somewhere.

I shook myself. If I nurtured thoughts like that for very long, I'd be seeing bogeymen in every dark corner.

'May I help you?'

The deep voice came out of a very dark corner and nearly scared me out of my skin. 'Um – I was looking for the sculpture studios. Actually, I'm trying to find Gillian – um – I'm afraid I don't know her last name . . .'

'Classes have been delayed this term. Come back next week.' It was a good voice, deep and musical, but its owner wasn't being obliging.

'I don't want to take a class. I simply want to speak to her.' Annoyance was beginning to dampen my fright. 'If she isn't here, I'll leave a note for her at the school office. Could you direct me there?'

'The office is closed. We've had a serious accident in the department.'

The owner of the voice had moved into the light, and I could see he was tall and good-looking, and nobody I'd met before. Whoever he was, he was being extremely rude.

'I do know about the accident. I was here when Mr—' (drat, what was the man's name?) '—when the body was discovered. Would you be so kind as to direct me to the sculpture studios, where *someone* might be able to help me find Gillian?'

I taught school in Indiana for many years. I'm capable of a commanding tone of voice when necessary. Usually the listener quails. Not this time.

'Madam, the school is closed until next week. I don't know who you are or what you're doing here, but you are trespassing and I must ask you to leave.'

'My name is Dorothy Martin, and I have several good friends here at the university, and it is necessary that I see Gillian. Who are you, for that matter, to order me around?'

'Not that it's any business of yours, but I'm W.T. Braithwaite. You may be familiar with the name. I paint.'

He said it as the Queen might have said, 'I reign,' obviously expecting me to doff my hat or curtsey. I did in fact recognize the name. He had won quite a lot of recognition for paintings that looked to me like bad freeway accidents rendered in screaming shades of neon.

'Oh, yes, I think I may have heard the name somewhere.' That was unkind of me, but my irritation was getting the best of me. 'Do you teach here?'

'I do. In fact, as the senior member of staff I am at the moment the acting head. And I say again, the school is closed—'

'What's up, Will?'

Another voice out of the gloom, but I recognized this one. 'Oh, good! You're Mr Singleton, aren't you?'

'Dennis. And you're the one who came to see poor Gillian and then squashed Chandler in the lift.'

I winced. 'Actually I believe he was dead long before he was – er – squashed, as you put it. But yes, my husband and I came to Gillian's reception, and I'm hoping to talk to her today, see how she's doing.'

'I've *told* her she'll have to come back next week. The school is not open until—'

'Oh, dry up, Will. This lady isn't doing anyone any harm. Come with me, dear, and we'll find her. She's in the studios somewhere.'

'Thank goodness you came along,' I said when we were well clear of the obstructive painter. 'I thought I was going to stand there all day arguing with that man.'

'Will's a right prat,' said Dennis, 'and loves to throw his weight about. Mind that puddle. The roof leaks, among other problems.'

'So does mine. Or actually, it's my windows and doors in a storm like yesterday's. But then my house is something like four hundred years old.'

'The Fine Arts building is something like fifty, but it's coming to pieces. Bad design from the start. Ah, here we are. *Gilly*!' he roared.

A head poked around a corner. It was clad in a welder's mask and looked rather like an invader from another world, except I assumed aliens didn't wear blue jeans. 'Oh. Hi,' it said, and doffed the mask to reveal Gillian's face, innocent of make-up and indeed streaked with what looked like clay.

'Did we catch you at a bad moment, love? Can you leave whatever it is for a little?'

'Sure. I was finished, really.' She looked a little uncomfortable. 'Just welding the arms on that one piece.'

Dennis shook a playful finger at her. 'Ah, my dear, still stuck in the figurative! Never mind, this place will soon cure you. This lady's come to see you. I'm sorry, I don't remember her name.'

'Dorothy Martin,' I said. 'I'm no good at names, either, so don't worry. I have this theory that names live in a particular part of the brain, and my name-spot has turned to cream cheese.'

'Well, I'll not forget you,' said Gillian, a shadow coming over her face. She pulled off her gloves. 'You're Inga's friend. And you were in the lift when . . . oh, yes, I certainly remember you.'

'That's why I came to see you. I wanted to see how you were doing. It was a pretty horrible experience for you, just starting out here and all. What a way to begin a career!'

'It wasn't exactly pleasant for you, either, was it? At least I'm not claustrophobic.'

'I do feel so foolish about that. I absolutely hate being at the mercy of irrationality, but I'm afraid I haven't been able to conquer it.'

'I've heard hypnotism can do the trick,' said Dennis. 'But look, we don't have to stand about. Why don't you both come to my office, and I'll see if I can find some coffee. There used to be a pot going all the time in the main office, but now we've no secretary, everything's at sixes and sevens.'

He started down a dimly lit corridor. 'No secretary?' I commented. 'That must be why my voicemails never got answered. Will she come back once the term has started?'

'She was sacked.' Dennis's voice was dry enough to vaporize the puddle in front of his office door. 'Mind you don't slip. Make yourself at home, and I'll see what I can do about coffee.'

'Don't go to a lot of trouble for me,' I said quickly, as I imagined the kind of coffee he might find. If it was out of a vending machine, I'd very much rather not.

'Nor me,' said Gillian. 'I don't actually drink coffee.'

'Well, then. The stuff I could come up with might be pretty vile, to tell the truth. Give bronze a nice patina, probably. So.' He sat in one of the two wooden chairs in front of his desk. 'Take my desk chair, ma'am,' he said to me. 'It's ancient, but it's comfortable. Just don't lean back. It has latent homicidal tendencies.' And then he looked very much as though he wished he hadn't said that.

I glanced at Gillian and decided to defer that subject for a little while. Casting about for something else to talk about, I said, 'So you said the secretary was sacked. Incompetent, was she?'

'She was supremely competent,' said Dennis, that odd tone back in his voice. 'She did everything expected of her and more. Her work was completed on time; she kept the staff informed; she reminded us when we'd forgotten some important report or that sort of thing. She was also a beautiful woman.'

That rang alarm bells. 'Uh-oh. Domestic problems of some kind?'

'Not exactly. I hadn't told you, Gillian, but you'd better know, if only for your self-protection.'

'I've heard some rumours,' the girl said quietly. 'She got in some sort of difficulty with one of the senior staff?'

'You could put it that way. To put it baldly, William Braithwaite made a pass at her. She was married with two children. So's he, for that matter. Married, I mean. She told him where he could get off. He's accustomed to getting what, and who, he wants. He kicked up a great shindy, made some entirely unwarranted accusations about her handling of the petty cash funds, and she was sacked without a reference.'

I made a noise of disgusted disbelief. 'But that's . . . in this day and age! It's unbelievable. Sounds like the nineteenth century, when the son of the house got a servant girl pregnant and she was the one who was punished.'

Gillian had gone white with anger. 'That man! I might have known. He's already tried it on with me. I told him where he could stuff it, and said I'd report him to the Head of Faculty if he didn't back off. That's sexual harassment of the very worst kind, and I'll not stand for it! And now you tell me he actually got that poor woman sacked!'

'And with two children!' I exclaimed. 'What does her husband do? Can he support them until she finds another job?'

'She doesn't have a husband now,' said Dennis. 'He was killed in a car smash a few days after she had to leave here. She's been getting along, barely, with a little insurance money and some government support.'

'That poor woman! Does she have to worry about school fees, too?'

'No. The kids aren't old enough for school yet. She brought them to the day nursery here. It's free for employees, one of the truly enlightened efforts of the university. Now, when she gets another job, *if* she gets one, with no reference, she'll have to pay for child care.'

'It's iniquitous! What was that man – the head – thinking of, to let it happen?'

'Oh, Will's his fair-haired boy. Was. He's had all sorts of honours showered on him for those appalling paintings of his, and it all redounds to the glory of the school. Or so Chandler apparently thought. He let Will nobble most of the budget, too. I tried and tried to make him see that paint and canvas cost a fair amount less than clay and bronze and marble and mahogany, but he wouldn't listen, just kept yammering on about found materials and the new wave of art, and all the tired old clichés, and let Will scoop the lot.'

'That might have been about to end,' said Gillian.

Dennis drew back and stared at her. 'End? What do you mean, child?'

'I heard something,' she said, scuffling her feet under her chair. She reminded me of an embarrassed schoolchild, the child she so recently was. 'I wasn't meant to hear it. It was after the staff meeting at the end of term. You'd said my teaching schedule would be in the office, so I went in and was just about to turn on the light – the whole building was dark – when I heard voices in the inner office. I didn't know whose they were, but they sounded angry, and I almost left, but the door squeaks so much, and somehow I didn't want them to know I'd been there.'

She took a deep breath. 'So I sort of skulked. I didn't mean to listen, truly, but they were shouting. And one of them said he didn't have the money, and the other said he'd have to find it, and said it in sort of a funny way. I didn't understand. Then they both left, and I escaped. Now I know, though, that the one who was sounding so strange was Braithwaite. And the other one must have been the head. Who else would have been in his office?'

'So you think Braithwaite was asking for yet more money, and Chandler turned him down?'

'Well, actually it didn't sound quite like that. It was more as if Braithwaite was making some sort of threat. But that doesn't make any sense. He already gets all he wants for his studio. Everyone's talking about how unfair it is. Braithwaite's a real scuzz, and I wish he'd been the one under that lift!'

SIX

I suppose I should have been shocked, but I wasn't. 'He sounds like a nasty man. I don't know that I'd wish him dead, but he certainly ought to get his just deserts. I still don't understand why he's tolerated around here. I'd have thought someone would have sued him long ago.'

'The man is a menace, but he's not stupid, Mrs Martin.'

'If you're Dennis, I'm Dorothy,' I interrupted.

'Dorothy, then. If a victim goes to law, she has to prove her case. Our William has made sure, over the years, that there could be no proof. There are never any witnesses to his advances. Nothing is ever put in writing. It's always the victim's word against his, and his argument has always been that he was more sinned against than sinning. He's an attractive chap, I suppose. Well, you've seen him.'

'In a dark hallway. Probably not to recognize again. I'd know his voice, though. And his attitude. Why was he so unwilling to give me a little help, back there? I was only asking directions.'

'Will doesn't need a reason to be disagreeable. It's his natural disposition. He no doubt calls it artistic temperament. Let's talk about something more pleasant. Or different, anyway. Has that husband of yours found our murderer yet, Dorothy?' He grinned at the look on my face. 'Aha! Surprised you! I may not remember names, but I don't forget *who* people are. I don't remember your husband's name, either, but I know he used to be the great white chief in the police here, and the whole town thinks he walks on water.'

I blinked at that. Of course I thought Alan was marvellous, but I'd never noticed him displaying any peculiar aquatic skills. 'I might not go quite that far, but yes, he's a very dear man, and he was a very good policeman. Of course he's long since retired.'

'But he was right here on the spot, and so were you. And I've heard about you, too. The Miss Marple of Sherebury.'

'I like to know what's happening,' I admitted. 'And I can tell you that no one apparently knows very much about Mr Chandler's death, so far. Of course Alan isn't officially involved, but as you say, both of us were here, so the police are bound to have some questions for us. I thought someone around here might know something, or at least have some ideas.'

'Oh, we have ideas. The staff has done almost no work since it happened. We're spending all our time speculating, and looking at each other crosswise. The fact is, Dorothy, that John Chandler was not a popular man. Virtually everyone in the department hated him, if that's enough reason to kill someone.'

'Murder has been done for hatred, Dennis. Many times. Or jealousy, or greed, or lust. Pick a motive.'

'Yes. You might, I suppose, just as well know mine straight off. I am a man of frustrated ambitions, and the source of the frustration was found under the lift. I submitted my application for promotion to principal lecturer. That was the first step on the path to what I really wanted, which in fact was John's job.'

'And you'd do a much better job than he ever did, if what I hear is true!' said Gillian passionately.

'Thank you, my dear. In fact, I think I would be a better administrator than John. That's not saying a great deal. Almost anyone would have done a better job. But he was the one who had to endorse my application, and he threw it out. He claimed I hadn't the qualifications. Which is a lie. So there you have it. Enraged, frustrated, I pushed him down the shaft.'

Gillian made a protesting noise. 'I see,' I said calmly. 'There's no point in confessing to me, but I'll be happy to call Inspector Morrison if you like. Or perhaps you'd like to tell me about your accomplices in the dastardly deed.'

He chuckled. 'No shortage of possibilities, but I'm not going to tell tales about my colleagues. They'll tell you themselves, I imagine. *De mortuis* and all that, but the only real sentiment being expressed about that man's death is general rejoicing, I can tell you. Gillian, why don't you take Dorothy off to some-place where she can get a decent cup of coffee and you can have whatever it is you do have, and then when you get back we can take a look at how badly you've mucked up your darling *Summer*.'

I must have looked my confusion, because Gillian giggled. 'That's the name of my bronze. You'll see why.'

We left the building by the nearest door, which left me hopelessly lost. 'I have no idea where I am. Or where my car is.'

'You probably came in the main door. I'll help you find your car. But we don't have to drive anywhere. If you don't mind Starbucks, there's one just around the corner.'

'I love their coffee, though I'm sorry they've wiped out so many proper English cafés and tea shops.'

'But you're not English!'

'No, but I'm a devout Anglophile, and I really hate the creeping Americanization of England. Like the convert who's more Catholic than the Pope, you know.'

She giggled again. I don't usually care much for gigglers, but hers was a pleasant laugh, very like a little girl.

'So why did you decide to be a sculptor?' I asked when we were settled with my double espresso and her hot chocolate.

'I'm not sure I decided. I mean, it sounds really affected and stupid, but it sort of chose me. There was never a time when I didn't know that was what I was going to do with my life.'

'A vocation.' I nodded. 'It doesn't sound stupid at all. It sounds fortunate. Not everyone finds their proper niche in life, but you obviously have.'

'Oh, if only it doesn't get spoilt! I was over the moon when I got this appointment, and now who knows what's going to happen! That rotten Braithwaite has the department in his own hands now, and there are fifty ways he could make my life miserable if I won't play his nasty little games.' She was near tears now, her emotions as volatile as a toddler's.

Really, I had to stop thinking of her as a child. 'Gillian, listen to me. You must protect yourself. Never be alone with Braithwaite. In fact, you might take to carrying some small recording device with you. Do they still make tiny tape recorders, or maybe some digital thing you can put in your handbag or pocket?'

'I think maybe my phone will do that. Or I know you can buy recorders.'

'Good. Get one. I'll buy it for you if you can't afford it. I want you to record every word that man says to you, especially, of course, the suggestive remarks.'

She shuddered. 'You couldn't call them suggestive. They were too overt for that.'

'Even better, because it wouldn't be subject to misinterpret-
ation. You mustn't entrap him, but if he does sneak a chance to
come on to you, make sure you get it recorded. Get a voice-
activated recorder, that's the best way, and make sure it's ready
to go anytime you're in the same room with him. The same
building. The same universe.'

'You're serious, aren't you?'

'You bet I am. I want to get this guy almost as much as you
do, for the sake of that poor secretary and her kids, if for no
other reason. And the only way we're going to do it is with
evidence that can be taken to the authorities.'

'You're right! I'll do it. And I can afford to buy it. I don't
make very much money here, but I have some savings, and my
parents – well – they can help. I just hope I wasn't so fierce with
Braithwaite that he'll give up on me.'

'That kind never gives up. They take rejection as a challenge,
and they never believe the woman really means it. No doesn't
mean no to them, it means maybe. Or later. Or whatever they
want it to mean. The danger is if you made him so angry that
he'll push for your dismissal before you can collect any ammuni-
tion to fight him. Maybe you'd better follow him when he's
around other attractive girls as well.'

'I don't know many of the students yet, but I'll try. Thanks,
Dorothy.'

'Good. Now, since this man is obviously not exactly an upright
citizen, what do you think about him as a possible for—' I looked
around and lowered my voice '—for what happened at the
reception?'

'I'm not sure. I've thought about it, actually. He's certainly
vicious enough, but I can't see that he'd have had any reason.
He was getting everything he wanted out of Chandler.'

'No names, please. It's noisy in here, but you never know who
might be listening. And you did say that you had some idea the
victim might have been cutting off the funds.'

'I wish I could remember exactly what was said. It was two
months ago, and I was sort of scared, if you want the truth. They
sounded . . . not just angry. Dangerous? Oh, that sounds stupid.'

'Gillian – what's your last name?'

'Roberts,' she said, surprised.

'Gillian Roberts, you have to stop saying you're stupid! You're an intelligent young woman, and it's time you learned to trust your own judgement! Forgive an old woman for lecturing you, but I hate to see people underestimating themselves. Now, I'm pumped up with caffeine, and I'd like to go see that sculpture of yours.'

'It's really not . . . no, I won't say that. You're right. I'll let you form your own opinion about it. Actually, I . . . I like it a lot!'

'Good for you.'

We walked in silence. It was a gorgeous day after the storm, crisp and cool with the promise of autumn to come. Here and there gardeners were at work on the campus, picking up downed limbs and other debris of the storm, but the university didn't seem to have suffered much damage. I thought of the yew tree in the close and was saddened, but all things have their lifespan, and the yew had certainly had a good run. It would be mourned, though. The English cherish their old trees.

I was grateful that we didn't run into William Braithwaite when we returned to the Fine Arts building. Knowing what I now knew about him, I doubted I could have been even civil, and I wasn't entirely convinced that he couldn't have murdered Chandler. His motive was obscure, I agreed, unless something else was going on that I didn't understand. But there was plenty of evil character, evil enough, I thought, to do the deed.

The sculpture studio was deserted, Dennis apparently about other business. Gillian shyly opened the door to the bronze workshop and turned on the lights.

There stood one of the loveliest pieces of sculpture I'd ever seen. About half life-size, the girl stood with her head and arms upraised. She was essentially nude, with only a suggestion of diaphanous draperies clinging to her taut young body. Her whole being expressed the joy of the warm sun, of abandonment of care, of sheer youthful exuberance.

Gillian was watching me anxiously. 'My dear,' I said at last, 'I don't know what to say. It's perfect. It's . . . I have no words.'

She sighed with relief. 'I haven't shown it to many people, only Dennis and Inga. Dennis picked it apart, of course. That's his job. And it isn't really finished yet. I have to grind down the

welds, and of course add the patina. She's going to be a bright
bronze, almost gold. I want her to look like sunlight.'

'She does already. It isn't the colour. It's the whole attitude.
She almost sings, Gillian. And how in the world did you manage
to make those scarves, or whatever they are, look so soft and
fine? This is metal, for heaven's sake, but I want to reach out
and touch to make sure it isn't really cloth.'

'Well, I work in clay, of course, and that's a softer material.
I – I can't tell you how I did it. There are techniques, but this
just sort of came, as if I wasn't really doing it myself.' She spoke
hesitantly, sounding almost ashamed.

'And don't you dare say that sounds stupid! It sounds awesome,
in the real sense of that word. You have a great gift, Gillian.'

She sighed deeply. 'And this may be the last bronze piece I
do for a long time. At least in this sort of size. I began this at
Hallam and brought it with me to finish. It's to go in their student
exhibition in the spring. But awful William says we can't afford
bronze here, and the horrible head said we were to concentrate
on found materials, and I don't know what I'm going to do.'

'I don't either, but I know it would be a crime if you couldn't
continue with what you do so well.'

'Mooning over *Summer* again, are you, love?'

Dennis had come into the room with that disconcerting quiet-
ness of his. I turned on him. 'I'll not hear a word against this
work of art,' I said indignantly. 'I'm not an art teacher, or critic,
but I'm old enough to have seen a lot of art, and I know this is
brilliant work.'

'And who said it wasn't?'

'Gillian said you picked it to pieces.'

'I pointed out where, in its earlier stages, she could make it
better. She did. She's a good craftsman and a good child, and
right now she needs to get busy setting up the studio for her
classes, which begin, I remind her, in two days. Off you go!' He
gave her a friendly slap on her shoulder, and she grinned and left.

'Don't think me a monster,' he said quietly when she'd gone.
'She's the best sculptor I've seen in thirty years of teaching,
which is why I ride her unmercifully. She has some things to
learn yet about technique, ways to make the work easier, tricks
of the trade. But her eye, her mind . . .'

'Her soul,' I said. 'You called her a craftsman. You know she's an artist.'

'She is. There will come a time, soon, when I have nothing more to teach her, and then she'll have to go on to the Slade or the Royal College, or simply take off on her career.'

'Dennis, why did she come here, where there's next to no budget for sculpture?'

'I didn't want her to. I saw what a tragedy it would be. If that child can't do what she was born to do, which is figurative work in bronze, she'll pine away. It was Will who pressured Chandler into making her a good offer. She's getting paid about twice what most graduate students draw. It's still not much, but it was enough to get her here.'

'I got an idea from something she said that her parents were wealthy and could afford to support her until her career takes off.'

'They are, and they could, but she's eager to be independent. She's an interesting character, childish in some ways, adult and assertive in others. If I *had* murdered Chandler, it would have been for that girl's sake. I suppose I should wish you luck in your efforts to find his killer, but quite honestly I wonder if the chap who did it shouldn't get a medal.'

SEVEN

And maybe he did, in fact, murder Chandler, I mused as I wandered aimlessly around the building, trying to find my way to my car. Gillian had promised to help, but I didn't want to talk to her just then. Suppose I found out that Dennis was guilty, and thereby helped put her friend and mentor in prison. I was afraid, if I met her, that these thoughts might show on my face, which I've been told is the sort that should never get involved in a poker game. No, I didn't want to see Gillian just now.

Dennis didn't seem the murdering type, but then Alan had told me again and again that there is no such thing. Certain kinds of murder can be identified with certain kinds of personalities, but there are too many variables to say, this man, or that woman, is incapable of killing. I liked Dennis. That had nothing to do with anything, either.

There was the chisel, of course. That was a piece of information that the police were keeping to themselves. If Dennis had said, 'I grabbed a chisel and went for him,' I'd have known for sure. But he didn't mention it. And the chisel wasn't the murder weapon, in any case. So why was it there?

That was a path I'd been down before, and it led nowhere. And speaking of paths, where on earth was I going? The corridor I'd chosen at random seemed to end abruptly, with no turning or exit. I began to feel a bit like Charlie on the MTA. Would I ever return?

'You look lost.' The voice apparently came out of nowhere. I was getting used to that, in this place. Not only was the design eccentric and the lighting inadequate, the acoustics were peculiar as well. I peered, and a figure materialized through a doorway.

'I am well and truly lost,' I admitted. 'I was trying to get to the main door so I can find my car, but I find the layout confusing!'

'And worse with all the lights out,' the man growled. 'Economy measure, when only the staff are here. Damn nonsense. I can see in the dark, though, so let me direct you.'

'Then you must be a photographer,' I said as he gave me his arm.

'Clever of you,' he said approvingly. 'How did you know?'

'My first husband was a photographer. Only an amateur, but he had his own darkroom and developed excellent lowlight vision. We used to say he was part cat. And you smell like a photographer.'

It was out before I realized how rude it sounded, but the man gave a shout of laughter. 'And how do photographers smell?'

'I'm sorry. I didn't mean it as an insult. You smell like hypo. Is that what they call it in this country?'

'I know the term. Sodium hyposulfite, a fixing agent. You're talking about a vanished era, you know.'

'I do know. The world has gone digital. But plainly you still use it, or you wouldn't have that distinctive aura. I quite like it, by the way. It brings happy memories. My uncles were photographers, too, back in Terre Haute, Indiana. They were professionals, and when my parents and I used to visit, they'd let me spend time with them in the darkroom. I loved those times.'

He stopped. 'You like darkrooms?'

'Love them.'

He turned around. 'Come see mine, while it still exists.'

'Is your department being threatened with budget problems, too?' The man had begun striding down the hall and I had to hurry to keep up.

He stopped and I almost cannoned into him. 'How do you know about budget cuts? You're not new staff or something, are you?'

'Or something. My name's Dorothy Martin and I'm a friend of Gillian Roberts, the new grad assistant in sculpture.'

He put out a hand. 'Sam Andrews. I teach photography here, as you will have gathered. So you've been talking to young what's-her-name about the budget?'

'To her and to her boss, Dennis – I've forgotten the rest.'

'Singleton. But I still don't understand why you were discussing the budget. We try to keep that information to ourselves.'

'To be frank, it came up in connection with the death of the head, Mr Chandler.' I was a little nervous. Here I was alone with a man I didn't know from Adam, who might have killed Chandler.

But could a man who smelled like hypo be a killer? That idiotic thought crossed my mind just as he snapped his fingers and said, 'Oh, now I know why your name sounded familiar! You're the one who discovered the body in the lift.'

'My husband and I, yes. In the shaft, actually. And it was really the firemen who found him, who got us out when we got stuck . . . look, let's back up. My husband, who is Alan Nesbitt, retired chief constable of this county, came with me to the reception for new staff. Some friends of ours know Gillian. She was showing us around the building when the elevator got stuck. I panicked, like a fool, because I'm claustrophobic, and the fire department had to come and get us out. They found the body.'

'So it was you that killed him, really, was it? The lift you were in, I mean.'

'No, thank the Lord! I thought that for a little while, but then everyone realized he'd been dead some time.' And that, I belatedly realized, was as much as I'd better say about what the police knew.

But Sam persisted. 'What did kill him, then? Fell down the shaft somehow? Damfool thing to do, larking about in a lift, and he wasn't the larking sort.'

'I really don't know how he got down there, and if you don't mind, I'd rather not talk about it. The whole thing was an experience I'd like to forget.'

'So you came back to where it happened.'

He let the statement lie there. We stood in the dark hallway, where he could presumably see far more than I could. There wasn't another sound in the building except for the pounding of my heart, which I was sure could be heard three streets away.

At last I sighed. 'All right. You've rumbled me. I came to talk to Gillian, to make sure she was all right, since she was with us in that awful elevator. And I came to nose around. I'm an unregenerate snoop, and I don't like leaving questions unanswered. I very much want to know how Mr Chandler got where he was found. Right now I also want very much to find someplace where there's light. Unlike you, I can't see in the dark, and it makes me nervous.'

'Right. The darkroom's straight ahead and up a flight of stairs. And it can also be a light room. Follow me.'

Said the spider to the fly. I tried to remember if my phone was fully charged. Would it be too obvious if I pulled it out of my purse to check?

But then we were in the darkroom, which I could have identified with no light at all, and Sam had turned on the light and I was surrounded by the familiar and friendly, and my fears felt foolish.

Sam pointed out his treasures in terms that sounded both familiar and incomprehensible. Thus had Frank told me about the new lens for his enlarger, the superior developing tanks, the film dryer he had concocted using an ancient hairdryer. This darkroom was larger and better equipped than Frank's very home-made one, but the ideas were the same, and Sam's enthusiasm was just as fervent as Frank's.

It shut off abruptly, though. 'You didn't understand a word I said, did you?'

'Not the words. I'm not a techie when it comes to photography. I understood that you've put your heart and soul into this dark-room, and everything is the best possible for its purpose.'

'And it's all going to come to an end. In a week or two, if I can't get materials, I'll have to close this darkroom down and go over entirely to digital.'

'That would be a great pity,' I said, meaning it. 'A digital print, be it ever so well done, can never have the same range of tone—'

'Exactly! Especially in black-and-white. You must have seen some of the prints on the walls of the studio when you came to that reception.'

'They were beautiful. Reminded me of Ansel Adams and Edward Weston at their best.'

'I made those prints,' said Sam with justifiable pride. 'And some of my students can do nearly as well. I teach them all the techniques, you know. I even used to teach tricolour carbro. Ever hear of that?'

'Yes. Colour prints made using a special camera and black-and-white film. Frank tried it once. The water wasn't quite the right temperature and the whole thing washed down the drain.'

'Yes, it was tricky. Made beautiful prints, though, when you got it right. Permanent colour. No one makes the materials anymore.'

'And no one processes Kodachrome. The world's changing, Sam.'

'Yes. Do you like it?'

'No. But they didn't consult me.'

He was silent, looking around at his precious darkroom, perhaps soon to be dark forever. Then he looked at me. 'Dorothy, are you afraid of me?'

'No, I don't believe I am,' I said after a moment's thought.

'You were jumpy a little while ago.'

'Yes. It was dark and I didn't know anything about you.'

'And old Chandler was probably murdered. Am I right about that?'

'Possibly. I really know very little about it.' I mentally crossed my fingers, though what I said was, technically, true. I didn't *know* very much at all. Surmises don't count, do they?

'I imagine you know more than you're saying. And I imagine you also know why I'd be a prime suspect.'

'From what I can gather, nearly everyone in the department had a reason to dislike him, at least.'

'The budget. Yes. But it wasn't just that.' He hitched one hip up on to the enlarging bench. 'You see, most of us in Fine Arts here are traditionalists, at least when it comes to technique. We believe in teaching our students the old ways first. They can learn the new methods anywhere, but the art school here at Sherebury has always been a bastion of conservatism. Just as Picasso had to learn to draw properly before he could branch out into Cubism, so we train young artists in traditional methods and then encourage them to march to their own drummers. But Chandler was changing all that. He hadn't been here very long, you know.'

'I didn't know, actually.'

'Oh, yes, it would have been three years at the beginning of this term. The old head was getting past it, and I know Dennis thought he'd be promoted, but it didn't work out that way. Chandler was an award-winning architect, won the Marlowe several years ago, so it was thought he'd bring prestige to the art school. I suppose he did. He was expected to bring in students, too, but that didn't go so well. A few new architecture students came, but they didn't stay long. That was when he began cutting the budget and making gentle and then not-so-gentle hints that our teaching methods were outmoded. It all came to a head at the last staff meeting, when he not only cut all our materials budgets by half – *half,* mind you – but also told us all, in so many words, that we were "mired in the backwater" of art, that our work was not "relevant" to today's world. Not content with insulting our art, he fired a nasty personal slur at . . . well, I'll let you find that out for yourself. But by the end of that meeting, when Dennis and I went out to drown our troubles, the only soul on this staff who wasn't ready to do murder was William Braithwaite.'

'Pity,' I said. 'He's the only one I've met so far that I'd like to nail.'

'Me, too. Now, dear lady-who-likes-photographers, who on the staff haven't you met?'

'I don't know who all is on the staff. I've met Dennis, and that painter person, and Gillian, and you.'

'That just leaves Matt, our printmaker, of the senior staff. And of course poor Amy. You know about her, do you?'

'That's the secretary? Yes, I've heard, and it makes my blood boil. Do you think there's any possibility she might get her job back?'

'Not so long as darling William is in charge.'

'Then I wish he'd be thrown *out* of charge.'

'Agreed, but it's not so easy. Anyway, would you like to meet Matt? I think he's working today, and that would round out your list of suspects.'

'Or non-suspects, as the case may be. Sure.'

Another half-blind trek through dark, labyrinthine corridors. The difference was that this time I had confidence in my guide. I remembered a sign my husband had once had hanging in his darkroom: Photographers do it in the dark. I giggled.

'What's funny?'

'Nothing. That was a half-sneeze. It's dusty in here.'

'The cleaners haven't been since term ended. Another austerity measure.'

'Not a very intelligent one, it seems to me.'

Sam grunted, apparently in agreement.

The print rooms were up one more floor. Sam made no attempt to take me up in the elevator, and I certainly didn't mention it.

I had been in the print department briefly on the day of Gillian's party, but I didn't remember a lot of the layout, so I let Sam lead me.

'Matt! A visitor!' Sam's voice was less stentorian than Dennis's, but just as effective. I gathered it was the done thing to shout for one's colleague rather than go in search. I could understand that when it came to photography. The cardinal sin is to open a darkroom door. But the other arts? I shrugged and let Sam do it his way.

After a bit a small, dark, intense young man came around a corner, wiping his hands on a rag. 'Sorry, I was pulling a print and couldn't stop in the midst of it.' He looked at me enquiringly.

'Matt, this is Dorothy Something, who found Chandler's body and wants to meet everyone who hated him.'

I've had more pleasant introductions, but Matt just laughed and extended a hand. 'Matt Thomas. Don't mind our Sam. He likes to twist tails.'

'Dorothy Martin's the name.'

'And you're American.'

'I was. I've lived in England for quite a while now, and I'm married to an Englishman, but apparently I'll never lose the accent. And you're Welsh.'

'By my accent or my name?'

'Both, and your appearance.'

'Most Americans can't tell the difference. They think everyone in the UK looks alike and speaks the same way.'

'Oh, come now! Even the first-time visitor can tell the difference between, say, the Queen and a Glaswegian.'

'Point taken. But you're more astute than some English. Of course the English have hated the Welsh for centuries.'

'And vice-versa, I believe. Why are we talking about ethnic differences?'

'You started it.' We both laughed.

'I'll leave you to it, then,' said Sam, and disappeared.

EIGHT

Once again I was alone with a strange man in a strange place. I was going to have to edit a lot when I told Alan where I'd been and what I'd been doing.

Or maybe not. Maybe I'd just tell him I had been a bit foolish, and let him fuss. It's rather pleasant, actually, to have someone care what I do.

'Are you really looking for a murderer, Ms Martin? Or is it Mrs?'

'Mrs, but I prefer Dorothy. And I don't honestly know quite what I'm doing. I don't even know for certain that Mr Chandler was murdered, but I'm finding it hard to escape the unhappy fact that I was in the elevator when it landed on the poor man's body. They say he'd been dead quite a time when that happened, but I still take some personal interest, if not a smidgen of guilt.'

'If you've been talking to the staff, I'm sure you've come to the conclusion that guilt isn't quite the term any of us would use.'

'I did get the impression that he wasn't popular,' I said cautiously.

'About as popular, my granny used to say, as an Alsatian in a room full of cats.'

'That's one I've never heard.'

'Not surprising, as I just made it up. Would you like to see some of my work?'

Of course there's only one answer to that, and I obligingly provided it. 'Very much.'

We went into the large classroom/studio where the paraphernalia for various printmaking methods littered tables and benches. Stone slabs I thought were probably lithograph stones were stacked in an open-shelved cupboard made of some very sturdy wood. A workbench had a shelf above it where small tools were ordered neatly. From my teaching days I recognized sharp knives of the sort I used to use for linoleum-block prints; I assumed these were used for the more professional woodcuts. Other tools I didn't recognize at all, but guessed they were part of the etching process, or engraving, or any of the many, many other ways to make reproducible works of art.

They all looked very clean. 'You said you were pulling a print just now. What's your favourite genre of printing?'

'I've grown to love monotypes. Do you know what a monotype is?'

'Just barely. Mono meaning one, it's a one-off print, but I don't know more than that, really.'

'One creates a painting on a hard surface, usually a zinc plate, but almost anything, really, so long as the surface is essentially impermeable. You don't want the paint or ink to soak in. And then you lay paper on top, put the thing in a press, and voilà. There's your print.'

'But why bother? You could just as well paint straight on to the paper, and it would be a lot easier.'

'True. But there's a quality to a monotype that simply can't be achieved with direct painting. Here, take a look.'

He walked me around the room, showing me prints that were certainly lovely, but to my untutored eye not very different from an ordinary watercolour. Then, in a different section, was a display of breathtaking woodcuts. 'But these are incredible!' I exclaimed. 'They remind me of Dürer.'

'Just imitation of his style,' said Matt, waving his hand. 'Nothing original about them.'

'Except of course the subject matter,' I said drily. 'I haven't seen too many Dürers featuring Volkswagens.'

'Oh, well, there's something about a Beetle that just seems to cry out for the technique, don't you think? Now would you like to see my etchings?' He twirled an imaginary moustache and spoke in as lecherous a tone as he could manage.

'Along with a little Madeira, m'dear? Lead on.' I couldn't have told you quite why, but by now I was convinced that I, or any other woman, would be perfectly safe viewing Matt's etchings, even in a more romantic setting.

The etchings, like all Matt's other work, were exquisite. Small in size and extremely delicate in workmanship, they reminded me of a tiny Renoir I'd seen once in a museum, of two women trying on hats, one helping the other. It had been somewhat fuzzy in outline, though, soft, like many of Renoir's paintings. Matt's were crisp and clean, and often featured nude or semi-nude men, which tended to confirm my suppositions.

When we'd completed the tour, I sat on a grubby chair in the studio. 'Matt, you're a superb artist. Was your horrible head after you to change your methods, like all the other staff?'

'Oh, yes. He wanted all this—' he swept a hand in a wide arc – 'done away with. Outmoded techniques. Time-consuming. Expensive. I was to teach the modern version of printmaking, the *zheeclay* print.'

I pictured the word in my mind as he had pronounced it. 'What on earth is that?'

'Highfalutin name for a computer printout. Spelt g-i-c-l-é-e, with an accent. French for squirt. Also French for . . . well, never mind. They're made on ink-jet printers, which squirt out the colour in tiny dots. If you have a good graphics program and a first-rate printer, you can get some good results. We have neither. The students do the best they can, and some of the work they produce looks gorgeous on the screen, and then they print it and it looks like a bad copy of a magazine page. An *old* magazine page.'

'How discouraging for them, after all that work.'

'And the worst of it is that the damn machines can make thousands of copies, so the concept of a limited edition turns to nonsense. Or no, that's not the worse of it. The worst is the soullessness. I make a woodcut, let's say, and I'm involved in it, start to finish. I choose the wood, and the tools I'll use. I draw the picture on the wood and cut it, and curse when the tool slips and I cut a gouge where I didn't want it. Put the spoiled block on the fire and start over. I make the print. It's mine, start to finish. If it's bad, I am solely to blame. If it's good, I can claim the honour.'

'I'll bet it's usually good. You're a gifted artist, Matt, and you know it perfectly well.'

'Yes, well,' he muttered, embarrassed by the compliment. 'I try to teach the students proper technique. Then it's up to them. If they have a good eye and a hand that will realize their vision, they produce good work, and they can take pride in it. Artists *and* craftsmen, following in the footsteps of all who came before.'

'That's a very English slant on the world. Or, sorry, British. You Brits revere the past, at least the good parts, and you have deep respect for tradition and those who passed it along, especially the artists and artisans. On the one hand, people like the thatchers, who have practised their craft for centuries and passed the secrets down to their successors, are honoured in villages all over the UK. At the other extreme are the great architects who planned and built the medieval cathedrals, whose names we may not even know, but whose work still stands, loved and admired and preserved at enormous cost. I think the abiding attribute of those workers was love. They loved their work and its results, and that love adds a quality that can never, never be seen in anything mass-produced. Oh, I'm saying this badly!'

'I know what you mean, though. Those old chaps not only loved their work, they respected it, and that meant they respected themselves and would never, could never, pass off anything shoddy. They'd work till they'd got it right.'

'Which is why it's lasted for centuries, and will for centuries longer. Whereas . . .' I looked at a corner of the studio, where the paint was cracking and peeling from damp. 'I must say, I don't understand why the head, who I'm told was an architect, didn't have something done about this building. He couldn't have made it beautiful, but he might have fought for some repairs. Surely he understood that things like this could end by making the whole place structurally unsound.'

'One might think so, but one might be wrong, mightn't one? Chandler won the Marlowe thirty years ago, and to my certain knowledge he's done nothing notable since. Those laurels he was resting on were getting most frightfully withered and crushed. The wonder isn't that someone heaved him down the shaft, it's that they took so perishing long to do it.'

'Is that what you think happened?'

'Well, he didn't get there all by himself, did he? I do assure you, our late unlamented head was not in the least suicidal. He thought entirely too much of himself for that. *And* he wouldn't have wanted to give us the satisfaction. He knew none of us could abide him, and the longer he remained among us, the longer he had to make our lives miserable.'

His tone had changed. I studied him for a moment and then

said, 'There's something else, isn't there? More than just his miserly ways and his aversion to traditional methods in art.'

'Yes. The man was an outright sadist, the sort who probably tore the wings off butterflies as a child. And an implacable homophobe.'

This time it was his gaze studying me, watching my reaction. I took a deep breath. 'What form did it take? Sleazy jokes? Veiled threats?'

'Neither. He couldn't threaten me with exposure; I came out years ago. And the man wouldn't have recognized a joke if it had come and bitten him on the bum. No, just barbed remarks. Constantly. At the last staff meeting he implied that I . . . sought relationships with my students. He knew perfectly well that I had lived in a committed relationship for many years. My partner was killed a few months ago. Chandler knew I was grieving, and yet he had the bloody cheek to accuse me of casual affairs, and with the students! I could have killed him then! I wish I had.'

'I'm glad you didn't, Matt. I won't say I can understand the temptation, because I've never had anyone hurt me that badly. I can imagine, though. I'm so sorry about your partner. How did he die? If you don't mind talking about it.'

'No. It's a bit of a relief, actually. At the time I couldn't even think about it, but I've begun to want to get it out, get the poison out of my system. It was all so sordid and unnecessary. We'd been out to dinner. There weren't a lot of places we could go together, because he was Kenyan, you see. Born in England, but of Kenyan parents.'

'Oh, my. Not just dark-skinned, but *very* dark?'

'Black as jet. The most beautiful skin . . .'

I waited.

'And there's still some prejudice of that sort, too. His people didn't like my colour; my people didn't like his. We had to be careful on that score, not to mention that we were a gay couple. There were a few little places where we always felt comfortable and they knew us, and mostly we went to one of those. But that night was my birthday, and Phil – his African name was Pili, but Phil was easier here – he wanted to take me someplace special, so we decided to try a new wine bar not far from here.'

'There was trouble?'

'From the first. We walked in, and we could see from the look on the proprietor's face that we weren't welcome. I don't know whether it was his colour, or because we were obviously a couple. I would have turned around and left, but Phil was in a funny mood, ready to brazen it out. We were told there was no table available, when we could see the room was three-quarters empty. Phil just started to walk to a table and sit down, but two men stood up and got in his way, and . . . .'

'You don't have to tell me the whole thing, Matt. There was a fight.'

'It turned into almost a riot. The two men pushed us out into the street and got into brawl with Phil, who's – who was a fine fighter. Strong. Muscular. He held his own, but then some louts from the neighbourhood joined in, and one of them had a knife, and before the police could get there . . .'

He made no attempt to wipe the tears from his eyes. They rolled down his cheeks. He swallowed a sob.

I rummaged in my purse for a tissue, and when he had his face under control, handed it to him. He took it without looking at me.

'I don't know what to say, Matt. That's a terrible story. And to have the head taunting you, so soon after . . . well, all I can say is, if anyone ever deserved his fate, it was Chandler. I've disturbed you long enough. I'll leave you to your work, and your grief.'

He murmured something, and I turned and left the room. I fumbled on the corridor wall and found a light switch, and kept finding them and turning them on as I made my way down the stairs and out of the building. Let someone else worry about the electricity that was being wasted.

I took a deep breath of lovely, crisp September air. It was good to get out of that mausoleum of slain hopes and shattered lives.

NINE

'Well, I met them all,' I said to Alan as we sat down to a late lunch. 'The whole staff, I mean. At least the full-time ones.'

'And?'

'And I like them all, a lot. Except for William Braithwaite, the painter.'

'Doesn't he do those abstract things in brilliant colours, sort of a cross between Jackson Pollock and Mondrian?'

'And oh, how he'd hate the comparison! The main difference, as far as I can see, is that both those painters had talent.'

'Ouch. But I agree. I can't abide his work, though I gather it sells like hot cakes. Why didn't you like him?'

'Other than the facts that he's conceited, rude, a bigot and a sexual predator?'

Alan blinked. 'I don't suppose you'd care to expand on those remarks?'

'Finish your sandwich first. You won't want it after you've heard all the stories. Let me tell you about the others, first. Well, you met Dennis, the sculptor and Gillian's mentor.'

I told him about Dennis's problems with Chandler, the man's refusal even to consider Dennis's promotion. 'I can't make myself feel sorry the man's dead, Alan. I kept uncovering one layer of nastiness after another. He was bleeding the budget white in all the areas except painting. He apparently thought Braithwaite was such an asset to the department that he should get the lion's share. And he killed, or tried to kill, the artistic integrity of everyone else on the staff, by insisting that they abandon the way they'd always taught and embrace new methods entirely foreign to their . . . I nearly said, to their beliefs, and I'm not sure that isn't the word. Art is a religion to all these men, and Chandler was, as far as they were concerned, preaching heresy.'

'Plenty of scope there for hatred to grow.'

'Even that wasn't all of it.' I started ticking off items on my fingers. 'Dennis's academic ambitions, dismissed as not even worth Chandler's notice. Then there's Sam, who loathed Chandler's insistence that the photography students abandon film and go entirely digital. Matt, the printmaker, is gay and lost his partner in a horrible incident in the spring, and Chandler kept taking swipes at him, suggesting in public that Matt was trying it on with his students. Matt told me about it this morning; I left the poor man in tears.'

'So.' Alan pushed aside his plate. 'You said I'd lose my appetite over stories about the painter. So far, Chandler's done pretty well in that department.'

'Yes. Sorry. But wait till you hear what William, well, he and Chandler together, did to a poor defenceless secretary.'

I told the story, growing more and more agitated. 'And Alan,' I finished, 'she lost her husband just after she was fired, and she has two young children to support, and no references. How's she ever going to get another job?'

Alan whistled. 'She should talk to a lawyer.'

'Of course she should, but lawyers cost money. Anyway, it's just a case of he said/she said. She can't prove anything. Oh, and Alan, I didn't tell you that now William's going after Gillian! I told her she should carry a recorder with her and try to tape him, or whatever they call it now. If she had solid evidence of inappropriate behaviour, maybe the sleaze could be brought down. Would that help the secretary at all, do you think?'

'Perhaps. These things are chancy, as I'm sure you know. Misconduct is, as you say, difficult to prove, absent pictures or recordings, and even if the victim has those, the defence is apt to claim entrapment. But to get back to the real problem—'

'This problem is real enough!'

'To the original problem, then, if you prefer – you got no sense of which of the staff might have murdered Chandler?'

'They all had reason to hate him. All except the painter, that is. Dear William was getting everything he wanted from Chandler. Although Gillian said a funny thing. Not amusing, I don't mean, but odd. She overheard a conversation just at the end of last term. She hadn't been around enough then to know who was speaking, but now she's sure Will was one of them, and Chandler must have been the other.' I related what Gillian had heard, and the conclusion she had drawn from it.

'Hmm. Odd, indeed. I wish she could remember the exact words.'

'Yes. But it was weeks ago, and she was nervous, afraid she shouldn't be there, someone would catch her, all that. What she seems quite sure about is that there was something wrong about the encounter, something just a little off-key, somehow.'

'And she's sure it was Braithwaite and Chandler.'

'She's sure about Braithwaite, since she's now heard his voice entirely too often. She had met Chandler only once, at her interview, and couldn't be certain. But the two men were in Chandler's office.'

'And she had the notion that Braithwaite was pressing Chandler for money.'

'That was what it sounded like to her. And Chandler was saying he couldn't – oh! You don't think . . .?'

'I think I should talk to Gillian myself. But it sounds uncommonly like it, doesn't it?'

'But . . . but then it's all wrong! A blackmailer doesn't kill the victim, the goose that's laying all those nice golden eggs. It's the goose who goes after the blackmailer.'

'Usually, I agree. But we know nothing of the circumstances. It sounds a bit as if the worm had turned. And before we get into any more zoological analogies, I think it might be a good idea to consult the SIA.'

I just looked at him.

'The Sherebury Intelligence Agency. In other words . . .'

'Jane!'

Jane Langland, our next-door neighbour, is, like me, a retired teacher. She combines the appearance of Winston Churchill, or the bulldogs she adores, with a gruff manner and the softest heart I've ever known. No human or animal in need has ever been turned away from her door. She's lived in Sherebury all her life and knows everyone; most of the residents were in her classroom at one time or another. She brings us baked goods now and then, bread and pastries fit for the gods. She gives me cuttings from her garden, and advice about how to talk Bob Finch into planting them. She takes in our mail and looks after our animals if we have to go away. She is invaluable.

And, as Alan implied, she is a one-woman information bureau.

I don't know how she does it. Of course her old-boys and old-girls network helps, but I've often said Jane knows everything that happens in Sherebury, sometimes even before it happens.

I found a box of chocolates someone had given me, that I'd put away to stave off temptation. When it comes to home-made goodies I'm no match for Jane, and I know it, but she loves good chocolates. With our offering, Alan and I walked through the back garden to Jane's kitchen door.

After the usual barrage of enthusiastic canine greetings, we settled down at Jane's kitchen table, where we'd had so many casual meals, so many conversations. I proffered the chocolates. 'In payment for services about to be rendered, we hope.'

'Thought you'd be coming round about now. Coffee's ready.'

Add clairvoyance to Jane's attributes.

'This business at the university, is it?' she said when she had poured the coffee, opened the chocolates and set them temptingly before us.

'Of course,' said Alan. 'This is one of those cases where there's unlikely to be much physical evidence. The general public doesn't know this, but the police aren't even at all sure what killed the man. They think it was some sort of poison, but they'll have to run a whole battery of tests to find out what, and even that may not produce results.'

'Not the fall or the stabbing,' said Jane. It wasn't a question. 'Stands to reason. One or t'other. Not both.'

'Exactly. So until they learn what it actually was – *if* they learn what it actually was – we've little to go on except the characters of the people involved. So what can you tell us about the staff at the Wolfson College of Art and Design?'

'Chandler. Met him once or twice, didn't know him well. Not from around here. Didn't care for what I saw. Bully.'

For Jane, that was an unusually stern judgement. 'Where was he from, then? Where did he get his education?'

'Came from the Midlands somewhere, studied for a while at Oxford, then went to America. Studied architecture there and then taught at . . . Harvard? Yale? One of that sort.'

'If he taught at either of those universities he must have been highly qualified. They're not Oxford or Cambridge, of course, but they're highly regarded.'

Thus spoke my husband, who occasionally displays his quite unconscious, and quite natural, bias toward all things English. Harvard and Yale are quite nice little schools, for the colonies. I kept a straight face. 'Yes, they do have rather good reputations. A good many American presidents have been graduated from one or the other. Which makes me wonder. Both those universities have very stringent entry requirements, and hundreds, if not thousands, of applicants for every one they accept. From what I've gathered, Chandler seemed to be a mediocre sort of person, at least academically. How in the world did he get into such a prestigious school?'

'Not sure it was one of those. Might have been one like them. Are there such places?'

Good heavens! We'd hit a vein of information about which Jane was less than fully informed. 'There's a group of colleges – sorry, universities to you – that are popularly known as the Ivy League. Harvard and Yale are two of them, the two oldest, I believe. I know for certain that Harvard is America's oldest university, founded in sixteen-something, if I'm correct. Then there's Dartmouth and Princeton and . . . oh, dear, I can't remember the rest. They're all in the east, all very well respected and all extremely expensive. Could Chandler have taught at one of those?'

Jane shrugged. Alan cleared his throat. 'I think we need to look into it. Surely the art school would have his credentials on record. As Dorothy says, it seems just a little peculiar that he should have been able to land a teaching position in that sort of university. However, let's press on.'

'Won the Marlowe Award for Architecture while he was in America. Designed some bank or whatnot in New York.'

'I've been meaning to ask,' I said. 'What's the Marlowe Award? I never heard of it.'

'Don't know. A lot of privately endowed awards in the art world. Ask at the college.'

'Whatever it is, it would explain the job at the celebrated university, if it happened before his appointment there,' said Alan. 'Did it?'

Jane shrugged again. 'Don't know. Don't think so. Think he came back to England directly after he collected the honours. Mooched around for a bit and then came to Sherebury as head.'

Alan had been making notes. 'Right. Anything juicy in his background?'

'Not that I've heard. You think there is?'

Jane was entirely trustworthy. I spoke up. 'Jane, we think it's possible that he was being blackmailed. We'd like to know why.'

She shook her head, somewhat regretfully, I thought. 'Haven't heard anything like that. Put out some feelers?'

'Please,' said Alan. He didn't have to tell her to be discreet. 'Now. The next man I'd like to know about is William Braithwaite.'

'Ah.' Jane settled back. 'W.T. Braithwaite. The "painter".'

I couldn't have said what about Jane's tone put quotation marks around the word, but they were certainly there. 'You don't like his work.'

'Masses of people do. Made a fortune off them.'

I hadn't thought about that aspect of it. 'But if he's made a fortune, what's he doing teaching in a small place like Sherebury? I mean, I think it's probably a pretty good art school, but it isn't exactly the Slade. For that matter, why's he teaching at all, if he could be making a lot more money devoting all his time to painting?'

Jane lifted her hands in an elaborate shrug. 'Only know what I'm told.'

I was reminded of Will Rogers, who reputedly only knew what he read in the papers. 'All right, what are you told about William Braithwaite?'

'Got an expensive wife. Isn't faithful to her. Expensive tastes, too. New car. New house. Travels. First-class swine.'

Translating from Jane's always moderate language, I could imagine several more pungent terms.

'Heard his paintings aren't selling as well. Might need to retrench.'

'That's very useful, Jane. He might be in financial difficulties?'

Again the shrug.

'Very well. Anything about the rest of the staff?'

'Well-liked, even if they are artistic. Lot of sympathy for Thomas.'

Alan looked at me questioningly.

'Matt Thomas, the printmaker whose partner was killed.'

'Nice chap,' said Jane. 'No excuse.'

No. There never is any excuse for mindless violence. I didn't even want to think about it. I wondered if Jeremy Sayers, the Cathedral organist, could supply any more insights about Matt and the tragedy. Jeremy's gay and in a long-term relationship, and in a small place like Sherebury, he would certainly have known of Matt and his partner.

'Don't know much about the rest. Try to find out.' Jane stood. 'Can't say I'm weeping over Chandler's death. Not a good man.'

And that, from Jane, was equivalent to calling him several highly unprintable names.

TEN

'Some useful pointers there,' said Alan as we walked back across the garden.

'Nothing to follow up on immediately, though.'

'Except Chandler's academic credentials. They sound ever so slightly dodgy to me. I shall suggest that Derek track them down.'

'And I'm going to go over and ask Jeremy what he knows about Matt and his partner, Phil. He'd know. The gay community isn't that big in Sherebury.'

'Good idea. I'll see you when I see you, then. Oh, and I meant to say. Pettifer's going to send one of his men over this afternoon to take a look at our water problem. He wasn't very encouraging. Said it might mean replacing the lot.'

'Oh, good grief, and they'll have to be custom-made to match the originals, and they'll cost a fortune. Why in the world did I ever want to live in a four-hundred-year-old listed building?'

'Because you love it, dear heart. Off you go.'

He went into the house and I made off across the close to the Cathedral.

I've always thought of it as the 'Cathedral', capital C. It isn't just a building, it's a living presence, a benevolent giant watching over Sherebury. The bells are its voice, chiming out the hours and joyously pealing on Sundays and special occasions, raising a glorious cacophony on the eight venerable bells that have praised God for time out of mind.

Only two bells were ringing as I crossed the grass, and as I approached the south door they stopped and the hour chimed. Three o'clock. Drat. I hadn't noticed that it was time for Evensong. No speaking to Jeremy now. I could sit in the back of the church and listen till the service was over, or perhaps the verger would let me linger in the choir transept. There was a convenient tomb I could lean on.

The verger, fortunately, was one I knew well. 'A bit late, Mrs

Martin,' he whispered. The procession had just entered, the choir singing lustily.

'I know. May I stay here?'

'Mind you don't let the tourists see you,' he said with a chuckle, and moved back down the aisle to ward some of them off. Touring the Cathedral is not allowed during a service, because the noise would interfere with worship.

I was content to lean on Lady Annabel, beloved wife of Sir Jonathan Brinton, whose eight children knelt at her side in unlikely proportion, having probably contributed to her death at age thirty-two in 1753. The children were a bit knobbly. I shifted my position slightly as the choir launched into a beautiful setting of the psalm for the day.

English cathedral choirs are known throughout the world for their superb musicianship, and the unique sound of the boy soprano voice lends an ethereal quality. No matter how well I know that the boys are anything but little angels, are indeed a torment to their director, I am wafted straight to heaven when they sing.

Much of the service is spoken, not sung, however, and I was getting a bit tired of Lady Annabel and her progeny by the time the presiding canon pronounced the final blessing and Jeremy took up a lively voluntary.

The choirboys filed past me, their impatience curbed by the stately pace of the verger leading them out. The choir men followed, then the clergy, and then Jeremy concluded with a final flourish and came down from the organ loft and out into the aisle where I lurked.

'Dorothy! I didn't see you in there.'

'I got here too late. Actually I hadn't realized it was time for Evensong. I wanted to talk to you. Do you have a few minutes?'

'I do, in fact. Christopher's busy at the uni, with the new term just beginning, and won't be home until quite late, so I'm on my lonesome the rest of the day.'

'In that case, why don't you come over as soon as you've divested – that sounds like a stock transaction. Disrobed? Even worse. Anyway, when you've got out of your vestments, come and have some tea with us.'

'You're sleuthing again, aren't you? That art teacher?'

'Come and find out.'

I'd barely had time to switch on the kettle and put some muffins in the toaster when Jeremy was knocking at the door, which was open. 'Come on in,' I called from the kitchen, 'and tell me what you'd like to eat.'

'Oh, some lovely cucumber sandwiches and perhaps an eclair or two would do nicely.'

'"I'm sorry, sir. There were no cucumbers in the market. Not even for ready money."'

He laughed and sat down at the kitchen table. 'Bread and butter, then?'

'With perhaps even a bit of jam.' I buttered the toasted muffins, made the tea and rummaged in the cupboard for a jar of homemade marmalade I'd bought at the last church fête and a pan of brownies I'd made the day before. If I do say so, I make excellent brownies.

Alan came to join us, and we settled down to enjoy our tea and far more carbohydrates than I needed in a week.

'Right,' said Jeremy briskly, 'now you want me to tell you all I know, and all Christopher knows, about the Art College Murder.'

'You're making it sound like the title of a thriller,' Alan objected. 'Nancy Drew, perhaps.'

'Oh, no,' I objected. 'Nobody was ever murdered in a Nancy Drew. They were written for children, remember. Nancy nearly bought it at least twice in every book, but she always foiled the villains by her combination of a clever mind with an intrepid spirit and amazing athletic abilities. Trust me. I read every one of them when I was young.'

'That,' said Alan drily, 'may help explain your present taste in literature and activity.'

I gave him an evil look. 'What I really wanted to ask, Jeremy, is what you know about Matt Thomas, the printmaker at the college, and his partner.'

Well, that darkened the atmosphere. Jeremy put his muffin back on the plate. 'Poor Matt! We all felt dreadful for him. Well, not quite all. There are bigots in the gay community, too, and a few had been spiteful about Phil all along. But when that frightful thing happened, anyone who hadn't thought Phil was quite the thing had the sense to keep quiet about it.'

'Do you think the attack was mostly on account of his race or his lifestyle?' I asked.

'Equal parts of both, I'd say, with drink to set the match to the fuse. My friends are just a teensy bit upset that no one has ever been arrested for it.'

'Bigotry exists in the police force, too, I'm sorry to say,' said Alan heavily. 'But to be fair, it's nearly impossible to pin down responsibility for the actions of a mob. No one will talk, or if they do, they claim they can't remember exactly what happened.'

'Which may be true, Alan. You know how confused things can get in the middle of a crowd. You can't see properly over everyone's heads. Well, maybe *you* can, but people of ordinary size can't. And there's noise, and lots of things happening at once. And I'm not even talking about a riot, just something like the Christmas sales in London, or a football game.'

'Our sort of football game,' Alan retorted, 'can be indistinguishable from a riot. I don't know about your American ones. But I take your point.'

'Jeremy, how is Matt dealing with it? I saw him today, and he seemed to be okay as long as we talked about art. But then he told me about Phil, and how horribly Chandler had been treating him, and he . . . well, he sort of fell apart.'

'I don't know him well. Christopher knows him better, though the Wolfson lot don't mix that much with the rest of the university staff.'

Christopher taught English literature, specializing in very early works in Middle English. I stood in awe of him. I've never been able to read Chaucer except in translation.

'I've heard, though,' Jeremy went on, 'that Matt is extremely depressed. As you gathered, he turns to art for solace, and with Chandler pulling the rug out from under his funding, and treating him like dirt into the bargain, his closest friends have begun to watch him pretty closely.'

'Suicide watch, you mean?' asked Alan sharply.

'We-ell . . .' Jeremy wriggled uncomfortably. 'Perhaps not quite that serious, but they're worried that he might do something . . . reckless, let's say.'

Alan leaned toward him. 'As reckless as throwing his boss down a lift shaft?'

Jeremy sighed. 'I have no idea. I just don't know him well enough, really. I'll ask Christopher. For what it's worth, I've had the impression that Matt's too sunk in his own misery to do anything more decisive than choose which wood to carve for his next print. He's quite good at woodcuts, by the way, did you know?'

'Quite good! Jeremy, he could give Dürer a run for his money.'

Alan cocked a sceptical eyebrow.

'Truly!' I insisted. 'You wait till you see them. Intricate, delicate, powerful . . . you just wait.'

Alan shook his head. 'And this is the man Chandler wanted to restrict to computer-generated prints. Dorothy, I think I'd like a little whisky instead of this tea.'

So of course that led to everyone having a drink, after which we invited Jeremy to supper, most of which he cooked. He's a superb cook, the sort who can walk into someone else's kitchen, find a little of this and some of that, and turn it all into a marvellous meal.

When he'd gone home and Alan and I had cleaned up the kitchen, we sat around the fire, for the evening had turned chilly. Watson snoozed at my feet and the cats chose a lap each and purred themselves to sleep. The humans sipped a little sherry and talked about John Chandler and Matt Thomas.

'That poor man. I'm worried about him, Alan. If his friends think he might be suicidal, no matter how Jeremy tried to gloss it over, he just may be. And apart from any humane considerations, it would be a dreadful loss to art. If he's this good at thirty or so, one can only dream of what he could still do. That's one reason I feel it's urgent that we help the police about this all we can.'

'And if he's the murderer? He has one of the best motives.'

'I know, but I'm still convinced he had nothing to do with it. You've not seen his work, but I have. You know art reveals an enormous amount about the artist. You take a look at those woodcuts and then tell me if the man who created them could do murder.'

'I'll do that, but I remain unconvinced. If he's devoted to his art, and knows he's good, and knew Chandler was virtually shutting him down . . . I don't know, Dorothy.'

'I'm trying to get a feeling for what made Chandler tick,' I mused after a long silence. 'Why would he gather a group of talented artists and teachers around him and then frustrate them at every turn?'

'Is that what he did? Gather them, that is? Or were they already there when he was plumped down in the midst of them?'

I tried to search my memory. 'I don't think Jane mentioned anything about it, and I can't recall what the rest of the college staff said.'

'One more thing to look into,' said Alan drowsily.

'I don't know that it makes a whole lot of difference, one way or another. The point is that he was perverting the whole notion of art, of creativity. I suppose it would make him even more cruel if he had brought them there with rosy promises, and then proceeded to cut them off at the knees. But why? And why give that ass William Braithwaite free rein, when for my money he's the least talented, and for anybody's money the most obnoxious, of the lot?'

It was a more-or-less rhetorical question, but I looked at Alan for his reaction.

His reaction was a light snore.

I carefully removed Emmy from my lap, which she did not appreciate, poked the fire to extinguish it, spread an afghan over Alan, and went to bed.

ELEVEN

Sometime after I'd gone to sleep, Alan came up and joined me. He barely woke me, but it must have been then that my dreams, which had been vaguely pleasant, changed to the uneasy 'mission unfulfilled' sort. I didn't remember the details in the morning, but they involved tasks that couldn't be completed because I hadn't the right tools or couldn't find the work site or whatever, or journeys that went nowhere because the road was closed or there was a flood in the way or I kept getting lost. I finally woke about five with a jerk, sitting straight up in bed and crying 'No!' and of course waking Alan.

He soothed me and went back to sleep. I tried, but after turning over and punching my pillow several times, I gave it up. I'd wakened Watson, anyway, who decided it was time to go out, and the cats, who were certain it was time to be fed.

Five a.m. is not my favourite time of day. I dealt with the animals, who were quite literally bright-eyed and bushy-tailed (except for Sam, who is mostly Siamese and has a slim, elegant tail that bushes only when she's furious), made myself coffee, and sat and brooded.

The list of suspects in Chandler's murder seemed extremely limited. He had to have been killed after the end of last term, which was in early July. I hadn't heard whether he went on his trip to Greece, but it didn't seem likely. He surely wouldn't go just for a week or two, not when he had a six-week break, and if he'd been gone longer and got back only a little while before term started, the body . . . . I swallowed. The autopsy would have revealed that.

So assume he died shortly after that unfortunate staff meeting. How shortly? If it was that same day, all the full-time staff and presumably some of the students would still be around. When, I wondered, had he planned to leave for Greece?

Well, Derek would find out all that. Watson whined outside the kitchen door; I let him in and gave him breakfast, which he wolfed down. He's learned that if he leaves any of his food, the cats will either eat it or scatter it all over the floor. His kibble comes in fairly big chunks, and they make wonderful cat toys.

Watson burped loudly and settled on his cushion for a nice little nap. I poured another cup of coffee and went back to my ruminating.

Four full-time staff. Three if you discount William, who was a rat but had no apparent motive. Four again, though, if you add in the secretary whose name I'd forgotten. She could have come back to plead with him, ask to be reinstated. He would have been flint-hearted, of course, and she could have lost her composure and lunged for him. And if the elevator shaft was open, for some reason . . .

It wouldn't work. A woman would have had a dreadful time hauling that body around. And why would the shaft be open?

Maybe someone was working on it. Gillian said it was 'wonky'. It was left open for the workmen and Chandler stumbled and fell through . . .

That wouldn't work, either. He wasn't killed by the fall. And if workmen had been around they would have done something about it.

Blast it all, what *did* kill the miserable man?

'I'm sure we'll know, sooner or later.' Alan came into the room and gave me a peck on the cheek.

'Oh, was I talking to myself?'

'And apparently with little satisfaction. Have you had breakfast?'

'No, just coffee. I couldn't get back to sleep, so I came down and fretted.' I craned my head around to see the kitchen clock. 'You're up early.'

'I rather thought I'd like to go to Early Service.'

'Oh! I'd forgotten it was Sunday. That's a good idea, Early Service.'

'Then you'd best get yourself moving, darling. I've showered; I'll organize breakfast.'

Alan not only *can* cook, he does. Frequently. Every woman's dream.

When I got down he'd made a fresh pot of coffee and was just finishing scrambled eggs. 'There's cinnamon toast in the oven keeping nice and warm for you. Comfort food, to cheer you up.' The dear man hates cinnamon toast, or any hot-buttered toast. Toast for him is served in a little rack to make sure it gets cold as soon as possible, and is then spread with nice cold butter and marmalade. But he indulges my peculiar American tastes, and even remembers, sometimes, to put ice in my cold drinks.

The bells began as we were clearing away, so we hurried a little through the misty morning and made it to our regular seats in the choir stalls just as the bells stopped.

There is no music at the early Eucharist. I love our superb choir, but there are times when the simple solemnity of the lovely old Book of Common Prayer is exactly what I need. Then, too, there is profound peace in a place where God has been worshipped for centuries. Whatever cares and woes have been brought to this place in the past hundreds of years are cured now, their sufferers at rest in the churchyard, or in heaven, depending on one's beliefs. Certainly they are in distress no more. The short years of a human lifetime are as nothing compared to the enduring stones of the great church.

In this exalted mood I stepped out, with Alan, into a morning as dismal as any England can produce, and that's saying something. The autumnal mist that had pearled the air earlier had turned to a dreary mizzle. Not as definite as rain, not as innocuous as mist, it can carry on for days on end at this time of year. One becomes wet to the skin in a matter of minutes, and an umbrella is of little use, since the slimy dampness is everywhere. I clung to Alan, hurrying as fast as we could over the treacherous paving stones to our gate.

A car pulled up in front of our house just as we reached the door, and a man stepped out. He was so swathed in mackintosh and black rain hat that it took me a moment to recognize him as Jeremy's partner, Christopher Lewis.

'Good grief, Christopher, come in and get warm. What a nasty day this turned out to be!'

He came in, but didn't take off his coat and hat. 'I'm quite warm, thank you. I wrapped up because I take a chill easily, and I wanted to avert it if possible. I won't stay. I just thought you'd want to know that Matt Thomas seems to have disappeared.'

*   *   *

The story, conveyed in the few minutes Christopher could spare before he went to sing in the Cathedral choir, was simple and profoundly unsatisfactory. Some friends had invited Matt to dinner the night before, determined to try to keep him cheerful and occupied. He didn't show up, didn't phone. The friends had gone round to his house, an old cottage on the edge of town. It was dark; his car was gone. He had no near neighbours; the closest house was barely within sight, and they knew nothing. The friends went to the university. The Fine Arts building was dark and locked, but someone found a sympathetic guard who went in and looked. The only occupant he found was a mouse nesting in a broom cupboard.

'Has anyone called the police?' Alan asked.

'I thought someone had to be missing for twenty-four hours before they'd take notice.'

'There are extenuating circumstances,' said Alan, and his tone was grim. 'There, the bells are starting. You'd better go. I'll take it from here.'

Christopher dashed off, and I turned to Alan. 'Do you think . . .?'

'I think I'd better speak to Derek straight away. This could be nothing, but it could be very serious indeed.'

He pulled out his phone, found Derek's direct number, and placed the call. I stood there wondering what I could do, besides worry.

There was nothing useful to do in the house. We'd had a good breakfast and it was a long time before I needed to start thinking about lunch. The house was in reasonable order. I'd done the laundry a day or two ago. Gardening was out of the question in this weather.

None of the things, in short, that women do to keep busy and keep our minds off disagreeable thoughts were available to me just now. I went into the room that I choose to call our parlour and sank down on the couch. Watson was too sound asleep in the warm kitchen to sense that I was in need of comfort, and the cats were invisible.

Alan came into the room and started to build a fire. That was one of the things he did to stave off uncomfortable thoughts.

'What did Derek say?'

'He's concerned. Several scenarios come to mind, some of them not very favourable.'

'Matt's committed suicide out of grief. Or because he can't face the guilt of murdering Chandler. Or he saw who did it, and the murderer has killed him. Or he thinks he knows who did it and he's gone off to confront whoever it is. Or—'

Alan held up his hand. 'Enough, love. All of those things are possible. It's equally possible that the boy simply couldn't stand the atmosphere around the college anymore and has gone to the seaside for a breather.'

'Right.'

The fire was going nicely. Alan sat down beside me and put his arm around my shoulders. 'Derek's putting someone on it. The police will do everything possible. There's no point in worrying.'

'Right,' I said again.

The distress in our voices got through to Watson, who came trotting in and sat on my feet.

It was a very long day. The weather stayed grey and wet and miserable. I bestirred myself to open a can of soup and make some cheese sandwiches for lunch, but neither of us ate much. I tried to read, and after I'd been on the same page for ten minutes, without taking in a word, I put the book carefully back on the shelf. I wandered into the kitchen and thought about making a batch of cookies, but we had no chocolate chips, or oatmeal, or peanut butter, which disposed of my three favourites. I certainly wasn't going out to Tesco's in such rotten weather. I pulled out a crossword book and tried to concentrate, with conspicuous failure.

Alan retired to his den, where he turned on his computer and sat, presumably working on his memoirs. He's been writing them for ages, more as busywork than anything else, I suspected. Whenever I glanced in, he was sitting staring at the screen, hands idle, which didn't seem to indicate much progress.

By tea time I simply couldn't stand it anymore. Derek hadn't called. Nobody'd called. The only sound was Watson's snores and the steady drip, drip of the sodden world outside. I nudged Watson aside and stood up.

'Alan, we're going over to the college.'

'Yes,' he said, and shut off the computer.

Neither of us knew what we expected to accomplish there, but it had become simply impossible to sit doing nothing.

TWELVE

'There won't be anyone here on a Sunday afternoon,' I said as Alan pulled the car into a parking space.

'Probably not.' He fished the umbrellas out of the back seat and handed me mine. I got out of the car and put up the brolly, though I knew it would do little good. Moisture was everywhere, seeping into one's clothes and hair, into one's very pores. Not for the first time, I wished the car park were closer to the Fine Arts building.

The main door was locked. That was no surprise. 'Shall we try one of the other doors?' Alan suggested.

'Might as well try them all,' I said, trying not to sound as morose as I felt. 'We can't get much wetter.'

The building had lots of doors, some of them hidden away at the end of narrow passageways between the cubes that made up the structure. I was about to give up when Alan spotted a loading dock around the back, with a steel roll-up door at the top of a slight ramp. 'That must be where they bring large sculptures in and out. It will be locked, but I'll just make certain.'

I stayed in the car, wet and shivering and thoroughly fed up, while Alan walked up the ramp and surveyed the door for any sort of opening mechanism. It looked like the sort that opens only from inside, electrically. He looked at me and shrugged. No hope there.

There was a concrete platform to the side of the steel barrier, though, and in the interest of thoroughness Alan stepped over to it. I couldn't see very well because of the angle, but he fumbled with something and then gave me a broad smile and wave.

He'd found an unlocked door.

If Alan hadn't been there, nothing could have made me enter that dark, apparently deserted building. I admit that doesn't make sense. If a building is deserted, it's harmless. It's the people inside who might be hazardous to one's health. But if anyone wants to make fun, let him enter, alone, a labyrinthine structure where someone has been murdered; let him, furthermore, enter late on a dark, misty afternoon, when no lights are visible and there are no passers-by to hear a possible cry for help – let that person say, if he dares, that fears are foolish.

Even with Alan right there, I wasn't wild about the idea. I hadn't much enjoyed my tour of discovery the day before, with corridors leading nowhere and people popping out of unseen doors.

I had a reputation to maintain. Dorothy the intrepid. My comments as I got out of the car and trudged up the ramp were unspoken ones, and I hoped that Alan wouldn't be able to read my face in the half-light of the deepening gloom.

Whether he could or not, he sensed my mood and tucked my hand firmly over his arm. 'We stick together,' he said very softly, 'and make as little noise as possible. The place may be empty, but I don't quite like that open door.'

Of course that raised my spirits immensely. I gripped his arm rather tighter than strictly necessary and wished my wet shoes wouldn't squeak so on the linoleum.

'What are we looking for?' I murmured.

'First, a way out of this confounded loading area.' It came out as a sort of growl and I almost giggled. Tension does that to me. I hoped I could behave myself.

Alan loosed my hand for a moment, groped in his pockets, and came up with, miracle of miracles, a flashlight. A bright, new one, too, with that penetrating blue light that LEDs supply. It wasn't very big, so the beam wasn't broad, but that almost windowless space was very dark indeed, so the light seemed powerful. It showed us another large garage-type door at the other side of the room, as firmly shut as the outer one, but with two prominent buttons to one side, a red one and a green one.

'I don't think we dare, Dorothy. It'll sound like Hannibal and all his elephants. There must be a human-sized door somewhere.'

If there had ever been one, some remodelling project or other had taken it away or covered it up. No matter how carefully Alan surveyed the room with his light, there was plainly no way out of the dock except the way we'd come in, or the electric door into the building.

'Shall we risk it? Or acknowledge ourselves defeated and go home to a thumping good tea?'

I was suddenly impatient with our precautions. The building was plainly empty. There was no danger. (I suspect that Alan's flashlight played a big part in my new courage. I've never liked the dark.) 'We've come this far. It would be too silly to turn tail and run. Let's risk it. The green button, I'd think.'

Alan pressed it. The door obediently rose, with little more noise than a low rumble, and we were free to roam as we wished.

The only lights visible were the green exit lights here and there over doors. The corridors had no windows, and although some of the rooms that opened off to left and right had windows, and glass-panelled doors, what little light penetrated those recesses had given up heart long before it reached the hallway.

'All right, Miss Braveheart. Shall we switch on some lights or make do with the torch?'

'I'm not quite that foolish. Lights, even in the corridors, could be seen from outside, and if someone like a campus guard came to investigate, we could be in a lot of trouble. Let's make do with your flashlight and what little I remember of the layout of this chamber of horrors. And I warn you, people can sneak up on you before you hear them. Something about the acoustics.'

'Ah, but there's no one to sneak, is there?'

'I certainly hope not. We'll be careful anyway, though, okay?'

Now that I was actually in the place, some of my trepidation returned. I resumed my tight grasp of Alan's arm. 'I think the sculpture studios are just ahead,' I said in barely audible tones. I knew they were on the ground floor, anyway, and surely they'd be as close as possible to the dock.

And yes, behind the first door we opened, here they were. Probably on a bright sunny day there'd be plenty of natural light here. Today we might as well have been at the bottom of an aquarium; the light was green and murky. We could see enough, with Alan's cautious use of the flashlight, to know that there was no one in any of the rooms, though Gillian's *Summer* gave me a nasty jolt for a second.

'Onward and upward?' I murmured.

'Let's just have a quick look at the offices first. I don't think we need bother with any of the lecture rooms.'

This wasn't the time or place for a lengthy discussion, but I wondered again what we thought we were doing here. If we were looking for Matt, the way to do it would be to bring in several friends, turn on all the lights, and make a systematic search of the building. Except the police had probably already done that. I couldn't explain why we both had the strong feeling that there was something important to be found here. Nor why we felt so uneasy about it that we were sneaking around like a couple of burglars.

Nobody in the main office. Nobody in Chandler's office. I made some excuse not to go in there, telling myself firmly I was not getting stupid ideas about ghosts. Nobody in a kind of work room, with a photocopier and stacks of paper and a couple of computers. Nobody under the table, nobody under the sofa, nobody under the bed . . . I wrenched my thoughts away from Ebenezer Scrooge and his uneasy ghost-hunt and directed Alan toward where I thought we'd find the stairs to the second floor and the photo studios.

For a wonder, I was right. Getting around the studios themselves was a bit trickier. We first found several darkrooms, which were indeed very dark. But we bumbled about, using Alan's light when we absolutely had to, and finally found ourselves in the large room where set pieces, or human models, could be photographed. It was full of windows, floor to ceiling, and also full of obstacles. Here a large silver umbrella on a stand loomed over one corner, there I nearly got myself tangled in a roll of background paper. Tripods thrust their wiry legs out to trip us up, and light stands were everywhere. I finally stood in the middle of the room and rotated slowly, surveying the room with the aid of a very occasional flash of light.

'No one,' I said at last.

Alan nodded. 'I checked the darkrooms while you were doing your slow pirouette. No one. And nothing. They're virtually cleaned out.'

'I know. Isn't it sad? Now shall we try the next floor?'

'That's the print department, isn't it? Matt's department?'

I nodded, swallowed, and gripped his arm again.

We found the stairs easily, and climbed them very quietly. My shoes were dry by this time, at least on the bottom, and no longer squeaked. I nearly held my breath. We were walking into Matt's world, the place where he was master, where he created such splendour. I didn't want to find him there, hurt or . . . I didn't want him to be there.

We came out of the stairwell, crept down the corridor, and opened the door to the main print studio.

I gasped and would have fallen if Alan hadn't supported me.

By the fading light we glimpsed a scene of utter chaos.

'The hell with this!' said Alan roughly, and found the light switches. By the glaring light of the overhead fluorescents, the mess was truly appalling.

Tables were overturned. Sharp tools lay all over the floor, presenting a very great hazard. Plastic bottles of acid for etching, rolls of silk, inks of every colour made a sort of mad collage. Even some of the lithograph stones lay broken on the floor. We just stood and looked for a moment, and then I gave a great cry. 'Alan! The prints!'

For the woodcuts, the glorious, miraculous woodcuts that I had so admired, had been torn from the walls and lay in ragged pieces, soaking up spilled ink.

Alan walked gingerly to one that had escaped the worst destruction. He stood looking at it for a long time, and then took his phone out of his pocket and punched in a number.

'Derek? You'd best come over to the Fine Arts building. There's been the most damnable vandalism.'

I stood there in tears. How could an artist, how could anyone destroy such beauty? Had Matt gone utterly out of his mind and done this himself? Was he . . . oh, God, was he lying dead in one of the printing rooms? Destruction of his work and then of himself?

'Alan, we'd better search—'

'No, love. We'll do nothing until Derek gets here. This is a murder scene.'

'Then you think . . .'

'I don't know if Matt is here somewhere, if that's what you mean. But if it's murder to destroy a man's very soul, then someone committed murder here.'

I drew a shaky breath. 'Could we at least turn out some of the lights? I don't think I can bear to look at this.'

'I suppose. I touched the switches once tonight. Once more won't make much of a difference.'

He turned to walk back to the switches, and a cold voice from the door said, 'I see that, not content with trespassing, you have now embraced mass destruction.' William Braithwaite started to walk into the room.

'I'll ask you to stay where you are, sir,' said Alan, in his most commanding voice. 'This is a crime scene. I have called the police, and they will be here very soon. Meanwhile no one must disturb anything.'

'I say! You're a cool customer, telling me what I can and can't do in my own college! I am W.T. Braithwaite, and I am the head of the school of art, and who the hell are you?' He strode past Alan, crushing plastic tubes of colour as he walked into the room.

Alan caught his shoulder and swung him around. 'NO FARTHER, SIR! My name is Alan Nesbitt, I am the former chief constable of Belleshire, and I am still a sworn police officer with every right to arrest you on the spot. I assure you I shall do so if you take one more step.'

Alan will never see seventy again. Braithwaite was probably in his forties. He was also six inches shorter than my husband, and soft around the middle. He shook off Alan's hand, with some language I tried hard not to hear, but he stayed where he was.

We waited in uncomfortable silence for Derek to arrive.

Alan's phone rang. Keeping a stern eye on Braithwaite, he pulled it out, listened a moment, and uttered an uninformative, 'Right. I'll see to it.' Then he turned to the unhappy painter and held out his hand. 'Your keys.'

The man started to protest, considered Alan's grim expression, and sullenly pulled a key ring out of his pocket.

'Main door?'

Braithwaite indicated it.

'Right. Dorothy, can you bear to go down and let Derek in? Can you find the door?'

'Yes, and yes, but I'll need your flashlight.'

He handed it to me. 'But go ahead and switch the lights on as you go. There's no need for caution now.'

I was thankful to get out of that terrible room. The carnage had sickened me. Alan was right, I thought. It was a massacre, the slaughter of hopes and dreams and brilliant achievement, and it would give me nightmares for a long time. I could only hope, as I threaded my way down the stairs and through the corridors, that Derek did not find Matt somewhere amongst that butchery.

Derek had brought two men with him. I tried to prepare them for what they would find, but no description could match the reality. Derek stood at the studio door in utter stillness and silence for a moment, then drew a deep breath. 'All right,' he said to one of his henchmen, 'send for the crew. Tell them to prepare for a long stint. We'll have to dig our way in. And who, sir, are you?'

Braithwaite, who had been fidgeting, now spoke with some of his former bluster. 'W.T. Braithwaite, head of the college.'

'Ah, yes. Some of my people spoke to you in connection with the earlier crime, I believe. Surely your title is Acting Head, or something of the sort? And why are you here today, sir?'

Derek's cool indifference punctured the little man's ego, but he still put up a fight. 'I am here on legitimate business, which is more than I can say for these two trespassers! Furthermore, this man physically accosted me as I tried to investigate this horror!'

Derek looked Braithwaite slowly up and down, noting his cashmere pullover, the pristine shirt under it, his unruffled hair, and his trim trousers stained at the cuffs with spots of bright inks. 'He doesn't seem to have done a great deal of damage. Do I understand that you wish to file a complaint?'

'He – I – oh, forget it!'

'Very wise, sir. Mr Nesbitt was acting entirely properly, you know. Now, let me escort you to the corridor, so that you won't do any more damage to the scene than you have already done, and you can wait there. I'll want to ask you a few questions in a bit.'

Derek spoke to Alan and me for a moment and inspected our shoes.

'I'm sorry,' I said, 'we went in before we really saw what had happened. But we didn't go far, so we shouldn't have messed the scene up too badly, do you think?' Derek gave me a quizzical look. 'I'm sorry, I'm babbling. This is all just so . . . Derek, Alan called it a kind of murder, and it is, isn't it?'

'It's frightful. And I can tell you this. It has happened since two o'clock this afternoon. We searched this building thoroughly then, and this studio was in perfect order.'

'Then . . . Matt came back, or . . . it doesn't make sense!'

'Nothing about this series of crimes makes sense.' He lowered his voice. 'Technically, you know, you two were in fact trespassing. Add breaking and entering to the charge, as well.'

'We entered, Derek,' said Alan. 'I'll confess to that. But we did not break. A door at the loading dock was unlocked.'

'Was it, now? That's interesting. Because when we left this afternoon, we made quite sure that the building was sealed up tight.'

THIRTEEN

After our apologies to Derek for our impulsive foray into the Fine Arts building, and his absolution in view of our discoveries, Alan and I left. I simply couldn't bear to stay near the print studio, and we were only in the way. If Derek and his crew found anything of any interest, if, God forbid, they found Matt's body, he'd let us know right away.

'I wonder,' I said as we got in the car, 'how long he's going to let that man cool his heels.'

'Long enough to teach him a lesson,' said Alan. 'He really is an insufferable git, isn't he? You do realize he blundered into that room on purpose, don't you?'

'I wondered. Very few people defy you when you talk like a chief constable. Why did he?'

'I can think of two possibilities. He wanted to plant something in the room, or alternatively to find and remove something. Or he wanted us to see him get ink all over his shoes and trousers.'

'You think he did it?'

'I think he's malicious enough to do almost anything. And he thinks he's clever enough to get away with almost anything.'

'Murder?'

'Oh, he could do murder. The only problem is—'

'He doesn't have a motive,' we said together. 'And we don't know how the man was killed, or when, or any of those little details,' I added. 'And now Derek and co. have this new atrocity to deal with. Alan!' I clutched at his arm, and the car swerved.

'Easy, Dorothy! You nearly had me on the pavement! What is it?'

'Gillian! Is she safe? If this horrible attack on the studio was someone gone crazy . . .'

'Where does she live?'

'I don't have her address with me!' I wailed. 'It's not far from here, and I got there once, but the roads are so confusing around here . . .'

Alan patted my knee. 'You got her address from Inga, didn't you? Why don't you phone her?'

He pulled to the side of the road while I made the call and then sighed with relief at the news I heard. 'Gillian's with Inga and Nigel. They invited her for tea, and Inga said we're to come over, too.'

'It's a bit late for tea,' said Alan, putting the car in gear.

'Yes, but we haven't had any, and I'm parched. And exhausted.'

'Right.' He turned in the direction of the Evans's house.

They lived in a small semi, what I would call a duplex, in a housing development near the university. It was bright and new, and Inga kept it shining, despite the unceasing demands of the Nipper. Today the garden was looking a trifle bedraggled, though. The constant fine rain had weighed down the shaggy heads of chrysanthemums till they fell over in the mud, and petals from the fading roses littered the mulch below the bushes. A well-kept bicycle was propped against the side of the house, and I surmised that Gillian had not yet invested in a car.

Nigel met us at the door. 'The girls are talking nineteen to the dozen,' he said with a smile, 'and I've just got the Nipper into bed for his nap. There's fresh tea in a minute or two.' He looked at us more closely and his manner changed. 'Something's wrong. Is it something to do with the murder?'

'Not exactly,' I said. 'We'll tell you about it, but we don't want to upset Inga.'

'She's tough, so long as it isn't another death.' He looked at us closely, to see if we took this as a joke, and was not reassured.

A scream from the tea kettle recalled him to his tea-making, and we went on into the minute front room, where Inga and Gillian sat side by side on the couch, tea cups and crumb-littered plates in front of them. 'We've been making pigs of ourselves, but Nigel's fetching more biscuits and cakes,' said Inga. Then she, too, saw the strain on our faces. 'Oh, dear.'

'Yes, but it's not as bad as it might be,' I said hastily. 'We've just been to the college, Gillian, and some madman has wrecked the print studio. It's . . . pretty awful, actually.' My voice started to shake and Alan took over.

'We went to the college to see if we could find any sign of

where Matt might be. A rather frail straw to cling to, but we had no other ideas.'

'No, Alan, we might as well admit it was sheer intuition. We knew the police would have been there, and there was no reason to believe . . . you three do know what we're talking about, don't you?'

'Not a clue,' said Gillian. She tried to sound flippant, but her face had gone white.

Alan smote his head. 'Fool that I am! How would you know? Christopher told us only this morning. Matt Thomas has gone missing. At least, he didn't show up at a dinner party last night, didn't notify his hosts, and still has not phoned. I called Derek straightaway, since this could be connected with Chandler's death.'

'And then we waited and waited to hear something,' I said, 'and finally decided to go to the college and see for ourselves. And I don't know why Alan wanted to go, but I had a strong feeling that something was wrong there. Idiotic, perhaps, but . . .'

'You told me not to say that sort of thing,' said Gillian quietly. 'Am I allowed to send your advice back to you?'

'Oh, my dear!'

It was a good thing Nigel came in with the tea tray just then, or I might have dissolved in a maudlin little puddle.

Tea is not just a beverage, or a light meal. It is a ritual, not perhaps as rigidly structured as the Japanese tea ceremony, but in its own way as formal. One of the unspoken rules is that unpleasant things are not discussed over tea. That means that tea provides a respite, an island of calm in the midst of trouble. So we drank our tea and ate our excellent biscuits (Inga is a great cook) and talked about the weather, and the exploits of Max, the venerable pub cat at the Rose and Crown, and the chances of Nigel's favourite football team in the season that had begun in August. And I felt refreshed and ready to face further discussion of Matt and the art school crimes.

'Gillian, do you know Matt at all?'

'We've met. I rather like him. I've seen his work, and he's brilliant, you know?'

'I do know. I've seen his work, too.' I decided not to tell her about the ruined prints unless I had to. If their destruction had nearly made me ill, I couldn't imagine what the news would do to an artist of Gillian's calibre. 'But you don't really know him as a person?'

'No. You know term hasn't actually begun. I've been around the college now and again, but working, not socializing. But Mrs Martin—'

'Dorothy,' I reminded her.

'Dorothy, why do you both say he's disappeared? Couldn't he have just decided to take a weekend holiday before term begins tomorrow?'

'He could,' said Alan, 'but his friends don't think he would have done without telling them. Especially as the dinner last night was organized for him, and they say he was never rude. He would have said something to them.'

'He did seem quite courteous,' said Gillian doubtfully. 'But why would he do a runner? You said it might have something to do with Chandler's death?'

'Might,' said Alan. 'Only might. There are any number of possibilities. A sudden family emergency. A sudden illness or accident. Even amnesia. That's rare, but it does happen, especially when a person has been under considerable strain.'

'I'm sure the police are checking hospitals, accident reports, that sort of thing,' said Inga.

'And checking with his family,' I added. 'All of those things are of course possible. But with the other things that have been happening at the college, we have to wonder if it's just a coincidence that Matt's gone. And as you're connected with the college, too, Gillian, we . . . well, mostly I, got worried about you and wanted to make sure you were all right.'

'I'm fine,' she said in the sort of small voice that puts the lie to the statement.

'She's scared,' said Inga. 'That's why we asked her to tea. Gilly, darling, they won't laugh at you. Tell them.'

'It's just . . . I've been getting phone calls.'

Alan recognized her tone of voice. 'Anonymous ones?' he asked gently. 'Obscene?'

'Not the first ones. They were just annoying. They always came in the middle of the night, and when I answered, there'd be no one there. I didn't want to unplug the phone, in case my

parents called. My father's not been very well. But after two or
three nights of very little sleep, I called Mum and told her I was
using my mobile for nearly everything, and she should use that
number, and I did unplug the landline.'

She took a deep breath. 'Then I started to get scared, because
the calls started to come in on the mobile. The only people who
have that number are my friends and family! And they've got
worse. Threats, obscenities . . . the lot.'

'Have you reported this to the police?'

'What could they do? It isn't a crime to make phone calls.'

'It is to make that sort, and the police can and will follow it up.'
Alan got a pad and pencil out of a pocket. 'When they did start?'

'Only a few days ago. The first one was just after . . . that
fateful ride in the lift.'

She was trying hard to maintain self-control. I smiled and gave
her a thumbs up.

'Less than a week, then.' Alan made a note. 'And when did
they change in character?'

'When I switched to my mobile, two days ago.'

'Caller ID?'

'Blocked.'

'Right. Now here's what you can do immediately: get another
mobile and give the old one to me. I'll give it to the chaps who
look after phone crimes, and with any luck they'll track down
your caller in a day or two.'

Wordlessly, she pulled it out of her handbag and gave it to
him.

'Excellent. Now, the new phone needn't be an expensive one.'
He looked with awe at the one she'd given him. 'Assuming you're
not planning a moon-launch or whatever else this thing can do,
a throwaway will do for now. You'll get this one back in due
time. You'll change the number when you do, of course. And the
other important thing is this: give the number of the new phone
to no one – *no one* – except your parents and two trusted friends.
Two, in case one is unavailable when someone needs to reach
you. And impress upon them all that they are to keep it absolutely
secure.'

'Gillian,' I asked, 'are your parents reliable, or are they inclined
to gossip?'

She smiled at that. 'My father was MI5 before his health forced an early retirement. And my mother, in the early days, was his secretary.'

Alan chuckled. 'Then presumably they both know how to keep a secret.'

'I haven't told them what's been happening, though. Didn't want to worry them. I suppose now I must do.'

'That's up to you,' said Alan. 'In your place I think I'd gloss it over, say something about prank calls that you want to stop. Your father will probably read between the lines, and with luck your mother won't be upset.'

'They're not fussy parents, thank God!' said Inga. 'Even if your mum works out what's going on, she won't have nervous prostration.'

'They're terrific,' agreed Nigel, 'from what I've seen of them. You're lucky, Gilly.'

Nigel had never met his father, who had died when Nigel was a tiny infant. His mother had done her best, but money had always been in short supply, and she'd had to work long hours away from her young son. He wasn't quite twelve when she died, too, and he was shifted from pillar to post until someone discovered he could sing and he got into a choir school. After that, he'd managed more or less on his own. Now he had a good job, about to get better, and a wife and family he adored, also about to get even better. But he could still appreciate the value of admirable parents.

'And if they do cut up rough about her being alone,' said Inga, 'we've told her she can move in with us until life calms down a bit. We're crowded, but till the new baby comes, we can manage.'

'Good,' said Alan, standing. 'Now that we know you're well looked after by your friends, Gilly, we'll leave you to them. Just one other thing. I'd like you to write down anything your offensive caller said, the exact words, as nearly as you can remember them. I do realize that will be unpleasant for you, but it's valuable to us, if you think you can bear it.'

'I'll do it straightaway. Shall I bring the notes to you, or leave them at the police station?'

'To me. I'll pass them on. Cheerio, then.'

'And thank you, Inga,' I added. 'For everything. Look after

Snicklefritz, there.' I nodded to her as-yet flat belly, and waved as we got into the car.

And to Alan, as we drove away, I said, 'I don't like it.'

'Nor do I. It's one more unsettling thing. I'm going to drop this off on the way home and have Guy, Derek's best IT man, get to work on it. They're slow to tackle phone crimes as a rule, particularly when anything major's going down, but I'll try to get Derek to ginger them up a bit. I don't care for this latest development one bit.'

'Any idea what's behind it?'

'Other than that someone's trying to frighten Gillian, and succeeding, no. Dorothy, what would you think of asking that child to stay with us for a bit? Nigel and Inga have their hands full, and their house, as well. We've plenty of room, and I'd rather like to have her under my eye.'

'I think that's a wonderful idea! I'll call right now and suggest it.'

Inga protested, of course, but she was ready to be persuaded. 'It's because of the baby, really,' I said. 'You need to get a lot of rest right now, and of course Nigel Peter doesn't cut you much slack.'

'Not much,' she admitted. 'He has some slight inkling of what's happening, I think, and he's already showing a little jealousy.'

'Well, not that I know a thing about it, but I understand that's likely to get worse before it gets better. I know Gillian's a good friend, but truly, if she's willing to come to us, it might work out better all the way round.'

'She's having a little rest right now. I think she's just a bit overwhelmed. Too much has happened in too short a time. Moving to Sherebury, and getting excited about her first job, and then all the beastliness. Shall I talk to her when she's feeling more like herself, and ring you back?'

We left it like that, and the minute we got home I went into action to prepare the guest room and plan meals for one more person.

FOURTEEN

nga talked her into it. Inga can be very persuasive, and I think Gillian was feeling somewhat awkward about staying with the Evanses anyway, given the tiny house and active little boy. They had stopped at Gillian's flat and packed a suitcase, and deposited her and it, and her bicycle, at our house a little before seven.

Nigel Peter was volubly unhappy about the situation. 'Aunt Gilly was wiv *us*. I want Aunt Gilly wiv *us*! She weads to me.'

'Gom and Gof need someone to read to them, darling. Aunt Gilly will be back soon.' Gom and Gof were Nigel Peter's renditions of godmother and godfather, and I chuckled inside every time he called us that.

'Want Aunt Gilly *now*!' he roared, as Nigel carried him off, red-faced and struggling.

'He's going to take after his father,' I commented as we escorted Gillian into the house. 'Excellent lungs.'

'I do feel awful about deserting him, but he can be a little distracting.'

'Dearly as we love him, Alan and I agree our godchild can be hell on wheels at times. I admire Nigel and Inga enormously for the way they deal with him. I wouldn't have the patience. And what poor Inga's going to do with a new baby in the house, I don't know. Now, here's your room. The bathroom's across the hall, and most of the time it's all yours. Alan and I will use the little loo off the kitchen. In the middle of the night, though, we probably won't risk the stairs. At your age, I doubt you'll ever notice.'

She laughed a little. 'No, I almost never need to get up in the night.'

'Oh, for the days when I could say the same! I'll leave you to get settled now, and supper's in about fifteen minutes. If you're not hungry, come down and join us anyway, and we can share a glass of wine, at least.'

I closed the door on her profuse thanks and went down to mash the potatoes while Alan grilled the pork chops and finished the salad. Comfort food. Gillian wasn't the only one in need of it.

I had set the table in the kitchen, and of course the animals all crowded in, eager to help us clean up anything that might fall to the floor. The cats can be somewhat critical and aloof with strangers, but they liked Gillian immediately. Emmy stropped herself against Gilly's ankles, and Sam uttered one of her best Siamese yowls, apparently meaning: 'I'm a wonderful cat. Pay attention to me. Better yet, feed me.'

'Just shoo them away if they get to be too much,' I said. 'I do hope you're not allergic. I forgot to ask.'

'No, I love cats. All animals, really,' she added, sitting down to pat Watson, who was feeling neglected.

So I introduced them, and darling Watson proffered a paw to shake. His former owner taught him that trick, but we were as proud as if we'd done it ourselves.

By the time the food was on the table, Gillian was a part of the family. 'I've missed this,' she said as I passed her the potatoes. 'Eating in the kitchen, with cats and dogs around. My parents have a big old farmhouse in Kent, with a huge kitchen where we spent most of our time. Then at Hallam I lived in rooms, and then I moved to the flat here. It's quite nice, really, but it's not . . .'

'Not home,' I finished for her. 'We practically live in this kitchen, too. When it's chilly outside, the Aga keeps this room blissfully warm.'

'And insufferably hot in high summer,' said Alan. 'Some salad?'

She made a good meal, slipping titbits now and then to whatever animal appeared by her chair. When I offered a dish of blackberry and apple crumble, though, still warm from the oven and smelling heavenly, she shook her head regretfully. 'I can't. It's my favourite, but there's no room. I shall grow out of all my clothes if you keep feeding me like this.'

'Don't worry. I'd turn to a blimp myself on this regime. We usually have something simple in the evening, but I thought this was appropriate for a trying day.' Trying, I thought to myself. I'm getting almost as good at understatement as the Brits. 'Tell me what you like to eat, and I'll provide it in future.'

'Or let me cook it myself,' said Gillian. 'I'm rather a good cook, actually. But I can't sponge off you forever. I'm sure I'll be okay at home. It was only . . . those phone calls . . . I felt a bit vulnerable.'

'And so you are.' Alan tented his fingers in his familiar 'lecturing' style. 'I don't want to frighten you, child, and I know you cherish your independence, but one member of the staff at your college is dead and another is missing. One of the studios has been viciously ravaged, and you've received quite nasty phone calls. Be sensible, Gillian. You're neither sponging nor imposing. There's a time to be bold and a time to take precautions. "She who fights and runs away . . ." you know . . .'

'I hate running away!'

'But I'm sure you'd like to live to fight another day,' I put in. 'Don't forget the rest of the quote: "But he who is in battle slain can never rise and fight again." Or to use a homelier bit of advice, choose your battles. And to go on to one of them, do you have any idea at all who might have trashed the print studio?'

'If it were term time, I'd say some disgruntled student. There were some incidents at Hallam while I was there that weren't very pretty. Art students can be very competitive, you know.'

'But it isn't term time, and I'd say there was a lot more damage than could be laid down to artistic temperament.'

'What actually was done? No one's told me.'

Alan forestalled me. 'I think the police will want the details kept quiet for the time being,' he said.

'Was anybody's work damaged?' she persisted.

'Yes,' I said, and had to control a shudder.

'Gillian, I'm sorry, but we really mustn't say any more,' said Alan. 'All we're asking is, can you think of anyone who hates Matt Thomas enough to damage his workplace? Or for that matter, anyone who hates the college? It could have been sheer blind malevolence directed against the school of art in general.'

She shook her head. 'You're asking the wrong person. I don't really know anyone except Dennis, who blusters a lot and looks fierce and is an absolute sweetie-pie. For the rest . . .' She spread her hands. 'I'm sorry I can't help. Oh, but I did write down what I could remember of the phone calls. Shall I run up and get it?'

'Time enough when you've let your dinner settle. Come in

and sit by the fire while Alan and I tidy up in here, and then you can tell us about yourself.'

But she insisted on helping, so I let her wash while Alan dried and I put everything away, and we were done in no time. 'If the art business doesn't work out,' I said, 'I'll recommend you as a domestic help.'

'I may take you up on that, if the college doesn't get its problems settled soon. It isn't just all the horrible things that have been happening. Even when we get beyond all this, I don't see how any of us can work with no budget. I don't understand how the college finances got into such a mess. The Wolfson's always had an excellent reputation.'

'Enrolments down, perhaps?' suggested Alan, shooing us into the parlour.

'Not that I've heard. I know there were several applicants for my position. I'm a student as well as a teacher, you know.'

'Is this something new?' asked Alan. 'I don't recall any such arrangements when I was at university. That was years ago, of course.'

'It's one of the American innovations the late unlamented head introduced. I don't know where he found the funding, but it's one of the few good things he did for the place. I suppose Braithwaite will try to change that, too.'

I shook my head. 'I hope not. It's a very common practice in America, Alan. We call them grad assistants or teaching assistants, TAs for short. They're generally viewed as slave labour, with stipends you can hardly find with a microscope.'

'It's much the same here. My fees are paid, and I'm given a tiny living allowance, about enough to support Emmy, here, if she went on a diet. Oof!' Emmy, all seventeen pounds of her, had landed in Gilly's lap. 'That diet might not be a bad idea, come to think of it,' she said, stroking the big grey cat's soft fur. 'Is she a British Blue?'

'Half. The other half was just plain tabby, but she looks exactly like her father. I'm sure you've met him, the Blue Max at the Rose and Crown. His children, like Abraham's, number as the stars. Sam is another one, though she's taken after her mother and stayed slim. Dump Emmy if she's too much of a nuisance.'

'Never! I'm well up on cat etiquette.'

'So Gilly, are you able to survive on your pittance? Are you thinking of taking another job?' I was trying to think of a subtle way to offer some aid.

'I couldn't manage without my parents' help. They insisted, but I hate to take it. I'm twenty-six. It's time I was supporting myself.'

'How, if I may ask without offence, did a very attractive young woman like yourself remain single for so long?' asked Alan in his most gallant manner.

'I've never had time for anything but art. Oh, there've been episodes. One chap at Hallam was really serious, but he was all about settling down and raising lots of kids and going to the seaside every summer for a holiday, with maybe an occasional daring jaunt to France. I just don't want that kind of life. I want to make beautiful bronzes and sell them all over the world. I want to travel and get ideas and then come home and make more beauty. If I ever meet a man who wants to share that sort of life, then I'll think about marriage. Right now the occasional dinner out, or a play in London, is all the amusement I'm interested in, and even then, if my work is going well, I don't want to leave it.'

'Well, then, we'd best see to the untangling of the mess at the college so you can get on with it,' said Alan cheerfully. 'For a start, might I see the notes you made for me?'

'They don't make pretty reading. Sorry, Emmy,' Gillian said as she picked the cat up and put her gently on the floor. Emmy growled and stalked away, high dudgeon written in every line of her body.

When she came back she also brought her new phone, a tiny flip-top that obviously amused her. 'The latest model. Want to know what it does, Dorothy?'

'I give up.'

'It makes phone calls! And receives them, as well. Imagine, a real live telephone you can put in your pocket. I want you to have the number, both of you, and I'm counting you as one of the two I'm allowed. Inga and Nigel combine as the other. Here's the number, if you want to program it into your phones.' She passed us a small piece of paper.

'But with no name on it, remember, love,' Alan put in,

unnecessarily, I thought. I do know the rudiments of modern communication.

'It won't take it without a name. "Friend" would be too obvious to anyone who stole my phone. So would "anonymous". I know, though. I'll put in Phyllis Loving. I once had a cousin with that name, so it's real, but she's long dead. She would have enjoyed standing in for you, Gilly.'

'And I'll choose a man's name. John Doe?'

'Talk about obvious!'

But Alan smiled. 'Jack, then. Jack . . . Roebuck. Close enough.' He punched the appropriate buttons and then began to read Gillian's notes, and grimaced as he read. 'Do you want to see, love? It's vile.'

'Gilly had to hear it, poor dear, and then remember it and write it down. I can bear to read it.'

Shorn of obscenities, which constituted the greater part of each message, the content comprised two themes: activities the caller planned to indulge in with Gillian, and what might happen if she refused. The latter concentrated on her position at the college. 'Can you afford to lose that?' was one often repeated threat, though larded in the original with expletives.

I handed the paper back to Alan with the feeling that I needed a bath.

'This is verbatim?' he asked.

'I wouldn't swear to it. I tried not to listen. It's as much as I remember.'

'And it was a noble effort! And I think we need something to wash the taste out. What's your tipple, Gilly?'

We settled down with drinks, and Emmy relented sufficiently to jump back into Gilly's lap, and we spent the rest of the evening talking of nothing in particular. But even a fairly stiff bourbon couldn't dim the horrors of the day sufficiently. As I'd predicted, I had nightmares. I woke in the night sweating, with my heart pounding, but I couldn't remember what had been so terrifying.

FIFTEEN

Monday, September 8

I'd remembered, before I went to bed, to ask Gillian when she needed to be up in the morning. In the blissful state of retirement, one sometimes forgets that the rest of the world is up and about at dawn or thereabouts. The sun had been up for half an hour or so when I stumbled out of bed, or so my sunrise/sunset chart said. You couldn't prove it in Sherebury. At seven o'clock the sun was obscured by thick clouds, and the air was full of the same sort of nasty wetness as the day before.

Watson went out, accomplished his mission, and hurried back in again, paws wet and muddy. The cats didn't even attempt it. Sam put her nose out the cat flap, backed into the room with some Siamese profanity, and demanded breakfast in atonement for the weather I had plainly created to annoy cats.

'It isn't my fault, Sam, and I can't do a thing about it!'

She stalked to her dish and swore again to find it empty.

I fed the animals, made a big pot of coffee, and then put the kettle on, remembering that Gilly didn't drink coffee. I had eggs and bacon at the ready, though Alan and I seldom had them for breakfast anymore, and got out several varieties of cereal from the cupboard. Bread for toasting, and butter, and marmalade – there, that should do it. I went to the stairs, heard the shower running, and sat down with a cup of coffee and the *Telegraph*.

When she came down a few minutes later, Gillian was as fresh and perky as any young woman should be on her first day in a new venture. Ah, the resilience of youth!

'I didn't know what you usually eat, so there's a bit of everything at hand.'

'You didn't have to do this, you know. I usually get a chai and a bite of something at Starbucks on my way.'

'A waste of your tiny stipend. Toast? Cereal? Something more substantial?'

'Wholegrain toast would be lovely, thank you, but let me make it.'

'Splendid, and put some in for me, too. Indian tea, or China?'

We were sipping and munching happily when Alan came down, looking only a little rumpled without his usual morning shower. 'What's on the agenda for today, my dear?'

It could have been addressed to either of us, but his smile was for Gillian.

'Administrative stuff, mostly, getting class rosters and schedules sorted out. Then I'm to teach one class in elementary figure modelling, *if* we have the model and the clay to work with, and then meet with Dennis to map out my work for this term. My own work, I mean.' Some of the light went out of her eyes. 'Whatever that turns out to be.'

She insisted on cycling to the college. 'The weather's no worse than yesterday, and I've perfectly good rain gear. I won't have you turning yourselves into my chauffeurs!' Stuffing what she needed for the day into her backpack, she blew us a kiss and spun off down the wet street.

'And what about *your* agenda for the day?' I asked when we sat back down over fresh cups of coffee.

'Go have a chat with Derek and his henchmen. I'd like to get up to speed on various details like their success in tracing Chandler's movements at the end of last term, and learn what they made of the vandalism.'

'Obviously they didn't find Matt's body in that mess anywhere, or Derek would have told you. What else do you think might have turned up?'

'God only knows. I'd love to learn that there was something to incriminate Mr W.T. Braithwaite, but I'm not expecting it. I also want to check with Guy and see what they were able to learn from Gilly's phone. What about you?'

'The first thing is some grocery shopping. If I'm to be catering for a young woman with a healthy appetite, as well as us two old fogeys, I need a lot more food in the house. That means I'll need the car, though. Shall I do the shopping first, or wait till you come home?'

'I can walk. The station's just the other side of the close, and the rain's not as bad as it was. So go when you like. And after that?'

'Then I've had a brilliant idea. At least, I think it's brilliant.' I paused expectantly. Alan did not disappoint me. 'And what might that be, delight of my heart?'

'Good heavens, what *have* you been reading? Victorian novels? Persian love poetry? Never mind, I don't think I want to know. Anyway, I'm going to call Penny Brannigan and see if she knows anything about any of these people. She's an artist; they're artists. She might have heard some dirt that even Jane doesn't know.'

'Not bad,' said Alan. 'But she's an amateur, and a Canadian ex-pat living in Wales. Do you really think she'd know any of the college people?'

'Wales is not all that far away. Nothing is all that far away in these scepter'd isles, not for people like Penny and me who're used to vast North American spaces. I bet she'll know somebody who knows somebody. Anyway, it's worth a try.'

'I'll give it three stars out of four on the brilliance scale,' said Alan, and left the room rapidly.

Well, I still thought it was a good idea. Alan just doesn't realize how small a world Britain is, and how interconnected groups of people are. I'm willing to bet that, for example, every person involved in theatre in the United Kingdom is connected to everybody else in that particular profession, at least at second or third remove. 'Oh, yes, my cousin's best friend was the set designer for that production. Eight or nine years ago it was, in Bath.' That sort of thing. And not just professionals, either. Somebody else's cousin helped every year with the Such-and-Such school production of Shakespeare, and So-and-So has seen every play Whosis was ever in.

And the same would be true of the art world, I was sure. So as soon as I'd cleared away breakfast, I picked up my phone and looked up Penny's number.

The call went to voicemail. That was disappointing, though I shouldn't have been surprised. Between the spa she runs and her painting, and a good many other activities in the charming Welsh village where she lives, she's a busy lady. I left a brief message just saying I had some art-related questions, and would she call me back.

Well. Here I'd been hoping to talk to her and get some ideas of a new direction for this frustrating inquiry. Never mind. She'd call back eventually, and meanwhile there was that shopping to do. I wrote out a list, made sure I had my carrier bags, and set out.

For a town of its size, Sherebury is remarkably well-supplied with shops. For clothing, we have, as well as the boutiques, a small Marks and Spencer in the High Street. Nearby, for food, is a small Sainsbury's, and in the new shopping centre at the edge of town there's a fine big Tesco. Now, in principle, I disapprove of supermarkets in England. They seem very un-English to me, another American invasion. They are, however, extremely convenient. I can get most of what I need at Sainsbury's, which is within easy walking distance of my home. I even have a little wheeled cart for bringing home my purchases if they're too bulky to carry. But for major shopping expeditions, or in bad weather, it's Tesco. I got the car, bundled Watson in, and took off through increasingly hard rain.

They'd changed the shelf arrangement since I'd been there last. It took me much longer than it should have to whittle my list down, and then there was a long line at the till. And just as I had packed the bulging bags in the boot, in driving rain, and was about to climb into the shelter of the car, my phone rang.

'Dorothy? Penny. How are you?'

'Wet. It's pouring here. Let me just unlock the car.' Of course I dropped the keys and then couldn't get the push-button thing to work, and Watson, who had been pent up in the car, greeted me enthusiastically, which didn't help. But eventually I landed safe in the driver's seat. 'Whew! Sorry about that, but I'm at the supermarket and had to get myself organized. And how are *you*, my dear? We haven't talked in a long time.'

'I'm fine, and I was about to call you even if you hadn't phoned. You see, I'm in Sherebury, or nearly.'

'You're what? Sorry, this line isn't too good. Watson, *hush*! I thought you said you were in Sherebury.'

'But I am. Or at least in Bellehurst. A friend of mine lives here, and we're going to an art exhibit at the Royal Academy day after tomorrow. And since I'm so close, I thought I might drop in, if it's all right with you.'

'It's perfect! Come as soon as you can, and stay as long as you can. Lunch? Tea? Dinner?'

Penny laughed. 'My friend expects me for dinner, as we're leaving quite early tomorrow morning. But lunch or tea would be lovely.'

'Come to lunch, then, and if we're still talking at teatime you can stay for that, too. I promise I won't stuff you so full of pastries you can't do justice to your friend's dinner. Actually, you could bring her along if you like. Or him, that is.' I sometimes forget that Penny is an attractive woman who has so far avoided marriage, but that doesn't mean there are no men in her life.

'Oh, no, it's her. It's she? Anyway, Louise is an old friend, and loves good painting as much as I do. But she's busy with various things today, so I'll come alone. Now, tell me how to get there. This part of England is a lot trickier to travel than North Wales!'

'I'm hopeless about directions. Call Alan.' I gave her the number. 'He may not be home right now either; that's his mobile. Oh, and tell him, if he's still at the station, I'll pick him up. It's way too wet to walk. I'll see you soon!'

Well, that added a couple of items to my shopping list, but I could get them at Sainsbury's. It was nearly next door to the police station, so if Alan was still there, I could easily swing by and get him.

He was standing in the shelter of the front door waiting for me, and sprinted for the car as I stopped in a clearly marked 'No Stopping or Standing' spot. 'Thank you, love,' he said. 'The Burberry would never have stood up to this. I understand we're having a guest for lunch.'

'Yes, isn't it lucky? But tell me what you learned from Derek and Guy.'

'Complications. They've traced Chandler, to a point. He was booked on a BA flight from Heathrow to Athens on July nineteenth. That was a Saturday, three days after that famous end-of-term meeting. And he caught that flight.'

'But . . . but then when was he killed? We thought it must have been just at the end of term. Or did he turn right around and come back, for some reason?'

'We don't know. He certainly left Heathrow, and arrived at ATH. Athens International Airport,' he added in response to my inquiring look. 'But we have no record of him after that. He did not pick up his luggage. He did not check into his hotel. He did not use the tickets for any of the island cruises he had booked. From the moment he presented his passport to the Greek authorities, he vanished into thin air.'

'But people don't vanish these days! All the security provisions, passport control . . . it's just not possible!'

'Nevertheless, it happened. And it's causing Derek and co. a good deal of consternation, I may tell you.'

'I'll just bet it is! It's giving me a headache. How in the world did he get back to England?'

'We don't know that, either. Not by any of the airlines or shipping lines. He could, just possibly, have travelled by rail. Within the EU the regulations are fairly lax. Derek is having the rail lines checked now, but there are so many of them, in so many countries, not all of them especially friendly to British authorities.'

'So the man walked out of Athens airport and was next seen under an elevator at Wolfson College of Art and Design.'

'So it appears.'

We were home by that time, so Alan helped me get the groceries into the house and then put the car away. Our garage is tiny and not connected to the house, so we both got pretty wet, and so did Watson. I tried to keep him in the hallway while he shook himself dry, but he was hungry and thirsty and headed straight for the kitchen, so the first thing I had to do, after putting the perishables away, was wipe down a good many surfaces. I tried to catch him to wipe off his paws, but he eluded me. The cats told us all what they thought of these proceedings, and I thought it was just as well we don't speak Cat.

'Oh, and I almost forgot,' I said as we were stowing away the rest of my purchases. 'Did Guy make any headway tracking down the obscene caller?'

'Dead end. He checked every number that had called Gilly's phone for the past month. There were several with blocked numbers, but the police have ways of retrieving those. All but one of them were telemarketers.'

'And the one?' I put some food down for the animals, though they didn't need it in the least. Anything for peace.

'The one had made calls on the right dates, and at about the right times. And when Guy tried it, he got a 'not a valid number' message. The man has chucked his phone!'

'But that means he must have known it was being checked. How?'

'Search me. The fellow's clever, Dorothy, damned clever. And is that Penny just pulling up in front? You look after her. I'll organize lunch.'

After we'd hugged and exchanged greetings, Penny said, 'Now before we do another thing, I want you to show me your house. You never told me you lived in such a wonderful old place!'

'Old, certainly. And wonderful when the windows aren't leaking, or the plumbing hasn't had a temper tantrum, or—'

'And you wouldn't trade it for a dozen lovely new homes.'

I laughed. 'You're right. I wouldn't. Let me just slip something into the oven, and then I'll take you on the grand tour.'

Our house was built early in the seventeenth century, intended to be the gate house for the great manor that was to be built on the grounds of the old abbey. Henry VIII, after closing all the abbeys, had sold some of them and given some to loyal followers. There was some dispute about exactly what had happened to Sherebury Abbey, but for whatever reason, the manor house was never built and the abbey was allowed to lie in peace, gently mouldering for over a hundred years until after the English Civil War, when it was restored and designated a Cathedral. The might-have-been lord of the manor had lived in a modest house, now demolished, somewhere in Sherebury and housed some of his servants in our house. They took good care of it, hoping perhaps to live there permanently themselves.

'So,' I concluded to Penny, 'the place is really in pretty good shape, considering its age. So far the leaks in the roof and windows and doors haven't damaged that gorgeous ceiling in our bedroom, which is probably the most vulnerable feature of the house.'

'I love the diamond-paned windows.'

I groaned. 'So do we, but they're murder to wash, and at least two of them have to be replaced. This is a listed building, so the repairs have to look authentic and use authentic materials as far as possible. It's going to cost us an arm and a leg.'

'Old houses do.'

'All houses do,' I said, thinking back to my World-War-Two-era house in Indiana. 'The difference is that old ones are worth the money and trouble. At least I think so. They have soul.'

'And they were well made to begin with.'

'Which reminds me. After lunch, if you have time, I want to take you over to the art college. There's a building that'll give you nightmares!'

Alan called us to lunch just then, and we spent the next hour catching up. We hadn't seen each other since Alan and I visited Wales some time ago, and we both had a lot of news.

'Now,' said Penny in businesslike fashion, 'you had some questions for me. Am I wrong, or is there a hint of something mysterious in the air?'

'A good many very mysterious things, and I think you can help me sort them out, because they all revolve around art and artists. Do you happen to know anyone who teaches at Sherebury?'

'I don't know. Give me some names.'

'Matthew Thomas, printmaker. Sam Andrews, photographer. Dennis Singleton, sculptor. William Braithwaite, painter. Those are all the full-time people.'

'W.T. Braithwaite?'

'Yes.'

'I don't know him. I've certainly heard of him.' Her voice was neutral. Carefully so, I thought.

'You don't like him.'

She made a disparaging gesture with her hands. 'As I say, I don't know him. I can't say I care for his work, and I've heard he's rather . . . full of himself.'

'Hmm. So other artists don't like him, either.'

'You're leading the witness, Dorothy,' said Alan, smiling.

'I'll tell you what I've heard. Mind you, I don't know many professional artists, so most of this comes from amateurs like me. They say he's not popular in the profession. Part of that could be jealousy, of course. He's climbed right to the top of the tree and made pots of money. But the scuttlebutt is also that his sales are going down, that people are losing interest in his style and turning more and more to representational work.' Again the gesture. 'I don't know, personally, how true any of this is.'

'I've heard some of it before, so it may in fact be true. At least it's a prevalent rumour. And you don't know anything about any of the others? The other teachers, I mean?'

'Not by name. I might recognize their work. Are you going to tell me what's going on?'

'Let's go over to the college, and we can talk on the way. Alan, do you want to come along?'

'Oh, yes. In view of what's been going on over there, yes, indeed. No, Watson, you can't come this time.'

The dog flumped down on the hall rug, the picture of an unloved, forsaken animal. The moment we left, I knew, he would go climb on our bed, muddy paws and all. I found umbrellas for the three of us, and we ventured out into the rain.

SIXTEEN

On our way, Alan and I gave Penny a brief version of what had been happening. When we'd finished she said, 'One murder, or presumed murder. One worrisome disappearance. One incidence of hideous vandalism. A possible case of blackmail. Along with assorted threats and obscene phone calls. Goodness, is that all that's been worrying you? No fires? No terrorist threats? Shrewsbury is certainly a quiet place, isn't it?'

Alan couldn't find a place to park anywhere near the Fine Arts building. Term had begun, and the campus was teeming with students and faculty, the latter walking huddled under umbrellas, the young ones with a fine disregard for colds and flu, running bareheaded and often bare-legged as well. It made me cold just to look at them.

He drove as close to the main entrance as he could. 'I'll let you out here and find a place for the car. Where shall I meet you?'

'The best thing would be if we left a trail of breadcrumbs, I suspect. I still have a hard time finding my way around that place. But I think we'll try the sculpture studios first, because I want Penny to meet Gillian, and see her work. And then if she's free for a while, she can show us around. But we'll wait for you in sculpture.'

Penny took a moment, standing under her umbrella, to gaze at the building. 'And you say the late head of this institution was an architect?' It was her only comment, but it spoke volumes.

'An award-winning one at that. Of course he didn't design this building.'

'I'm glad to hear that.'

'I think you'll like the work of most of the faculty, though. Some of it is brilliant, to my untutored eye, anyway.'

'Your eye may be untutored, but your taste is good, if your house is any example. Goodness, this place is confusing! That hallway doesn't seem to lead anywhere.'

'A lot of them don't. It's been remodelled so much over the years that nothing makes much sense. But I do know how to find the sculpture studios.'

I remembered that Gillian was teaching a class today, but I couldn't remember if it was scheduled for morning or afternoon. In fact, it had apparently been in the morning, for the main studio had, in one corner, a litter of platforms with twisted bits of metal on them.

'Oh, dear! I thought she was going to work with clay, but I guess the supplies ran out.'

'Dorothy, those are armatures. You have to have something to hold the clay in place. I'm not a sculptor, but I do know that much.'

'Oh. Goodness, I do feel ignorant! Anyway, I want you to see what Gillian's working on just now. Well, it's almost finished, actually.' I knocked on the door of what I thought was the room where *Summer* was being completed, and was surprised when Dennis opened it.

'Oh, I'm sorry! I just remembered Gillian said she was having a conference with you this afternoon. I just wanted to show her sculpture to a friend of mine, but we can come back later.'

'No, no, we've finished, don't worry. Come in and admire. Cheerio, Gilly.' He left, and with some trepidation, I led Penny into the room. If the conference had gone badly, if there'd been no good news about the sculpture program, Gillian would be in no mood to deal with a couple of visitors.

But she rose to greet us, all smiles. 'Dorothy! I was just going to call you with some good news!'

'Well, that's a welcome change, I must say. Good news has been in short supply of late. Gillian, I want you to meet my friend Penny Brannigan. Penny, Gillian Roberts. And Penny, this is *Summer*.'

The two women shook hands, and then Penny turned to look at the sculpture, and the look on her face told Gillian all she needed to know about public reaction to her work. She said nothing, just stood and looked.

'It's perfect,' she said at last. 'But of course you know that.'

Gillian laughed. 'I know it isn't. I can spot every flaw, and of course it's still not quite finished. But it seems other people like it quite a lot. That's my good news, Dorothy. A London gallery wants it, and wants more of my work as soon as I can get it to them. Isn't it amazing?'

'It's wonderful, but there's nothing amazing about it! You're in a class by yourself, you know. And speaking of classes, how did yours go today? Penny had to tell me what those bits of twisted wire were for. I thought you were having to abandon clay for the beer can and chewing gum school of sculpture.'

Her smile faded a little. 'Well, we still don't know what we're going to do about supplies for the students. My parents are willing to keep me in clay and bronze for my own work, until the fees start flowing in, if they do, but the college is another matter. Dennis is working himself up to go and talk to Braithwaite about the budget situation, and if he doesn't get any satisfaction, he may go over his head. The situation is untenable as it stands. But you didn't come to hear me moan! Penny, are you interested in art?'

'I paint a bit, and I enjoy all the arts. All the media, I should say. I'm not wild about the use some of them are put to these days.'

Gillian tilted her head to one side, as if listening. 'Are you American?'

'Canadian,' she said, and I could hear her suppressing the slight annoyance that Canadians always feel at that question. 'But I've lived in Wales for years.'

'Ooh, where in Wales? We did a holiday in Anglesey one summer, when I was young, and I've always longed to go back.'

Penny glanced at her watch. 'Do you have time to show me around the rest of the school? We could talk about Wales as we go.'

'Of course. There are three more storeys. Do you share Dorothy's anxiety about the lift?'

'She's told me what happened, but I don't think lightning's apt to strike twice. The lift by all means. Unless it really terrified you, Dorothy?'

'I'll stay here. Alan promised to join us soon.' And besides, I wanted Penny's impression of the whole set-up, untainted by my comments.

While I waited, I took a look around the studios. Nothing was happening yet in the carving area, apparently, for it was as clean as a sculpture studio can well be. Dennis's spiral of clay was taking shape, an elegant shape with sharp edges and smoothly curved planes, and still that odd look of anger. I had no idea how an abstract form could be made to look angry, but I knew now the source of that anger.

I thought about that, uncomfortably. Dennis had so many reasons to be angry with Chandler, and now with Braithwaite. Was it at all possible that he had done something about it? Even in my mind, I shied away from the word murder. And, I reminded myself, Dennis worked in clay, not any material that required a chisel. And anyway, the chisel had nothing to do with the case.

I was humming Gilbert and Sullivan when Alan found me.

'You sound cheerful.'

'Just a stray thought that reminded me of "The Flowers That Bloom in the Spring".'

'"Tra-la." Where's Penny?'

'Off on a tour with Gillian. I wanted her to see the place with her own eyes, not just through mine. She's already commented on the architecture.'

'Ah. Modified rapture, possibly?'

'Politely expressed loathing. Sensible woman. Oh, but Alan, there's good news for a change!' I told him about Gillian's good fortune.

'Well done Gillian! I hope she sells them all for lots and lots of lovely lolly. Did you talk to Penny about the crimes?'

'No more than we did in the car. I'm hoping something might strike her, some anomaly, some . . . oh, I don't know. Something a bit off that it would take another artist to notice.'

'And if she doesn't?'

'Then we've had a pleasant visit and we're no worse off than we were before.'

Penny was voluble in her praise of the prints and photographs she'd seen. 'Both those men are outstanding artists,' she said. 'It's such a pity about those prints that were destroyed. I do hope the printmaker . . . what's his name?'

'Thomas. Matthew Thomas.'

'A Welshman! Anyway, I hope he comes back soon to pull some more of those astounding woodcuts.'

'Oh, good grief, I hadn't thought about that.' I smacked my forehead. 'The blocks are still there, then?'

'There were a good many of them stacked on shelves in the printing room. I suggested to Gillian that she see to having them locked up. Most of the destruction you described had been cleaned up, but I could still see that it was vicious. If it was aimed at the printmaker in particular, rather than being just blind rage, whoever did it might well go for the blocks as well, and that would be a great loss to art.'

'Not to mention to Matt. Oh, I do wish we could find him!'

'Me, too.' Alan's voice was calm, but I could hear the tension in it. 'They're working as fast as they can, love.'

'When I get back home, I know a few people who'd be happy to help look. Do you know exactly where he's from?'

'No, but Derek will,' said Alan. 'I'll ring him as soon as we get home.'

Alan never uses his phone while he's driving, partly because it's illegal, but also because he's a sensible man.

We had a quick tea, as Penny needed to get back soon to her friend in the neighbouring village. I tried to steer the conversation away from the college of art and its problems. If she had any insight for me, I wanted it to come of its own accord, without any prompting. Penny was happy to tell us about her spa, its triumphs and disasters, and the quiet tempests in her teapot village of Llanelen.

'I hope Gillian will come for a visit soon,' she said. 'I did invite her, and maybe you could let her know it wasn't just a polite invitation. I really meant it. North Wales is so beautiful, and we have a number of galleries who'd be very interested in her work, if that London one doesn't decide they want exclusive rights to it.'

I assured Penny that I would try to convince Gillian to accept the sincere invitation. 'She needs a break, poor dear. She had so looked forward to beginning this new chapter of her life, but so far it's been one disaster after another. I don't know when she could find the time, though.'

'Any time. It doesn't matter.' She put down her teacup. 'Now I really must go. Thank you for a lovely lunch and such a pleasant afternoon, looking at all that marvellous art. Even Braithwaite seems to be doing a bit better than he used to.'

'Really? I admit I hadn't looked closely at any of the stuff he had on display, knowing I'd hate it.'

'I still hate it,' said Penny with a smile, 'but he's painting much more carefully now. Better brushwork, more attention to the effect of colour.'

'I bow to your expert knowledge. Maybe he's trying to ramp up his sales. Not that he'd ever admit there was ever anything wrong with his work.'

'Not he! I was so glad he wasn't in his studio. I've never met the man, but from what I've heard, I'd have had a hard time being civil to him.' She stood, gathered her things together, and then pulled an envelope out of her leather portfolio. 'I thought you might like this by way of a memory of Wales.'

It was a watercolour of Conwy Castle, light shimmering on the old stone and reflecting from the surrounding River Conwy. 'It's beautiful, Penny! We'll hang it in the kitchen, if you don't think that's insulting it. We spend so much time there, and I want this where I can look at it often.'

'The kitchen it is, and a compliment rather than an insult.' She gave us both a hug. 'Keep in touch, and don't forget to tell Gillian how welcome she'll be in Llanelen.'

Then she was gone, leaving me with several thoughts to try to put together.

SEVENTEEN

When Gillian came home that evening she was still full of excitement about the London gallery and its implications. As she helped me prepare dinner, she talked of extravagant plans.

'I'm thinking about buying a house. A farmhouse, with a good big barn I can turn into a studio. Then I could have animals, too, and space to work, and a lovely big kitchen with a slate floor and an Aga, and geraniums on the window sills.'

'Hand me that head of lettuce, will you, Gilly? And you could chop up a scallion or two, if you don't mind them in your salad. The cutting board's over there, and here's the sharpest knife. And Gilly, my dear, my first husband used to have a saying: "It is unwise to calculate the quantity of juvenile poultry before the period of incubation has been completed".'

She blinked. 'What does that mean?'

'"Don't count your chickens before they hatch." Frank liked to make things funny. But what I'm trying to say is, it's all right to have dreams. In fact, it's necessary. Those who never dream will never have their dreams come true. But don't start believing the good things will all come at once. There are probably a lot of disappointments in store before you achieve your ambitions.'

She grinned. 'I do know that, really. And honestly, I was just dreaming. But someday, I'm going to have that house and that barn, and a warm, friendly kitchen with red-checked curtains and a fat tabby cat asleep in a chair.'

Emmy, who was in fact asleep in a nearby chair, heard the word 'cat' and woke, stretching. When humans talk about cats, in her experience, they often feed them. She jumped down with loud meows, and of course Sam and Watson heard and came running. Gillian abandoned her preparation of human food and concentrated on the demands of the animals.

* * *

We heard very little in the way of progress on the case for the next few days. Alan found out from Derek where Matt was born and raised, and phoned the information to Penny. It was a tiny village in North Wales, in the slate-mining district, and as Penny had done some painting near there, she knew a few people, and promised to ask them to keep an eye open for Matt. Derek had also examined the personnel records at the college and learned that all the staff had been in place when Chandler was hired. Which didn't seem to get us anywhere, one way or another.

Beyond that, things appeared to be at stalemate. Gillian put the final touches on *Summer* and sent her off to London, with high hopes. She bought masses of clay, storing it in our cellar until her living arrangements were a bit more secure. She wanted to return to her flat, but Alan quite firmly discouraged her. 'You don't,' he said in the authoritative voice he seldom used, 'want to be a burden to an already overworked police force. So long as you're here, you're in little danger. Alone, you might very well be.' She saw the sense in that and acquiesced, and I thought she was secretly relieved.

September turned sunny again, but quite chilly. I searched out the heavy sweaters I'd put away in the spring, finally finding them, along with a couple of deceased moths, in a box under the spare room bed. I did a little work in the garden, helping Bob clear away summer plants to make more room for the asters and chrysanthemums of autumn. In truth, Bob would have made more progress without me, but he was in one of his kindly moods and allowed me to get in his way without too much grumbling.

'You don't want to pull up them geraniums,' he said sharply one afternoon, 'afore you takes cuttings.'

My blank look displayed my ignorance.

Bob leaned on his spade and delivered himself of a little lecture on gardening. 'No need to buy new plants every spring. You takes cuttings, see, and puts 'em in water for the winter, and when they root, you plants 'em in pots. Indoors, mind,' he added, doubtful of my grasp of botanical matters. 'You don't want 'em to freeze. Then when they're big enough to set out, and the weather's warm enough, I plants 'em for you, and bob's yer uncle.'

'Do I have any pots?' I asked humbly. Where plants and gardening are concerned, Bob is my infinite superior, and I know it.

'Stacks of 'em, in yer shed. Tell you what, I'll find some jars to start 'em in, and show you what to do next.'

'Thank you, Bob.' I knew the cuttings would probably die under my tender care. I can kill a philodendron. A *plastic* philodendron. But I'd try, if only to keep Bob happy.

'That's a nice girl you've got stayin' with you,' he said, returning to his spading. 'From over to the college, ain't she?'

'Yes, she teaches there.'

'Little trouble over there, eh?'

'You could say that. Is this about right?' I held up a severed piece of geranium.

'No, you wants 'em shorter than that.' He held his fingers about four inches apart. 'And healthy-lookin'. Don't want no scrawny ones. Me mum works over there, y'know.'

'No, I didn't know.' I rose creakily from the bench I use when gardening. My days of kneeling in a garden are long past, but I can reach most of what I need to from a low bench, and Bob does the rest. Getting up is sometimes a challenge. 'So Ada cleans at the college?'

'Now and again. Used to be twice a week, regular, but two, three years ago they started cuttin' back, and now it's only three, four times a month. Place is a tip, she says.'

'Did she help clean up the mess in the print studio?' I asked, and then wished I'd kept my mouth shut.

''Ere! 'Ow'd you know about that?'

I can lie like Ananias when it seems necessary, but I'm uncomfortable about lying to Bob. He's as honest a man as I've ever met, and somehow, lying to him seems a sort of betrayal. 'Um . . . actually, I saw the vandalism.' I hoped he would leave it at that. I didn't really want to explain what Alan and I were doing there, quite probably illegally.

Bob looked away from his digging, straight at me. 'Did you, now?' he said, with a speculative gleam in his eye. 'Ah.'

I had the feeling he saw the whole situation, but he said no more about it. 'Found some interesting stuff in all that clobber, she did.'

'Oh?' I tried to sound casual.

Again he fixed me with that watery blue eye, and again I felt he knew exactly why I was asking.

'Paints, you know, or inks or whatever they are. And paper enough to cover the room. And nasty sharp little knives and that. Wonder she didn't cut herself to ribbons.'

'I'm certainly glad she didn't.' And what else, I asked silently. What else?

'And a plane ticket. Or one o' them computer things, what does instead of a proper ticket. Wasn't torn nor nothin', but it was too old to use.'

'What a pity.' It was, too. I was hoping for something really incriminating. A cufflink, now. (Did men wear cufflinks anymore?) The butt of a particular brand of cigarette. Anything that would link the vandalism to any particular person, preferably the detestable W.T. Braithwaite.

'A real pity,' Bob went on. 'Me mum would've liked a nice little trip to Greece.'

I nearly dropped my pitiful bits of geranium. 'Greece?' I said in something nearer a squeak than my usual tone of voice. I cleared my throat. 'Sorry. Frog in my throat. Greece, did you say? A ticket to Greece?'

'Somethin' o' that. You'd want to ask her. I only know it was no use to her. Here, d'you still want this here barberry? It don't grow too good here. I can 'oick it out fer ya and put in a nice hydrangea as'll bloom beautiful next summer.'

'Whatever you think is best, Bob. You know this garden and what it needs. Here are the geranium cuttings, if you think they'll do. I think I need a shower.'

Bob took the cuttings with no more than a dubious look, and I escaped inside to think.

A ticket to Greece? But Chandler had used his. *Another* ticket to Greece? Was there to have been a companion? Then why didn't he – or she! – go on the trip?

I would have liked to discuss it with Alan, but he had gone to buy something mysterious for his computer. I had that shower and then went back to speak to Bob for a moment.

Bob had gone. The garden was looking much tidier. The small barberry bush had been 'hoicked out', and the resulting hole neatly covered and raked. As always, Bob had done a great job. But I had wanted to ask where I might find Ada just now. She had a heavy schedule, for she was such a good cleaner she was in great demand.

Oh, well. She was coming to clean for me in the morning. I would just have to wait until then.

'Bless you, I don't rightly remember! It was Bob what noticed it. I stuffed it in me bag, cause it looked valuable-like, and showed it to 'im when I got 'ome. He saw it said Athens, and then some word in heathen writin'.'

'That'd be Greek, I expect. They use a different alphabet from ours.'

'It was Greek to me, anyway! But as to what else it said, I couldn't say. If I didn't throw it in the dustbin, I'll bring it to you next time I come round.'

'It could be important, Ada. Would you mind if I came home with you when you leave here?'

'Not goin' 'ome from here. Got some shoppin' to do, and then I do the deanery this afternoon. But Bob'll be 'ome abaht lunchtime. He could mebbe find it for you. Now, I'll get a start on the kitchen. That dresser needs a good turn-out.'

I left her to it. Ada is neat-fingered and never breaks anything, but her whirlwind speed when handling my good china makes me nervous. I went upstairs to tackle the bedrooms.

I kept a close eye on the clock, though, and when noon rolled around and Mrs Finch shouted her farewells, I was on her heels. 'Can I give you a lift?' Mrs Finch had never learned to drive, and the only vehicle in the family was Bob's truck, which had been on its last legs for at least five years.

'Don't mind if I do, dearie. These pegs ain't gettin' any younger.'

I left a note for Alan, who was at his computer deep in his memoirs, and took Ada to the High Street. Then I went on to the oldest part of town, twisty little medieval streets with small houses. Ada's, as one might expect, was a little gem, with lace curtains of a bridal white, a front door with gleaming brown paint and a brass knob and knocker that shone like gold. The front steps were freshly scrubbed, and the pocket handkerchief of a front garden held flourishing chrysanthemums and annuals, and not so much as a single leaf of a weed. With Bob at the ready, one felt, weeds wouldn't dare show their heads.

Bob answered my knock, looking surprised. 'Did I get me days mixed? Did I ought to be at your place?'

'No, nothing's wrong, Bob. I'm just curious about that airline ticket. I talked to Ada, but she didn't remember much about it. She thought you might know where to lay your hands on it.'

'Ah. Thought you'd be interested. Me mum tossed it, but I scrabbled about in the dustbin and found it. Pongs a bit.'

Bob reached in a pocket and pulled out a greasy, crumpled piece of paper which was indeed smelly. I surmised it had shared the bin with the remains of yesterday's dinner, but at the moment I cared only that it was still marginally legible. I scanned it eagerly.

'Look, Bob.' I pointed. 'This is a ticket *from* Greece, not to. See: ATH – that's Athens airport – to LHR. London Heathrow. Someone was flying from Greece to England.'

'Huh. Would this be somethin' leftover, then? A ticket stub, like?'

'I don't think so. Every time I've flown I had to trade something like this for a proper boarding pass.'

'Why didn't they, then? Why buy a ticket and not use it? Must've been somebody rich. Ya don't fly to foreign parts for tuppence.'

'I can't imagine. I wish I could read the name, or even the date.' That information was obliterated by grease, and no matter how I squinted and held it up to the light, I was no wiser. 'Do you mind if I take this? I'd like to show it to Alan and see what he makes of it.'

Bob made a courtly bow. 'Welcome to it, m'lady. Wouldn't be my idea of a little present, but anyfink you like.'

Alan, by this time, would have come out of his den, flexing shoulders sore from too much computer work, and hungry for lunch. I hurried home and found him in the kitchen setting out sandwich makings.

'Oh, good. I'll get that potato soup out of the freezer. And while it heats, Alan, I have something interesting to show you.' I laid a paper towel on the counter and put the unlovely document on top of it. 'I wouldn't touch it, not when you're going to eat lunch in a few minutes. Just take a look and see if it tells you anything.'

He wrinkled his nose and picked up the paper towel. 'It tells me it's been keeping bad company. I'm moving it to the parlour, out of range of food preparation.'

'But do take a look while I stir the soup.'

'Where did you get it?' he called from the other room.

I told him. 'I'll tell you the whole story when I don't have to shout.'

As we ate our lunch, I told him as much as I knew. He frowned. 'Derek's men should have found this when they searched through the mess.'

'They're not professional cleaners. It must have been hidden under something, or in a crack. You know Ada never lets anything escape her.'

He was still frowning. 'And having found it, she should have turned it over to the police.'

'How was she to know it was important? Be reasonable, Alan, and stop being such a policeman. Bob thought it might be useful and saved it for me, so we have it now. What do you think it means?'

Alan pulled himself together and stopped grumbling. 'It could mean nothing at all, but it's curious. Sometimes the airlines give these things back to you after they've issued the boarding passes. They're useless at that point, but I've seen people tuck them into pockets for some reason or other.'

'But that would mean that someone returned to the college from Greece. And the only person from the college who went to Greece never came back. And yet he had to come back, didn't he, because he was found dead here. Alan, none of it makes sense!'

'Chandler is the only person we *know* went to Greece recently,' Alan pointed out with that annoying logic of his. 'There could have been any number of others. And this piece of paper could have been lying about for any length of time. Didn't someone say that the studios weren't cleaned very often?'

'I think someone at the college mentioned it, and Bob says Ada only works there a few times a month now, except of course when there's a disaster like the one in the print room. Budget problems again, I suppose. I *wish* we could read the date!'

'And the name. I'll take this to Derek this afternoon and see if he can send it to a lab. They can do amazing things with filters and so on.' He patted my hand. 'Sorry I was cross. It's an important find, and I'm happy you managed to retrieve it.'

I grinned. 'I'm happy you're over the sulks! Now, how about helping me finish off that crumble from the other night?'

We hadn't seen a lot of Gillian the past few days. She was out of the house before we got up, most days, and staying at the college until quite late, working frantically on new sculptures for the London gallery. Tonight she came home for a supper break, before going back to work some more, and we told her all about the find. She was only mildly interested. 'Probably something someone dropped ages ago. Students are forever going to Greece. Well, it's a Mecca for anyone interested in classical art, isn't it? And I don't see that it's going to help find Matt. We're all getting really worried about him, you know?'

'No one's heard anything from him, then?' I put down my fork, not very hungry anymore.

'Not as far as I know. His students are getting upset, too. He's not just a super artist, you know, he's a terrific teacher, too. No one else in the department knows a lot about woodcuts or lithographs or etchings or any of that, so they're all working on those giclée prints, which isn't really proper printmaking at all, is it? And nasty Will is trying to talk them into dropping printmaking and enrolling in his painting classes.'

'Is he any better at teaching than he is at painting?' asked Alan, one eyebrow raised.

'Not really. Some of his students are pretty good, but it's more or less in spite of him. He doesn't spend a lot of time in class, which isn't such a bad thing, actually. He's always off to galleries or shows or other pathetic attempts to promote his work.'

'Penny said his latest work is better than his older stuff.'

'She mentioned that to me, too. She's nice, isn't she? I try never to look at Will's paintings if I can help it. They give me indigestion.'

'Well, then, how about your own work? How's it coming?'

Alan and I had been ferrying quite a lot of clay to the college at intervals.

'Oh, it's just super! I don't mean the finished products. They're not far enough along yet that I can judge, though Dennis is less critical than usual, so I have hopes. I'm doing a series of heads, did I tell you?'

She had, but I smiled and gestured for her to go on.

'They're different nationalities, and it's such a challenge! Did you know that a Japanese head is usually slightly wider side to side than from front to back? Europeans are just the opposite, and Africans vary a lot from country to country. So it isn't just the facial features that have to be right! And then there are the clothes, not much, of course, for just a head, but the Japanese woman – I've named her Masako, after a friend – she has to have the suggestion of a kimono, and her hair has to be in a geisha style. And the Ethiopian man is so splendid, old, but strong and proud, with a beard and a turban – oh, it's just so great to have my hands in clay all the time, to be doing what I want to do!'

'What you were born to do,' said Alan gently.

Gillian got up from the table and gave him a hug. 'Thank you for that! And thanks, Dorothy, for another marvellous meal. And now I need to get on my bike.'

'She's a different girl from the dejected one of a while back,' I commented as we washed dishes.

'She's doing work she loves. But if we can't work out what's gone so badly wrong at the college, she may not be able to keep on doing it. Derek thinks the lab can get some good results from that disgusting printout, and that may give us some sort of direction.'

'And how long will that take?'

'You know the story, love. The lab always has more work than it can get through, and more urgent cases take priority.'

'But this is connected to a murder! How much more urgent can it get?'

'We think there's a connection. Derek thinks there's a connection. But there's no proof of that so far, and unless or until they can work out how Chandler died, there's no absolute proof that a murder has in fact taken place.'

I slapped my sponge down in the dishwater and created a miniature geyser that soaked the front of my apron. 'Drat! But this is so frustrating!'

Alan handed me the dish towel. 'Most criminal investigation is.'

EIGHTEEN

That evening, as we sat around watching a really boring western movie on TV, I had an idea. 'Alan, are Derek and co. doing anything about looking into Chandler's background? You remember, you had some questions about how he managed to get a professorship, or whatever it was, at an Ivy League college. And exactly when he won that architecture award. And so on.'

'He's put out feelers. I don't know that he's had any replies. As I said earlier, there are never enough resources to do the job in a hurry.'

'As you've said for years, in fact, beloved. That's why I think, tomorrow, I'm going to look up that secretary. I can't remember her name. The one who got fired?'

Alan made one of his equivocal noises that can mean almost anything, but usually implies a degree of scepticism.

'She's bound to have seen his papers, from when he was hired. And she probably knows where they are now. I think she might have some very useful information.'

'She has no reason to love Chandler. We don't know that she'd tell the truth about him.'

'No, we don't. But I'm predisposed to trust her, if only because she's been handed such a rotten deal.'

'A victim is always one of the good guys in the white hats?' said Alan, glancing at the screen where several white hats and black hats were shooting it out.

'Not always, except in the movies. But in this case I'm presuming innocence until proven guilty of something.'

'Ah, the great basis of English jurisprudence. I think that chap has just fired seventeen bullets from his six-shooter. Who edits these films, I wonder? And how do you propose to find a nameless woman who hasn't worked at the college in quite some time?'

'I'll ask Dennis,' I said smugly. 'He'll know. He's sorry for her. And you can't possibly have been counting shots and talking at the same time.'

'A policeman,' said Alan, 'can count shots in his sleep. Would you care for a nightcap before we go up?'

Alan obviously had little faith in my ability to find the secretary, but I was sure I could. Whether she'd talk to me was another matter. I don't suppose she had much reason to care who killed John Chandler, but she might be interested in telling me anything she knew to his discredit. If there was anything. But darn it all, we were pretty sure Braithwaite had been blackmailing him, so there had to be something he wanted to hide.

I woke well before dawn on Tuesday to a torrent of rain on the roof. That meant puddles to mop up. It also meant Gillian would be glad of a ride to the campus. I would have loved to snuggle back with my soft pillows and my lovely warm husband. It was that sort of morning. But duty called, so I slid out from under the covers, and Watson, as unobtrusively as I could and shrugged into my bathrobe.

Gillian came down just as the coffee was done. I made toast and tea and we sipped and nibbled in a sleepy early-morning silence which Gillian finally broke after a stretch and a yawn. 'I really, really do not want to get out in that rain today.'

'That's why I got up early,' I said. 'I have an errand to the college, and I thought I'd drive you, if you can wait a couple of minutes for me to get dressed.'

'Brilliant! Take all the time you need; I'm in no hurry.'

The sound of our voices had brought the animals to the kitchen. I asked Gilly to feed them and went up to get into some clothes. I found Alan half awake but, like me, showing no eagerness to rise and shine.

'I'm driving Gilly to the college,' I said, 'and then going to try to talk to Dennis. Expect me back when you see me.'

My reply was an inarticulate grunt.

Gilly was truly awake by the time we got on our way. 'What's your mission at the college today, Dorothy?' she asked.

'I need to talk to Dennis. I hope he'll be there.'

'He won't be happy, but he'll be there. He doesn't like early mornings, but Charming Chandler arranged his schedule this term to have early classes four days a week. He wasn't best pleased when he found out.'

I grinned. 'That's a wonderful example of the British understatement I enjoy so much. Will he be too grumpy to talk to me?'

'Not if you take him some coffee. He really misses the office coffee pot.'

So I made a quick stop at Starbucks for a cup of coffee and an insulated mug to keep it warm, dropped Gilly as close to the Fine Arts building as I could, and searched for a parking space, which took me another fifteen minutes. I was glad I'd bought the mug.

The campus hummed with activity. Students, dressed in everything from shorts and tees to full rain gear, trotted from one building to another. Actually, the ones in waterproofs were probably staff, old enough to worry about chills. The young never seem to mind being soaking wet or freezing cold. I suppose looking cool, or whatever the current word was, was more important to them than being comfortable. One's willingness to tolerate discomfort wanes, I had found, with increasing years.

I was quite wet enough myself by the time I walked into the building. My shoes were squishing. It would, I mused, have made more sense to wait until a bit later in the day, when the rain might have slacked off and Dennis might be in a better mood. Too late now. I found my way to the sculpture studios and walked into a class in progress.

In my long experience in the classroom, first as a child, then in college, and then teaching myself, a class was a well-organized affair, with recognizable patterns. The teacher was up front, demonstrating or explaining or lecturing. The students sat at desks and listened (or didn't), took notes (or didn't), put into practice what they had been taught (or goofed off). I had never, at any stage of my life, had the slightest degree of artistic ability, so had never taken an art class beyond the kindergarten painting with huge brushes and tempera paints. In my own teaching career, my art lessons were fairly pathetic efforts more aptly described as crafts.

So this class was a revelation to me. These were plainly advanced students, working in clay to be cast in whatever material was available. Dennis roamed about the room, suggesting here, correcting there, calling everyone to attention to demonstrate something that most of the students needed to see. I stood in the back and watched. I couldn't make sense of what the students were doing for the most part, but they were hard at work and seemed themselves to know what they were doing. One of them looked up at me, smiled, and shouted, 'Dennis! One of your lady friends!'

I would have flown out the classroom window before I'd addressed one of my college professors by his first name. As Gillian had so rightly said, '*autres temps, autres moeurs*'.

Dennis, after taking a swipe or two at a student's work with a small tool of some sort, came over to me. 'And what's my lady friend up to?'

'Not much, and I'm hoping you can get me going. Is there somewhere we can talk?'

He shrugged and gestured to the big room.

I shook my head, only a slight gesture, but the student who had noticed me caught it and gave us a knowing look.

'Oh, for heaven's sake, Dennis, I need to sit down in a proper chair!' I pitched my voice a little louder than necessary and in more of an old-lady croak than necessary. The student lost interest as Dennis led me into small room used apparently to store that miscellany of things that just might come in handy sometime. There was in fact a chair, though 'proper' wasn't exactly the adjective I'd have chosen for it. I stayed standing.

'I didn't want the students to hear,' I said very quietly. 'Things get so badly distorted. But I'm checking into a few things about Chandler, and I wondered if you had an address and or phone number for the former secretary. I've forgotten her name.'

He looked at me with suspicion. 'You don't think she had anything to do with his death, do you? Because I can tell you right now, she didn't. She couldn't.'

I didn't argue with him, though Alan has drilled it into me that almost anyone can kill, given the right (or probably the wrong) circumstances. 'No, I'm just wanting to learn more about the man's background, and I thought she might know where his credentials would be filed. You know, the paperwork submitted when he was first hired, that sort of thing.'

'Haven't the police looked at that?'

'They haven't got around to it yet. They will, in time, but I thought I might speed things up a bit. Being married to a retired policeman, I know just how understaffed they are.'

'And being a Miss Marple, you want to snoop.'

It was said with the hint of a smile, and I smiled back. 'Exactly! So do you have contact information for Mrs What's-her-name?'

'MacInnes. Amy MacInnes. And yes, I have her address, in my office. This lot is about to move on, so if you can wait a few minutes, I'll get it for you.'

'Thank you *very* much. And oh, before I forget, I brought you something.' I fished in the small bag I was carrying over my wrist and brought out the mug. 'Still hot, I hope.'

He bent to it and inhaled deeply. 'Heaven! For that I'll leave these budding geniuses to their own devices and get what you need right this minute.' He took off the lid and took a deep swig. 'God, I needed that. I don't know what sadistic idiot invented eight o'clock classes. Come along.'

When we had reached the privacy of his office, he said, 'Okay, what's really on your mind?'

'What I said. I want more information about Chandler's background.'

'Something dicey about it?'

'Oh, no, you don't. I have no idea.' Well, I had ideas, but they were only that, and I had no intention of discussing them with someone I barely knew. I liked Dennis, but I couldn't afford to trust him or anyone else in the department just yet. 'I'm grasping at straws. So if you have that address . . .'

After searching various drawers, he finally found a piece of paper and handed it to me. 'Here, but you'll have to copy it. And the office copy machine is down. Again.'

I found a scrap of paper and the stub of a pencil, and wrote down the address and phone number. 'I don't suppose you could tell me where this is. I ought to know my way around Sherebury after all these years, but I confess that I don't, apart from a few well-travelled rounds. I still find English roads extremely confusing.'

He gave me a thoughtful look. 'I could tell you, but as I have a break just now, why don't I take you there? I'll drive, and you can follow.'

It didn't take much insight to read his mind. He wanted to make sure I didn't browbeat Mrs MacInnes or accuse her of crimes or whatever dastardly deeds he thought I might commit. I smiled sweetly. 'That would be lovely. In that case, I'll leave my thumbscrews in the car when we go in.'

He just shook his head and gestured for me to leave the office first.

He drove me to my car. His was closer, in a staff-only parking area, and the rain was still pouring down in Niagara fashion. He might not think much of me, but he was thoughtful. When I got into my own car and set out to follow him, I appreciated his slow pace and careful signals. My windshield wipers were hard put to keep up with the floods of water sweeping over the glass.

I was glad he'd made the offer to show me the way, whatever his motives. I'd have got lost several times in the twisting streets, even if I had been able to see properly. We wound up at a biggish house near the edge of town. From what I could see of it through the rain, it looked like a once proud house now definitely in need of attention. Flaking paint on the trim, front steps in poor repair, a roof tile missing here and there. And it seemed way too large for an impoverished widow and two small children.

I pulled my hood over my head and got out, heading for the front steps. Dennis got out of his car and took my arm. 'Basement flat,' he said. 'Round this way.'

He led me around to what must, long ago, have been the tradesmen's entrance, and rang the bell. There was no roof over the door, no shelter from the rain and wind. I huddled in my rain gear and hoped Mrs MacInnes was home.

She was. I heard the sound of someone climbing stairs, and the wail of a fretful child. There was a pause, then the door opened.

The woman who stood there had certainly been beautiful once. Now her skin and hair were neglected. Her clothes hung on her, and she wore the expression of someone very nearly at the end of her rope.

'Dennis! It's good to see you, but why are you out on such a dreadful day? And have you had the measles? I think David is coming down with them.'

Dennis looked at me, and I nodded. 'We both have. May we come in?'

'Of course, but mind the stairs, they're frightfully dark. The light burnt out last week and Charlie hasn't replaced it yet.'

They were dark. They were also worn and uneven. I held tightly to the railing, though it quivered a bit under my hand and I hoped it wasn't going to give way.

Downstairs there was a little more light. Not a lot. A single, low-wattage bulb was burning in a lamp in the single large room. Two day beds and a crib took up most of the available space. A tiny kitchen alcove held a miniature fridge, a three-burner gas stove, a minute sink, a card table, and two cardboard boxes, one half-full of food, the other holding tableware. A closed door presumably concealed a bathroom.

The place was spotlessly clean. A little boy asleep in the crib had that scrubbed, shiny look of a well cared-for child, and so did the bigger boy his mother scooped up in her arms. He whimpered and turned his face to nestle on her shoulder. 'He really needs to see a doctor, I think, but I daren't take him out in this awful weather, and the new doctor won't come here.' She spoke softly.

'I'll drive you to the doctor as soon as we leave,' said Dennis in a low, gentle voice. 'You certainly can't wait for a bus in this monsoon. David would get pneumonia, and you probably would, too. Amy, this is Mrs Martin. She and her husband are looking into the mess at the college, and she thought you might be able to help.'

'And I'd be happy to stay with the little one while you're gone, if that would be some help.' I, too, spoke quietly. None of us wanted to wake the baby.

'That would be a very great help,' she said with dignity. 'Now, please sit down and tell me what I can do for you. Hush, darling, I'll give you some water in a minute.'

Without a word Dennis went to the kitchen, found a glass, filled it, and brought it to Mrs MacInnes.

'I'll only take a minute or two,' I said. 'This is obviously not the best time for you to talk. I'm just wondering where I can find the paperwork about Mr Chandler's hiring. There must be transcripts from his university work, letters of recommendation, that sort of thing.'

Mrs MacInnes frowned and looked at Dennis.

'It's on the up and up, Amy. Mrs Martin was the one who found John's body in the lift shaft, she and her husband, and he's a retired chief constable, so they're doing a little burrowing to save the official police some time.'

'Oh, you're that Mrs Martin. Dr Temple's friend.'

'Why yes! Did you know Dr Temple?'

'He was still very much a presence on campus when I first started working there. Everyone loved him, and I was no exception. I miss him.'

'So do I.' I blinked back sudden tears at the memory of the dear man who had been such a good friend long ago when my first husband came to the university to teach for a year on an Anglo-American exchange, and to me when I moved to Sherebury as a new widow. 'It was a privilege to know him.'

'Well, you need Chandler's credentials. I think I know where to find them, unless they've been moved, but it would be a bit hard to tell you. Dennis, do you remember the big filing cabinet that used to be in the copy room?'

'The one that was moved somewhere?'

'Yes, and very inconvenient it was, too, but someone decided it took up too much space. There's a sort of cupboard just down the hall from the small lecture room, and that's where they put it. I had to walk all that way when I needed a file. Fortunately I didn't need any of those very often. The information was entered into the central university computer files, naturally, but we keep the paper records just in case. The CVs and other staff materials were in the bottom drawer.'

'Excellent! So far as I know, that cabinet is still gathering dust in that same room. When we get back here, Dorothy, I'll take you to them.'

'Are you quite sure you don't mind looking after Bruce? It might be quite a long time if the doctor is busy.'

'I don't mind at all. Just show me where to find anything I might need.'

There was milk in the fridge and a packet of digestive biscuits in the box, and Mrs MacInnes showed me a small pile of diapers in the bathroom. 'He's almost trained, but I give him a nappy when he sleeps, just in case. He may not even wake up until we're back.'

'We'll be fine either way. Now wrap yourself up well, and David, too. It's dreadful out there.'

I was glad that David didn't fuss much about being inserted into a raincoat that was too small for him. A full-throated bellow might have wakened Bruce, and no matter how bravely I spoke, I hadn't babysat very much since my nephews and nieces were tiny, except for Nigel Peter. I wasn't sure how well I'd cope with a very young stranger.

They got safely out to the door. Bruce never noticed his mother had left. Relieved, I looked around for something to read.

There wasn't much. A few tattered children's books made up the library, housed in yet another cardboard box. There was a three-day-old newspaper in a rubbish bin. Mrs MacInnes struck me as the sort of woman who would want to keep up with the world around here, so I guessed that she had to wait until a neighbour or a local shop threw out papers.

I picked up one of the children's books and found a folding chair leaning against one wall. I sat down to read in the inadequate light.

On a bright day there would be more light. Two windows near the ceiling were very dirty on the outside, but clean inside, and though obscured by weeds, would let in some sunlight. Today there was no sunlight.

I found myself torn between pity and anger. It was iniquitous that a nice woman like Amy MacInnes should be reduced to such dire poverty. She was obviously trying to keep up some sort of life for the children. There were only children's books in the flat. The sparse store of food was all designed to appeal to children. The boys were well-dressed, even though David's coat was too small. Amy's jeans were darned and her shirt well-worn and baggy.

'Mummy?' The voice was soft and tremulous.

I stood and went to the crib. 'Mummy's had to go out for a little while, Bruce. She'll be back very soon, and I'll look after you until then.'

He considered that with a baby's intense frown. Something was puzzling him. I suddenly realized it was probably my speech. 'I sound funny, don't I? I used to live very far away where they talk differently. Now, let's see if you need a clean nappy.'

There are, after all, things one doesn't forget. I lifted him out of his crib and discovered that he was, indeed, slightly damp. 'No nappy,' he said firmly. 'On'y in bed.' I removed the wet one, and before I could catch him he trotted across the room, bare-bottomed, to point out a small pile of minute jockey shorts. 'Big boy!' he said with satisfaction.

After ablutions I helped him get into the fresh underwear and long pants, despite his preference for short ones. 'It's a cold day, sweetheart. You'll be warmer in the long ones. They're for big boys, too,' I added by way of enticement. He remained dubious, but acquiesced. What a love this child was! He could have been upset to find his mother gone, could have had a tantrum about being tended by a stranger. Instead he was polite and cooperative.

I had no illusions that my own child-minding skills had anything to do with it.

He sat down happily to some milk and a biscuit, and then I let him choose a book for me to read to him. We were happily ensconced in the folding chair with *Peter Rabbit* when Dennis and Amy came back.

'Where's David?' Bruce and I asked at the same moment.

'Being looked after,' said Dennis, with one eye on Bruce. 'And that's not the only bad news.'

NINETEEN

Bruce might not have understood the implications of what Dennis had so carefully left unsaid, but he caught the emotional tenor. 'Mummy?' he said in a near-wail, and wriggled out of my lap.

Amy hurried over and picked him up. 'And how's my little lamb, then? Were you a good boy while Mummy was gone?'

'David,' he said. It was a request both for information and for his brother's presence.

'David's got a bad itchy,' said his mother, 'and so he wanted to stay where they can help him feel better. Did Mrs Martin give you some nice milk?'

He nodded, his lower lip beginning to protrude. 'Want David.'

'I thought you might be a bit lonely, old boy,' said Dennis, 'so I brought you a little friend.' From an inside pocket of his coat he brought out a tiny kitten and put it on the floor near Bruce. It tottered on unsteady legs straight to the little boy and uttered a miniature mew.

'Pussy!' said Bruce, and smiled. He held out his hand. The cat licked a finger. The smile turned to a broad grin. 'Funny!' he said in reaction to the kitten's sandpaper tongue. The kitten mewed again, demandingly this time.

Bruce assessed the situation at once. 'Pussy hungry,' he said. 'Biscuit, Mummy.'

'I expect she'd rather have a little milk,' said Dennis, 'and perhaps some of this.'

Out of another pocket he produced a box of kitten kibble. He showed it to Bruce. 'For Pussy. *Not* for little boys. Nasty!' He grimaced and stuck out his tongue to cement the point.

In two minutes Dennis and Bruce had organized a meal for the kitten, and Bruce sat on his haunches watching intently as the little creature ate. Meanwhile Dennis brought out his final purchases, a small litter box, the appropriate filler, and a scoop. He set it up in a corner and, when the kitten had eaten all she wanted, carried her over and set her down in the box. She sniffed, scratched a small depression, and proceeded to use her nice new loo with, again, the fascinated supervision of her new master.

'I imagine you're going to have to explain that the box, too, is only for the use of the kitten,' I said to Amy.

She smiled. 'I'm sure. But perhaps only once. He learns quickly.'

'He's an adorable child,' I said. 'I'll babysit any time you like. He behaved like an angel.'

'He usually does,' she said. 'But he's going to miss David. They're very close. I only hope he can come home soon.'

'It's the hospital, then? Measles, as you thought?'

'And a very bad case, the doctor said. That's why they wanted him in hospital for a day or two. That, and to make it less likely that Bruce will catch them. I don't know what I'm going to do without David.' She sounded near tears.

'My dear, can I make you some tea? You look tired to death.'

'I don't think there is any.'

'I always carry a tea bag or two with me,' said Dennis, searching again in his pockets. 'Ah, yes. Darjeeling suit you?'

He busied himself putting the kettle on, finding the pot and cups, pouring milk into them while the tea steeped. He seemed very much at home.

'I hope no one takes sugar,' said Amy. 'I'm afraid I've run out.'

'Not I,' I lied.

The kitten by now had settled down with Bruce, who was sitting splay-legged on the floor, gently patting the soft fur as the animal purred itself to sleep.

'That was brilliant,' I said to Dennis as he handed us our tea. 'Where did you ever come up with a kitten on such short notice?'

'In my office,' he said. 'One of the students found it outside this morning, soaking wet and shivering. I said I'd try to find it a home. Well, a home presented itself.'

'Oh, so you stopped at the college?'

'Yes, and while we were there Amy showed me where the staff credentials ought to be.'

Uh-oh. 'Ought to be?'

'The file cabinet was exactly where she thought it was.

Everything was exactly as she had left it the day she left the
office, except for the staff records. The bottom drawer was empty.'

'It's a pity the drawer was touched,' said Alan when I told him
at lunchtime. We sat in the kitchen over steaming bowls of soup,
grateful for the warmth of the Aga.

'Fingerprints,' I said, nodding. 'On the other hand, if they
hadn't touched it, they wouldn't have known the records were
missing.'

We thought about that for a while. 'I didn't think to ask,' I
went on, 'but I don't imagine Dennis touched any of the other
drawers. He knew exactly where the records were supposed to
be. Whoever took them, though, might have tried all the drawers
. . .' I trailed off, and Alan shook his head.

'What do you do when you find that something isn't where
you thought you put it?'

'You look everywhere else,' I said with a sigh. 'Dennis probably tried all the drawers. Well, maybe the thief left fingerprints
elsewhere.'

'Dorothy, any of the staff might have needed to get materials
out of that file. We don't know what else is in it. Fingerprints will
prove nothing. So it doesn't actually matter much about Dennis's.'

'We're not getting anywhere, are we?'

Alan's answer to that was a shrug. I sat and finished my soup.

Over the dishes, I changed the subject. 'Alan, you've lived
here all your life. You know the way English people think, as I
never will, quite. Do you think I would offend Mrs MacInnes if
I offered her some assistance? Her living situation is pretty dire.' I
described it. 'And she's starving herself in order to feed the
children. Her jeans were at least two sizes too big, and there was
almost no food in the house.'

Alan considered. 'Love, I haven't met the woman. Does she
strike you as proud?'

'Self-respecting, at least. She accepted Dennis's tea, though.
He said he always carries some with him, but I wasn't convinced.'

'Hmm.'

There was something about the way he said it that made me
look at him sharply. 'You don't think . . . he must be twice her
age!'

'Perhaps it's a fatherly feeling.'

I considered. 'Well . . . he did seem very much at home in her kitchen. You could be on to something.'

'Then he's the one to ask about offering her help. You'll have to be careful, though. If he thinks you're in any way implying that he should be doing something, he could be very angry. The lad has a temper, as I recall. And we must never forget . . .'

'That any of the staff could be a murderer. Even Mrs MacInnes. I refuse to believe it of her, though.'

'A mother defending her young . . .' Alan didn't have to finish the thought.

I drained the sink and rinsed out my sponge while Alan dried the last few dishes. 'I don't know about you,' I said, 'but I think it's time to make some lists.'

Alan has sometimes smiled at my inveterate habit of list-making, but it's my one organizational tool. I don't know how anyone manages at the supermarket without a list. Christmas lists, lists of errands, lists of chores to be done. There's a lovely (if spurious) sense of accomplishment even in making the lists, let alone checking off items. And in the various criminal investigations in which I've somehow become involved over the years, my lists have often guided me on the path to new ideas and new discoveries.

So we sat down in the parlour with a small fire to cheer us and pads of paper on our laps. We also, of course, had cats on our laps, but their backs make reasonably good writing desks, and they're used to serving as such. Watson learned some time ago, to his regret, that he's not a lap dog, so he curled up at my feet.

'Right. Where shall we start?'

'How about with a list of the crimes?'

'They may not all be crimes.'

I waved that away as the pedantic comment of a policeman. 'Whatever you want to call them. First, of course, Chandler's death.'

'Then the next thing is Matt's disappearance, followed closely by the vandalism in the print studio.'

'Oh! You don't suppose—'

'Save the suppositions for later, love. What's next?'

'Gillian's phone calls. And then the disappearance of the

personnel files. Goodness! What a lot of different sorts of incidents! And they may not even all be related.'

'They all revolve around the College, though, and specifically the Fine Arts staff. Suppose we try to write down all we know about each of them.'

That took a while, and involved a good deal of discussion about what we actually knew (as Alan insisted) versus what we could reasonably assume (according to me). What we finally came up with was a trifle discouraging:

Chandler's Death
1. Found at bottom of lift shaft.
2. Dead approximately six weeks.
3. Cause of death unknown.
4. Flew to Greece three days after end of term.
5. Not seen or heard of since, in Greece or elsewhere.
6. (Added at my insistence) Someone brought back an apparently unused plane ticket for a return trip from Athens.
7. He was heartily disliked by almost everyone in the department.
8. (Also at my insistence) He was being blackmailed by someone.
9. (Alan did not dispute, but considered it irrelevant) He won an important prize for architecture years ago, but has done nothing important since.

Matt's Disappearance
1. He was expected at a party in his honour. Didn't call, didn't show up.
2. Had been very depressed since the murder of his partner. Friends feared suicide.
3. No signs of foul play at his cottage. His car gone. (I interrupted at that point to ask Alan if the police had found any signs that he had left voluntarily, missing clothes, or whatever.)
4. (Alan's reply to my query:) His cottage was in perfect order, with no suitcase in evidence, but no one could say whether any of his clothes had been taken.

Vandalism
1. It was done after 2:00 when the police finished searching the building, and before 4:30 or so when we arrived.

(There we stuck. We knew almost nothing more, unless the airline ticket meant something. As far as we knew, Derek and his crew had no clues to who had trashed the studio, much less why.)

Gillian's Phone Calls
1. Made by someone who knew her mobile phone number.
2. Someone who also knew when the police had taken her phone.

Missing Files
(There was nothing to note; we had no clues at all.)

'Well, that didn't get us very far, did it? I'm ready for some tea.' I stood and stretched, dislodging Emmy, who protested bitterly.

'So am I, but I think you're being overly pessimistic, love. We've cleared the decks. Now we can work out a plan of action.' Alan gently lifted Sam from his lap and followed me to the kitchen. 'Derek is working in a number of directions, those areas where the police organization can do much more than we can on our own. But let's not forget where you, in particular, excel: talking to people. You have a disarming way of encouraging people to tell you things.'

'But I've been talking to all sorts of people, and haven't learned much of anything.'

'I wouldn't say that. You've learned about the grudges against Chandler, and the possible blackmail, and the budget kerfuffle. I'd say it's time to go back and talk some more and see what you can nose out.'

'But term has begun. None of the staff have much free time.'

'There's one person who has a great deal of time on her hands. And who knows more about the inner life of an organization than—'

'The secretary! Of course. I could go and talk with Mrs

MacInnes. Maybe I could offer to drive her to the hospital to visit David.'

'And I could come along, and stay with young Bruce. Don't look so sceptical. He sounds an engaging child, and don't forget I have grandsons. I'll manage quite well.'

The kettle had boiled by that time, and we sat down to our tea. 'It's too late today,' I said, 'and besides, I want to talk to Dennis about what help we might be able to give her. I'm sure Gillian will have his phone number, so when she gets home, I'll be able to call him. And that reminds me, I wanted to make a pie for dinner, so I'd best get at it.'

As I rolled out pastry, I remembered the first time I had tasted an apple pie in England, at an upscale pub in Cambridge. My husband had had an evening lecture, so I was on my own, and found a likely-looking establishment and ordered what sounded like a typical American meal: steak and a baked potato and apple pie. Everything sounded familiar, but was in fact entirely different. The steak was the tenderest I'd ever eaten, and the tastiest. The waiter explained something I didn't quite understand about the way meat is aged. The potato was, of course, not an Idaho, and was waxy, not mealy. And the pie was made, also of course, with English apples, so much tarter than the American ones I was used to that I had to lift the crust and sprinkle on sugar.

I put a lot of sugar in the pie I was concocting, and hoped that Gillian would like it. I knew Alan would; he's become accustomed to my cooking.

Gillian was not destined to eat it, however, or at least not for dinner. She phoned shortly after I'd put it in the oven and said she'd be working late and would snatch a bite at Starbucks.

'I'll save something for you. You can put it in the microwave when you get home. And while I have you on the phone, do you have Dennis's phone number? I know it's no good calling the office there, with no secretary.'

'They're going to have to find someone soon. It's absolute chaos with no one to sort things out! I'll just find . . . yes.' She gave me the number.

'Is he working late, too, or will he be at home this evening, do you know?'

'He's left the building. Of course I don't know what his plans are for the evening.'

She said it so primly I was sure she had a good idea of his plans, and didn't altogether approve. I wondered again about him and Amy MacInnes, but I didn't think it was a good idea to discuss it with Gillian. 'Well, then, I'll just have to take my chances. Gilly, will you phone us when you need a ride home? It's much too far to walk, and this rain isn't ever going to stop, looks like.'

'Oh, someone will take me home. Don't worry.'

'Gilly, I hate to remind you, but someone at that school is doing some very nasty things, and we don't know who it is. I know you want to be independent and don't want to be a bother and all that, but please say you'll call us.'

She agreed reluctantly and I went back to preparing dinner, a quick chicken casserole that could be served almost any time.

As I slid it into the oven I had a thought. I picked up my phone.

'Dennis? This is Dorothy Martin. I hope I'm not interrupting your meal. Oh, good. The thing is, Alan and I have a few questions for you, mostly about Mrs MacInnes and her boys. We'd like to help, but we're not sure if she'd be offended. We wondered if you'd like to come over for a drink and some dinner, and we could talk about it. Well, yes, now if you can manage it. I know it's very rude to give you such short notice, but . . . oh, lovely. We live in Monkswell Lodge, at the end of the street by the gate . . . oh, you know it. Good. And you can park in front of the garage. We'll see you soon, then.'

I went to tell Alan we were having a dinner guest, and that Gillian wouldn't be with us till late.

'Ah. I'd better see if we've enough whisky.'

'And if you have to go get some, pick up some white wine while you're at it. We're running a little low.'

He decided to play it safe, and had just returned from his errand when the doorbell rang.

Alan replenished the fire, we settled with drinks, and I wondered how to begin. Dennis took the initiative.

'I suppose you were shocked to see the way Amy lives,' he said.

'I was upset, certainly. No one should have to live that way. I do admire her greatly for the way she's bringing up the boys. Even poor David, as awful as he must have been feeling, was well-behaved, and I fell in love with Bruce. But I can see the toll it's taking on her.'

'Yes. She's aged ten years since she left the college. And you wonder why I've done nothing about it, since plainly we're friends.'

'I don't know that I thought about it at all,' I said, somewhat less than truthfully, 'but now that you mention it, I suppose she won't let you. And I suppose she won't let us help, either, but I'd certainly like to try.'

'You think I haven't tried? I'll answer the question you haven't asked, too. No, we're not lovers. I love her, but not that way. I've never married, you see, so I never had a daughter. If I had, I'd want her to be just like Amy. Strong, intelligent, kind . . .' He became very interested in his glass of Glenfiddich.

'Oh, dear. Then there's probably nothing we can do. Except, she must get lonely sometimes. I mean, she can't really go anywhere with two young children and no money, and that flat is so dark and dreary. If I were to visit now and then, do you think she'd like that?'

'I'll ask. But I'll tell you what would be the most help. Find out what's going on at the college, so we can go back to normal and give her job back to her!'

TWENTY

We talked of other things over dinner. I felt that Dennis couldn't take much more talk about Amy without breaking down, and men get so upset about showing emotion. Especially Englishmen. The 'stiff upper lip' cliché holds a good deal of truth.

When he'd absorbed chicken and vegetables and was starting on his second piece of apple pie, though, I thought it might be safe to get back to part of our problem.

'I've wondered what the college is doing about Matt's classes until he comes back,' I said, passing the cream.

He poured a good dollop of it on the pie. 'If he comes back,' he said. 'That lad's in some sort of trouble, or he'd never stay away. He's the best artist at the college, and that's counting myself in. The students are at loose ends, and upset, because they're not learning anything. Our students are serious about what they do, and they've paid for instruction they're not getting. And I'm upset about Matt.'

'He's been very unhappy,' I said. 'You don't think he's . . .'

'Done away with himself. No, I don't. For one thing, he's a churchgoer, and the Church frowns on suicide.'

'I hope you're right, but I do wish the police would find him. I can't help wondering, with all the dreadful things that have been happening, if he's been hurt or – or killed. Dennis, did you see the print studio before they cleaned it up?'

'No. I've been told it was frightful.'

'It was beyond frightful,' said Alan, who had been listening intently. 'It was savage. I said at the time that it was a murderous attack, though the victim wasn't a human body, but his soul. I think someone went in there intending to kill Matthew Thomas, and when he wasn't there, the murderer killed the centre of his life and work.'

Dennis was shaken. 'That means,' he said slowly, 'that there's a madman at large in our college.'

'I'm sorry to say that I think it does mean exactly that. That's why Gillian is staying here for the time being. If she hasn't told you about some disquieting incidents, I won't betray her trust, but I think it possible that she could be a victim, too.'

'The phone calls? She's told me. She won't give me her new phone number. She said she was told not to let anyone know. But why would anyone want to harm Gilly? She's not been at the Wolfson for long enough to create any ill will.'

'And she's not that kind of person anyway,' I said. 'I can't imagine anyone hating her. And speaking of Gilly,' I added, looking into the kitchen at the clock, 'she surely should have called by now. I took her to school this morning and made her promise to call us to pick her up. She was working late.'

'Not this late,' said Dennis, and tension suddenly filled the room.

I pulled out my phone, found her number under the alias I'd chosen, and punched it in.

It rang and rang and finally went to the canned 'not available' message.

'Right,' said Alan, getting to his feet. 'Dennis, do you want to come with us or follow?'

'I'll follow, or rather lead. See you there.' He was out the door.

Watson, who had stayed courteously in the parlour while we ate, appeared and whined a little, sensing our disquiet. 'Alan, let's take him along. Because we don't know . . .'

He nodded and went to get the car out.

We didn't speak on that short ride to the campus. Watson, in the back seat, whined now and then. I was feeling the same way.

Alan ignored the parking regulations and left the car behind the Fine Arts building, in the dock area. The rain had diminished to a steady, persistent drizzle. Watson was soaked by the time we found an open door, not on the dock this time, but one of the side doors. He shook himself energetically when we got inside, and for once I didn't care.

Dennis was nowhere in sight. The building was dark save for an occasional corridor light. I took Alan's arm with one hand

and Watson's leash with the other, and kept a firm grip of both.
'Where are we?' I whispered. Watson whined.

'I don't know. This confounded building! I wish we'd brought
something of Gilly's. Watson might be able to find her.'

'Oh! I have a scarf. She left it in the car this morning, and I
put it in my pocket to return to her. Not as good as a shoe or
sock, but something.' I handed it over.

Alan took Watson's leash and held the scarf to his nose. 'Find
Gilly, old boy. Find Gilly!'

Now Watson is a spaniel mix, mostly mix. He's no bloodhound.
He has no training in search procedures. But like all dogs, he has
a nose that's something like a thousand times more sensitive than
anything we paltry humans can claim. Once before he had helped
us find someone, and I was hoping that this time he'd come through.

We could have roamed through that building calling Gilly's
name. Somehow I didn't want to. There was a feeling about the
place . . . I wished Dennis would show up.

Watson showed no signs of following a trail. He stood there,
looking up at Alan as if to question what he was supposed to
do. 'Right,' said Alan quietly. 'Let's try to find the main corridor.
That'll take us to the sculpture studio.'

On the maze principle – when in doubt, turn left – we eventually found it. We also found Dennis, waiting for us by the front
door in an agony of impatience.

'Where have you been?' He didn't bother to keep his voice
down. 'I've been all over the studio. She's not there.'

'Did you see her rain gear anywhere?' I, too, spoke in a normal
voice. It felt wrong, in that dark, silent place, but if Dennis
thought it was okay, I supposed it was.

'Didn't look. I'll see.'

He led us at a near-run to the niche where coats were hung.
There was Gilly's waterproof, bone dry. Her umbrella was
propped in a corner, barely damp. 'She hasn't been out at all
today,' I said, stating the obvious. 'She's here somewhere.'

Dennis gave voice to a full-throated roar. '*GILLY!*'

Watson quivered. Somewhere in the vast building footsteps
pounded down a stair and a door banged shut.

The humans looked at each other. Watson gave one short, sharp
bark.

'Oh, Watson,' said Gilly's voice, followed by Gilly, coming out of the stairwell.

Watson trotted over to meet her, quivering with joy. She patted him and spoke love words, but then gently pushed him aside. 'I almost had him,' she said. 'And then you all charged in and he ran away.'

'Almost had who?' I asked ungrammatically.

'I don't know.' She ran her fingers through her long hair, which was dishevelled, with clay stuck here and there. 'The one who's been doing all these dreadful things. I heard him in the photo studios. I thought it must be Sam, because what student would be here this late? Somehow, though, I didn't like to call to him.'

'It's spooky in here at night,' I agreed. 'You want to watch your back.'

'Exactly. Especially with all that's been happening. And anyway one never opens a darkroom door without permission. So I crept up the stairs and saw that the safe light was on in one of the darkrooms – the red light, you know?'

I nodded.

'But the door was open, which was all wrong. I saw someone in there, throwing things about. Then I knew it couldn't be Sam, so I waited in a dark corner. I thought when he came out I'd recognize him, and then we'd know.'

Dennis couldn't contain himself any longer. 'Damn it, girl, have you no sense at all? This chap is a murderer! If you could see him, he could see you! The Lord alone knows what he'd have done to you. Why didn't you call for help? Is your mobile dead? Or is it your brain?'

She put her hand on his arm. 'Don't you see? If I'd used the mobile, even in a whisper, he could have heard me. I wanted to catch him.'

'But I called you, just a little while ago. You didn't answer, but the man must have heard it ringing. That would have told him there was someone else in the building.'

'I'd turned it to mute earlier, when classes were going on, and forgot to turn it back to normal. Fortunately, in the event.'

'Next time,' said Alan, 'if there is a next time, speed-dial the number I'm going to give you. It's a direct line to Derek Morrison, who's investigating this series of crimes. You met him.'

She nodded.

'You don't have to say a word, just keep the line open. He'll know who it is, and that it's an emergency, and he'll be here at the double.' He watched her program in the number he recited. 'Now, shall we go and see what damage has been done? Don't go into the darkroom, and don't touch anything.'

We went soberly up the stairs, my hand on Watson's leash. The last thing we needed was a dog blundering into a crime scene.

Alan used his pen to flip a light switch in the outer studio, and we stood around the darkroom door.

It wasn't as bad as the print studio. There was less space to work with, for one thing, and fewer destructible objects. But it was bad enough.

The vandal had pulled photographic paper out of the lightproof container and scattered it about the floor. He had poured out the contents of some of the bottles. There was an overwhelming reek of hypo mixed with other noxious odours.

'Stand back,' said Alan sharply. 'Well back. Dorothy, get Watson out of here. And open all the windows, someone. That's potassium cyanide he's spilled, among the rest.' He took out his phone and called Derek. 'There's been another,' he said when he was connected. 'A darkroom this time. Cyanide spilled on the floor, and mixed with something acid. Yes, of course. Right.'

He put the phone back. 'He says we're to clear out and lock the doors behind us. I'll leave the windows open for ventilation. We're on the first floor here; no one can get in that way. Check your shoes. Anyone step in anything?'

All our shoes were dry, or at least only damp from our sojourn in the rain. Anxiously, I checked Watson's feet, but they were nearly dry, thank goodness.

I was glad to go with all the others down to the main floor. It was good to escape the sights and smells of that ruined darkroom, but I couldn't banish them from my mind. I kept thinking of how my first husband would have reacted to a scene like that, and the thought made me shake.

'Alan, did you notice the enlarger?'

'I know very little about photographic equipment, love.'

'The lens. The lens and its mount. They were lying on the floor, shattered.'

He took my trembling hand and held it firmly. 'We'll get him, my dear. We'll capture him. Don't worry.'

I went on worrying, but I was somewhat comforted.

TWENTY-ONE

The four of us – well, five counting Watson – huddled together near the front door, too shaken to say much. As soon as the police got there, the atmosphere changed. For one thing, they switched on lights everywhere, and the pervading gloom was conquered. The air of competent purposefulness helped as much. These men and women were clearly professionals who knew what they were doing and knew they were good at it. Derek issued a few brief orders and then came over to talk to us.

'Is there a place where we could sit?' he asked Dennis. 'Perhaps with coffee?'

'The only fluid that goes by that name here is unfit to give to Watson, let along humans. But we can certainly sit. My office is down this way. The chairs aren't comfortable, but they're better than standing.'

Derek called back one of his crew on her way to the stairs. 'Caroline, love, could you do us all a great favour? Apparently the nearest drinkable coffee is at Starbucks. I hate to send you out in the rain, and truly I'd send one of the men if they were within hail—'

'It's all right, chief. I know you're not sexist. And the rain isn't that bad. Four coffees?'

'Why don't you get one of those boxes and a supply of cups and so on? Then everyone can have some, as and when they need it.' He pulled some money out of his pocket and handed it to her with a pat on the back.

We settled in Dennis's office. As he had said, the chairs weren't great, but we were all weary from excess of emotion, and I for one was very glad to sit down. Alan pulled his chair close to mine, and Watson sat on my feet. I felt my heart and breathing begin to slow to normal.

'Well, then. Tell me, from the beginning.'

Gillian related her evening absorbed in her work, until noises from the photo studios upstairs caught her attention.

'What sort of noises?'

She closed her eyes in thought. 'Someone moving about. And then something heavy fell on the floor.'

'The lens,' I said. Alan shushed me.

'Were you making noise yourself?'

'Not a great deal, I imagine. Clay isn't exactly a noisy material, and I wasn't tramping about or singing to myself, or anything of that sort.'

'You had lights on, of course.'

'The lights in the big studio had been on all day. The rain made the world so gloomy. But I wasn't working in the big studio. These heads I'm doing are small, so I moved the current one – a young African woman, Dorothy, you'll love her – into that little room off the main studio. It doesn't have any windows.'

'And did you leave the lights on in the bigger room?'

'Inspector, have you seen the signs at all the light switches in this building? I was sure I should be set before a firing squad at dawn if I dared leave a light on one second longer than was required.'

'I hope they have their weapons in good order for me, then,' he said calmly. 'Go on. You heard noises.'

She told the rest of the story, sighing at the end. 'And I came so close! And then – oh, I know you all meant well, but I still don't believe I was ever in danger.'

'If you weren't then, you are now,' said Derek.

I looked from him to Alan, who wore the identical expression. 'I don't understand.'

Alan shook his head. 'He, whoever it was, knows now that he was observed. And thanks to our loud cries, he knows by whom.'

'All he doesn't know, we presume,' said Derek, 'is how much you saw, Gillian. But I imagine he'll be very eager to find out.'

We talked that over, Alan and I, after Gillian had eaten a piece of pie and gone to bed.

'Won't he know, when the police don't come knocking at his door, that she couldn't have seen enough to make problems for him?'

'A sensible person would do. I'm not certain this person is sensible. He may have begun with a plan that, however horrific, was conceived logically. Now I believe we're dealing with a rat in a trap, striking viciously in every direction, whether logical or not.'

I took a healthy swig of my bourbon. 'Alan, that's a terrible image!'

'Yes,' he said, and finished his whisky. 'I believe Gillian is in great danger. In fact, I believe everyone connected with that college is in danger, but especially Gillian.'

'Because she saw him.'

'And because she's young and female and thus presumably defenceless.'

'What can we do to keep her safe?'

'Nothing, unless we put her in protective custody.' I started to protest, but he held up a hand. 'Dorothy, the only way to be completely safe from a dangerous criminal is to stay in an inaccessible place. There aren't many of those. Some of the medieval castles were very nearly impregnable, but even there, foes could launch flaming missiles from a trebuchet. Modern maximum security prisons have been the site of riots and murders. Modern potentates have been assassinated despite elaborate security precautions. We could ask Gillian to stay in this house, all the time, see no one, speak to no one—'

'Which she'd never agree to.'

He nodded. 'Which she'd never agree to. But even if she did, with a little thought I could come up with perhaps a dozen ways she could be hurt or killed, within these walls. The only way she, or the rest, can be protected is if the murderer is captured.'

'And we're as far from doing that as from launching a rocket to the moon.'

'Well, perhaps not quite, but there hasn't been a lot of progress. I suggest we go to bed and think about it in the morning.'

'Thank you, Scarlett.' I polished off the bourbon, removed Sam from my lap and Watson from my feet, and did as suggested.

Wednesday, September 17

I had expected to sleep badly, but somehow I fell into deep dreamlessness and didn't wake until Alan brought me a cup of coffee.

'The rain has gone,' he said as he presented me with a steaming mug. 'The sun is shining, and Bob is already at work in the garden. A better day today, my love.'

Then he left me to complete my slow process of coming to full consciousness, but he'd cheered me considerably. I showered and dressed in record time, and went down to a sunny kitchen with a full complement of animals and Gillian feeding them titbits.

Alan looked up from his *Telegraph*. 'Eggs and bacon?'

'No, just toast and cereal this morning, thanks. I'm getting fat. I'll get it. Morning, Gilly.'

'Good morning. Fine day.'

'Beautiful. I wouldn't mind this kind of weather all year round.'

'Yes, you would,' said Alan. 'You'd be frightfully bored. And what would one talk about in trains and queues without the weather?'

'True, I suppose. "Another fine day" repeated for the forty-seventh time in a row would be a trifle monotonous. What are your plans for the day, Gilly?'

I tried to keep the anxiety out of my voice, but she must have read my face. 'Don't worry. Dennis is taking me to the college and home again. He insisted, last night. He's my designated mother-hen for the day. I've promised him I won't be alone with anyone except him today, and I'm not to work late. What are you two going to be doing?'

Alan, who had ignored me and prepared my meagre breakfast, sat down with us. 'I have a suggestion about that. Dorothy, how would you like to go with me on a hunt for Matthew?'

'Sounds great, only where do we start? Seems to me we have all of England to choose from, and the Continent's not all that far away.' I applied myself to my cereal.

'And what about Wales?'

'But surely the police have checked his home town.'

'They've made inquiries. That's not quite the same as going there.'

'You want to go to Wales?'

'Why not? It's a beautiful day, we can get there by lunchtime if we don't waste time, and we'll enjoy the drive, if nothing else.'

'Um.' Spur-of-the-moment travel has grown less and less appealing with the passing years. I like to plan. I sat and tried to think of what I was supposed to do in the next few days. 'How long do you think we might be gone?' I spread marmalade on my toast.

'If we have no luck in two or three days, there's no point in staying longer.'

'Oh. Well. If Jane can look after the animals . . .'

'I'll be here,' Gillian reminded me. 'I can see to them. You know I love animals.'

'And we'll take Watson with us,' said Alan.

Watson grasped that idea immediately, and barked his enthusiastic agreement.

I sighed and pushed aside what little remained of my breakfast. 'Okay, then. But I'll have to do a load of laundry first, and pack, and get in some groceries for Gilly . . .'

'The laundry is in the tumble drier, almost ready,' said Alan smugly.

'And I can buy whatever groceries I need,' said Gilly. 'I do want you to find Matt, if you can. Please agree to go.'

Three eager faces looked at me. (The cats, of course, paid no attention whatever. The conversation didn't concern their food or comfort.) Watson came up and licked my hand and gave me the full force of his pleading eyes.

I had to laugh. 'Oh, very well. I'll pack as fast as I can. And somebody make me a sandwich or something. I can't travel across the country on toast and cereal.'

'I'll do that,' said Alan, 'if you'll help her pack, Gilly.'

With Gillian fetching and carrying, it didn't take me long to assemble enough underwear, slacks, shirts and sweaters for four days. 'And if you stay longer, you can buy anything you need,' said Gilly. 'Now. Toothpaste, shampoo?'

'In that little bag at the top of the cupboard in the bathroom. It's all there; I keep that one packed in case of emergency.'

'I think this just might be an emergency,' said Gilly seriously, and then spoiled it by giggling at the toiletries kit, which had cartoon cats all over it. She tossed it into the suitcase. 'Extra shoes? It might be very wet.'

'Good thought. Those old sneakers – sorry, trainers – at the back of the closet should do in a pinch. They don't actually have holes in them.' I looked around. 'I think that does it. Oh, my bathrobe.'

'I put it in already.'

'Then I'm ready. Well, I'm probably not, but as you say, I'm not exactly leaving civilization as we know it.'

Still feeling rushed and somewhat out of sorts, I let Gilly carry the suitcase downstairs and out to the car, where Alan was waiting with Watson.

'You have your key?'

'Yes, and I'll be fine. Don't worry about me. Call me if you need anything.'

'And Gilly.' Alan leaned out the car window. 'Just to be on the safe side, don't tell anyone where we've gone or why. I think we took a sudden notion to visit . . . where, Dorothy?'

'The Lake District,' I said promptly. 'I've been told autumn is beautiful there.'

She agreed, waved goodbye, and we drove off.

I was still trying to sort out my feelings. 'Alan,' I said once he had negotiated several roundabouts and was on the open road, 'I agree that this is a good idea. But what's the big hurry? Wales will still be there tomorrow. If Matt is there, he'll presumably still be there tomorrow.'

'I don't know,' said Alan calmly, passing a slow-moving truck.

'Then why . . .?'

'I could give you reasons. The threat to Gillian is the biggest one. It's a beautiful day, I had an itch to travel. But the truth is, I have a notion in the back of my mind that this is the thing to do, and that now is the time to do it.'

'A hunch.'

'If you like.'

'Hunches are my specialty.'

'Perhaps they're contagious.' He grinned and took one hand off the wheel to pat mine. Watson, who had been a little upset by the tone of this exchange, sighed and settled down to sleep.

We weren't there by lunchtime. We had to go around both London and Birmingham, and the traffic was no better than usual. I was starving before we hit Wales, so we stopped for a quick bite in Shrewsbury. I knew a little about the city, at least the medieval city, from the wonderful Brother Cadfael books by Ellis Peters, but we didn't take time for any exploring. Alan was still possessed of this odd sense of urgency, and I was beginning to catch it from him.

When we had left Shrewsbury behind I said meekly, 'Did you happen to mention exactly where we're going? "Wales" is a fairly inclusive word.'

'Oh, sorry, didn't I say? The village where Matt was born is near Caernarfon, so I thought we'd find a place to stay there. Have you ever visited the castle?'

'My dearest love, I'd never been to Wales at all until we went to that music festival a while back. I've seen pictures. Isn't that where Charles was crowned Prince of Wales?'

'Indeed. It's quite impressive, actually.'

'The castle or the ceremony?'

'Both.' He concentrated on his driving then, trying to read the road signs, which are in both English and Welsh, with the language at the top varying from one sign to the next. I could make no sense of the Welsh ones, which seemed to bear no resemblance to the English names. But then, a country which calls itself Cymru (pronounced something like 'Kumry'), when the rest of the world calls it Wales, is plainly interested in presenting a challenge to visitors.

It was the castle itself which eventually led us to the city. It sits on the edge of town, the far edge, hard by the Menai Strait, but its towers are taller than anything else in even the modern city, so it was visible from a little distance and was quite unmistakable. Alan saw it the same moment I did, and considerately pulled off to the side of the road so I could gape.

I hadn't had nearly enough of it when Alan got going again. 'It's getting on for teatime, love,' he said as he got into the town and began manoeuvring its narrow streets cautiously. 'Look for signs to the tourist information office.'

It didn't take long to spot one. Finding the office itself, and then a place to park, was trickier. I was extremely glad Alan was driving.

'And it isn't even high tourist season,' I remarked.

'And a jolly good thing, too.' He turned another corner, and there, amazingly, was a car park with a space or two left.

He left me in the car while he sprinted for the TI office, which was probably about to close. The day was drawing in. I sat in the car for a moment, and then Watson reminded me that he needed out. I put on his leash, and we wandered a bit. Not far.

I didn't want Alan to come back and find me missing. He is not the sort to panic, but with everything that had been going on, he might get a little uneasy.

Caernarfon was clearly a tourist town. Every second shop was devoted to souvenirs, and the ones in between were either tea shops or antique shops, with now and then an art gallery. I peered into one or two of the latter. Most of the art was predictable. Watercolours of the castle. Oils of the castle. Photographs of the castle. Some of them were good; many were mediocre.

I was walking to one just down the street when I heard Alan calling me, and turned back.

'Success!' he said. 'We're booked into a pleasant guest house for three nights, and I got directions to the village where Matt's family lived.'

'Lived, or lives?'

'I don't know, but it's a tiny place, only about four miles from here. It's getting dark, though, so I think we'll wait until tomorrow to visit.'

'What's the name of the place?'

With a mischievous smile, Alan showed me the paper where the tourist people had written directions.

LLANGODFAN, it read.

I just looked at Alan. He pronounced it for me. 'More or less,' he added.

'I'll take your word for it. Right now I want to find a meal, and then our bed for the night.'

TWENTY-TWO

Thursday, September 18

'Now what?'

We had all finished our breakfasts. Watson was looking out the French door, watching the resident cat as it picked its way delicately through the damp grass. It was still early, with an autumnal mist in the air, but it would be a fine day.

'Now we go in search of Matt's village.'

'Right. I've named it Landon. Much easier. I wonder if anyone there speaks English. I wonder if it's there at all, in this fog. Maybe it's another Brigadoon.'

'Maybe you need a second cup of coffee to snap out of it.'

'I've had two already. I'd better hit the bathroom before we hit the road.'

Alan and Watson were waiting when I came back downstairs.

'He'll be all right in the car?'

'He's done his duty. He's a very fine dog, aren't you, old chap?'

Watson responded with his silly doggy smile and several wags of a sleepy tail, and then settled down for a snooze.

'How far are we going?'

'Only a few miles. It's within walking distance, really, but I didn't want to waste time.'

There was that odd urgency again. I never thought I'd hear my stalwart English husband refer to a country walk as a waste of time.

Oh, well. It was turning into a beautiful day, and this part of Wales was breathtaking, so I sat back to enjoy the ride.

It lasted for only a few minutes. Alan pulled the car over to the side and stopped.

'Something wrong with the car?' I asked.

'No. We're there.'

I was reminded of the judgement some sophisticated type pronounced on an American town: 'There isn't any *there* there.' We were stopped at what couldn't, by the wildest stretch of the imagination, be called a village. It couldn't even be described as a wide spot in the road. A few houses were clustered together. There was no pub or church or shop or garage. Just houses. Small, bleak houses. 'It looks very poor,' I said. 'Are you sure this is the place?'

'The sign says so.' He pointed to a road sign a few yards back. 'I'm sure it is very poor. This was a slate-quarrying village. Even when the quarries were working, the poverty was bad, but they played out decades ago, and you can see the result.'

'Does anyone still live here?' The only sign of life I could see was a seabird of some sort sitting on the peak of a roof.

'We shall see. I hope they do speak English. I have no Welsh at all.' He got out of the car and opened the back door for Watson, who bounded out, not at all daunted by the depressing scene before us. I got out with less enthusiasm. This was looking more and more like a wild goose chase.

Alan put Watson on the leash and walked up to the first door. Knocked. Knocked again. No response.

It was the same at the second house. And the third. I came up, took Watson's leash, and walked up the street. We might as well get some exercise out of this fruitless excursion.

Alan was trying the fifth house, the next-to-last, when I turned around with Watson and saw a car approaching. As it neared, I saw it was a truck, actually, a pick-up truck. It was dented and dusty, and its engine was making unhealthy sounds.

I pulled Watson to one side of the narrow road, but the driver slowed and stopped. The truck continued to shudder and clank. The driver leaned out, nodded his head toward Alan, and asked something. From the intonation I knew it was a question, but I couldn't understand a word. 'I'm sorry, I don't speak Welsh,' I said.

'Ah,' he replied, 'would you be looking for someone?'

'Oh, I'm so glad you speak English! Yes, we're looking for a friend, Matthew Thomas. He used to live here.'

The driver nodded. 'His people lived here once, but no one lives here now. There's no work.'

'Are they still living, his family?'

The driver shook his head. 'The slate's not so healthy for the lungs. His da worked it till he died, then his ma went on after him. No one lives here now.'

The repeated phrase was a dirge, a solemn tolling of a funeral bell. I nodded my thanks for the information, and as he drove off he called out to Alan, 'No one lives here now.'

We got back in the car and headed back towards Caernarfon.

'Not the most cheerful chap,' said Alan after a time.

'No. He'd have been a great hit marching in a Victorian funeral behind horses with black plumes. But Alan, even though we didn't find Matt, he did live there once, or his family did. They're all dead. Something about lungs?'

'Silicosis. When the working of slate was mechanized, the labourers breathed in the dust, and it killed them in the end, those who had survived the harsh working conditions. It's not a pretty story.'

'No. But Alan, why would Matt have come here, if his family are all dead and the place he lived in is dead, too?'

'I don't know. And I don't know that he did. It was an idea, but apparently not a practical one.'

The urgency was gone, and I, who had not been eager to take this trip in the first place, felt stricken. Alan is right so often, and despondent so seldom.

'Well, but look. It's a beautiful day, and Caernarfon is a magnificent castle. Why don't we go back and tour the castle and then the town? You booked the room for three nights. We might as well use at least two of them. And,' I added as I saw the look on his face, 'if you're worried about what's going on back home, you can always call Jane and Derek. Between the two of them they should know everything.'

He sighed. 'You're right, love. We can have a little holiday. Perhaps it'll give us a new perspective on the problems at the college.'

We left our car at the guest house. It was at the edge of town, but the town was so small, and driving so difficult, it was much easier to walk. Watson, we had learned, was not allowed in the castle, so we left him snoozing happily enough in our hostess's garden and set out.

Castles all have a family resemblance. They are not, as I used to think back in the States, fairy-tale places with romance written all over them. They were built as fortresses, made to withstand almost any attack, so they're massive, solid affairs. Of course, they're many centuries old, and they show their age. To me, although they ooze glamour, they're also somewhat frightening.

This one was especially so. For one thing, it's much bigger than the others I had seen and loved in Wales. Here, I felt, an army could withstand a siege for long enough that the besiegers would grow weary and go away. And they could stay in some comfort, for Caernarfon, I read in the guide book, was built to be also a royal palace, and Edward I actually lived there from time to time. Or at least his wife did, for his son, the first English Prince of Wales, was born there in the thirteenth century.

The huge size of the place intimidates. As, of course, it was meant to do. Octagonal towers and decorative bands of coloured stone set it apart from the others. It's in rather better repair than most, since it's still used on occasion by the Prince of Wales for various ceremonies since his investiture there over forty years ago.

It's a big tourist attraction. On a lovely day there were children running about; one toddler sat astride an ancient cannon. Yet for all its size and interest, it began after a while to make me feel claustrophobic. What would it have been like, I pondered, to be garrisoned there, or even living there in the relative luxury of the royal apartments, during a siege, when one couldn't get out?

I shivered, and was happy when Alan asked if I was ready for lunch.

'More than ready. I think I'm suffering from castle fatigue.'

'Never did I think I hear you say you were tired of a castle!' He offered me his arm and escorted me to freedom.

We found a pleasant place that served reasonable food and then went to pick up poor neglected Watson for a good walk around the town.

It didn't take long to reach the street where Alan had parked the day before. I recognized the second-rate art in the galleries. Neither of us was attracted by the souvenir shops, but the one gallery I hadn't had a chance to see was just on down the street. Literally down. The street at that point sloped steeply down toward the river. I handed Watson's leash over to Alan; when the dog gets enthusiastic he exerts quite a pull, and I didn't want to lose my balance.

I was glad we'd gone as far as the gallery. Gwyneth Davies, it said in gold letters on the window – apparently the name of the owner. It was several notches above the others. Yes, there were paintings of the castle and the town, in various media, but they were well done, and didn't constitute the entire stock of the shop. Displayed near the front window were—

'Alan! Look!' I pointed. 'Those are Matt's woodcuts or I'm a Chinaman!'

They were scenes of the town as it might have looked when the castle was built. No modern buildings. No suburbs. Just the walled town, the castle dominating even more than it seemed to now. They were done with amazing clarity and delicacy, and they conveyed far more than a picture of history. There was also the strong sense of how the Welsh felt about this stronghold of the English looming over their city.

Alan looped Watson's leash over a bicycle stanchion on the pavement outside the gallery, and we went in.

I had read somewhere that Caernarfon was a centre of Welsh nationalistic sentiment. The Welsh (with good historical reason) are sometimes not terribly friendly toward the English. Without even consulting Alan, whose accent was unmistakably English, I took the initiative, making an effort to inject as much Hoosier into my speech as possible.

'We're very interested in the woodcuts of old Caernarfon,' I said to the proprietor. 'I don't remember seeing them in here before.'

'Have you visited the gallery before, then?' she asked in a strong Welsh accent.

'No, but I've passed by and glanced in the window.' Half a lie is better than a whole one, and this woman looked very sharp. She'd remember who'd been here recently.

'You are right. These came in just a few days ago. They're lovely, are they not?'

'They are. They look new, though the views are old. Are they by a local artist?'

'He is from a local village. He does not live here now, but he came to visit and brought these to me. I have sold three already, and I am hoping he will be bringing me more. They are very fine.'

'They certainly are! Would I have heard of his name? They're so good, I'd think he'd be famous.'

'His name is Thomas, Matthew Thomas in the English – and here he is!' We turned around as Matt walked in the door with a portfolio under his arm. He stopped, saw us, dropped the portfolio, and ran out the door and down the street.

The proprietor said something in Welsh, and though I couldn't follow the words I understood that they expressed the same astonishment I was feeling.

'I must say I didn't expect that, any of it!' I said to Alan. 'How utterly frustrating, to find him and then lose him again. I don't suppose there's any point in going after him?'

'He's far younger and fitter than I am,' said Alan. 'But this proves what we already surmised.'

'Which is?'

'He's very much afraid.'

'But, Alan, why would he be afraid of us?'

'It's only a guess, but perhaps he's afraid we've come to take him back to the college. And it's not much of a stretch from that to suppose that whatever he fears is at the college.'

'It's not a stretch at all. It's only reasonable, given all the things that have been going on there. Something is rotten in the state of the Wolfson College of Art and Design.'

The proprietor had given up trying to follow our rapid English, concentrating instead on picking up the papers that had fallen from Matt's portfolio. Now she turned to us.

'Is it that Matthew is afraid? Is that what you are saying? Why should he be afraid, a fine young man, a fine artist as he is? He cannot have done anything wrong.'

'No,' said Alan reassuringly. 'Some odd things have been happening at the college where he teaches, and we think he may be worried about them.'

'Are those more woodcuts?' I asked. I wasn't sure, but I thought Alan would be happier with a change of subject.

'Indeed, and fine they are.' She held one out for us to see, and I gasped.

'But it's Sherebury! The Cathedral – and look, Alan.' I pointed to one corner. Matthew had chosen to show the Cathedral from an angle that showed also the vast expanse of close, and just on the other side of the wall—

'Our house!' Alan was as delighted as I. He pulled out his wallet. 'I think we must have this, Mrs Davies.'

She named a price that took my breath away, but Alan didn't bat an eyelash. He handed over a credit card, saying, 'And can you recommend a good framers' shop? I don't like to risk taking it home unprotected.'

Mrs Davies shook her head. 'No, that is the price with the matt and the frame. Come.' She led us to a counter at the back of the shop, where various matts and frame mouldings were on display. I let Alan work out the details of the transaction while I pondered the implications of Matt's appearance and rapid disappearance.

It was a great relief to find him, I had been desperately afraid he was dead, either by his own hand or another's. The fact that he had come back to his native heath made me think that his depression was easing a bit. He had sought the friendly, the familiar, the comforting. Further, he was showing initiative, selling his work to keep him going. Perhaps he meant never to go back to his teaching job. Perhaps he thought he'd be sacked for disappearing without notice.

One thing was perfectly plain, at least to me. Matthew Thomas knew something, something that would damage someone at the college. And Alan and I had to find him and get him to tell us what that was.

TWENTY-THREE

'It won't be ready until tomorrow,' said Alan, leaving the shop. An ecstatic Watson greeted us as if we'd been missing for days.

'That gives us one more day to find him. Do you think we can?'

'I gave Mrs Davies our phone numbers, yours and mine, and asked her to have him call us if he came back to the gallery. I tried to convince her that Matt had no reason to fear us, quite the contrary. I'm not sure I succeeded.'

'Well, what is the poor woman to think when he takes one look at us and flees as from all the devils in hell? Added to the fact that her English is a bit limited, and it's no wonder she doesn't quite trust us. Where would he be staying, do you think? Obviously not at his old home.'

'Probably not, though he could use it as a squat, if he's not fussy about his comforts.'

'But someone would notice. I know the village is deserted, but that makes it all the more likely that someone like the old fellow in the truck would spot any comings and goings. I'll bet he's holed up somewhere with one of his friends. And I have absolutely no idea how we could find out who they are.'

Alan got that faraway look in his eyes that may mean he's tuned me out completely. In that case his next words would be 'Yes, dear'. But what he said was, 'I wonder.'

That meant something I'd said had started him thinking. I waited.

'Darling, you remember the policeman who investigated those deaths when we were in Wales before? The competent, helpful one?'

'Mm. More or less. Wasn't his name Owen?'

'Probably. Every fifth inhabitant of Wales is named Owen. But I wonder if he'd know anything about Matt's family and friends.'

'But he's in a whole 'nother part of the country. Why would he know people here?'

'As you so frequently remind me, dear heart, every part of the UK is small. Wales is especially so, and we're still in North Wales. The big political division in Wales is between north and south, not so much east to west. It's true that Mold and Flint, where Inspector Owen has jurisdiction, are in a different county, but they're only about fifty miles from here. Some of you Americans commute that far to your jobs every day. And given that Owen has the name he does, he probably has cousins who live in these parts. We've nothing to lose by phoning him.'

I couldn't argue with that, so I wandered with Watson on down the street while Alan went through the tedious business of finding the inspector's number and calling him. There wasn't a lot to see, but apparently there were all sorts of entrancing smells, so Watson was happy. 'You're a useless mutt, you know,' I told him. 'Why didn't you stop Matt when he went hightailing it down the street?'

Watson grinned his happy doggy grin at me. I was talking to him. I was taking notice of him. Only if I offered him a treat could life be any sweeter. I ruffled his soft ears and turned back to Alan.

'Any luck?'

'I left a message. What would you like to do while we wait for him to ring back?'

'Find some tea! That lunch was fairly sketchy.'

'That probably means a hotel.'

He took my arm and we made our way to the Black Boy Inn, where it was just warm enough to eat outside at a table in the sun. We weren't sure Watson would be welcome inside, and we didn't want to abandon him again.

We'd just poured our tea, and I'd had one bite of a lovely piece of bara brith (a delightful Welsh tea bread), when Alan's phone rang. He looked at the number, said 'Owen', and moved away from the table to a sheltered spot where he could be relatively private. I didn't even try to listen. He'd tell me when he came back and meanwhile there was a plateful of my favourite kind of food in front of me.

I had time to demolish very little of it, though, before Alan came back. 'Any luck?'

'Some. He knows some people who know some people who

might have known the family. I have a few names to start with. *After* I have my tea.'

We had seen Matt. We knew he wasn't dead or a prisoner. Talking to him could wait a little.

I buttered another piece of bara brith.

When all of us, including Watson, had had enough to eat, we strolled back to our guest house. It was getting chilly, and I wanted a sweater. While I brushed my teeth, Alan busied himself copying some of the names and numbers Inspector Owen had given him. 'Why don't we divide them up, love? We can get through the list quicker that way.'

It didn't sound like a lot of fun. There were five names on my list. 'What if they don't speak English?'

'Almost everyone here does, as a second language at least. And I'll fare no better than you, if someone doesn't. I have about three words of Welsh.'

'Is this what the police call "routine"?'

'Usually with some unpleasant adjective before the word, yes.'

'Okay. What am I supposed to say, assuming I actually reach someone I can talk to?'

We worked out a script, and with a sigh, I began to work.

As a way of spending a late afternoon, it was somewhat more interesting than watching the grass grow. My first two calls were picked up by voicemail. I left a brief message, giving my name and saying that I was a friend of Matthew Thomas, that I was in Wales wanting to see him, and would they call me back. I thought as I hung up the second time that if I were a Welsh friend of Matt's, and he was hiding out with me, I would never in this world reply to a message like that, much less one in a slight American accent.

The third number I tried was answered by a man who either spoke only Welsh, or was defeated by my American-accented English. We gave up trying to communicate.

Doggedly I punched in the next number. This time it was answered by a woman. I could hear a radio or television playing loudly in the background. 'Hello, my name is Dorothy Martin. I'm a friend of Matthew Thomas's, from Shrewsbury—'

'*Who?*' A spate of canned laughter. Television, then.

'Matthew Thomas. He used to live in this area—'

'Never heard of him, sorry.' The phone was clicked off.

One more number. I looked over to see if Alan was having any luck, but from his expression I didn't think so. He was punching in a number. I sighed and did the same.

Another voicemail. I was batting zero. I left my message and put my phone down.

'Nothing?' asked Alan.

'Nothing. I left some messages.' My voice told Alan what I thought of the chances of joy from that.

He nodded. 'It was worth a try. There was never a lot of hope—' His phone rang. Both our faces brightened. 'Alan Nesbitt here. Yes. Yes, we are, very much so. We're at a guest house.' He gave the name. 'Any time; we'll be here.' He clicked off and smiled broadly at me.

'A lead?'

'Better. Much better. That was Matt. He's agreed to meet with us.'

The first thing Matt said when we opened the door to him was, 'I'm not going back.'

'Not if you don't want to,' said Alan agreeably, and Matt relaxed a little. 'Why don't we talk about it over a drink at the Black Boy?'

'I'm chapel. I don't drink.'

'Well, have some orange juice or tonic and lime to keep us company, then.'

We had to leave Watson behind, to his distress, but it had become much too cold to sit outside. On the way to the inn, Matt said, 'You bought one of my woodcuts. Thank you. Gwyneth charges far too much, you know.'

'Matt, we had to have it. It has a little sliver of our house in it!'

So then we had to explain where we lived, and the difficulties of maintaining a Grade II listed building, and that lasted us nicely until we were seated with drinks in front of us.

I lifted my glass. 'Matt, here's to you, and our joy at finding you safe.'

He looked surprised. 'Safe?'

'My dear boy, didn't you know everyone would be worried about you? The last time I saw you, you were terribly depressed, and then you disappeared without telling your friends you wouldn't be at the dinner party, or cancelling your classes. Of course we were afraid something dreadful had happened.'

But he had stopped listening and put his hands to his mouth in the classic 'oh, no!' gesture. 'The party! I forgot all about it! How could I forget to tell anyone? But all I could think about was getting away.'

'You do realize,' said Alan with commendable patience, 'that you still haven't told us why you felt you had to leave in such a rush.'

Matt toyed with his orange juice for a moment. 'Who else knows I'm here?' he asked finally.

'No one except Mrs Davies at the gallery,' I said.

'We've made some phone calls to people in this area who might have known you or your family,' Alan added, 'but we didn't say we thought you were here, or near here, only that we wanted to speak to you. In fact everyone I was able to talk to claimed not to know you at all. Dorothy?'

I nodded. 'Some of them didn't even speak English,' I added.

He smiled at that. 'Everyone knows some English, but they're rather like the French, linguistically, at least. They understand only what they want to. But no one back in Sherebury knows where I am?'

'Not from us,' said Alan, 'though we're going to have to tell them something when we get back. We told Gillian we were going to look for you, and where, but left strict instructions that she was not to talk about it.'

'I think, Matt,' I said, 'you'd better phone one of your friends, maybe Christopher, whom we know too, and tell him you're quite safe and not coming back for a while. And when we get home we can tell anyone who asked that we had no luck, which is true enough if we were trying to bring you back with us. But you never answered Alan's question. What drove you away?'

He took a deep breath. 'I know something that could be very dangerous. At the moment I can't prove it, so I'm not going to tell you what it is. No, I know,' he said, holding up a hand against our protests. 'I'm not going to tell you because if you let anyone else see that you know, it could mean harm, even death, to someone else. I've thought about this while I've been away, and there's only one safe thing to do. And even then . . . well. Does either of you know an art expert? I mean a real expert, like a conservator, or someone who authenticates paintings for auction houses, anyone like that?'

We looked at each other. 'I don't think we do,' I said at last, 'but I know where we could probably find one. We know quite a few people at the British Museum, and though they don't have paintings in the collection, museum people stick together. I'm sure one of our friends would know a conservator.'

'Then bring him, or her, to Sherebury to have a look at some of Braithwaite's recent paintings, and some of the older ones. I don't know how you'll explain it.'

'Are you going to explain it to us?' asked Alan.

'No. Just make sure the chap is discreet. If at all possible, Braithwaite shouldn't know he's there.'

And he finished his orange juice, shook hands with us, and vanished into the autumn evening.

TWENTY-FOUR

I was all for getting home as fast as possible, but Alan reminded me about the picture we needed to pick up in the morning. 'We can call some of our BM contacts just as easily from here,' he reminded me. 'And no art expert could possibly get to Shrebury before tomorrow, more likely several days from now. So we might as well stay right here where we are, order dinner, have a leisurely evening, and go on our way refreshed tomorrow.'

So while we waited for our meal, I phoned, or tried to phone, in order: Walter Tubbs, Jane's grandson, who had done a lot of volunteer work at the BM (voicemail); his wife Sue, who worked at the Bethnal Green Museum of Childhood (voicemail); and Charles Lambert, a fellow American and old friend who had spent many months doing research at the BM. That was years ago, now, but he had eventually moved to London for good, and would still know museum people. That call wasn't answered at all, didn't ring, in fact. Which meant he'd forgotten to charge his phone again, or lost it, or bought a new one and forgotten to give me the number.

Our food arrived, and it looked and smelled wonderful, so I put aside my frustration for the moment and refuelled, but when I'd finished every bite of my dinner, including the calorie-laden trifle (and sworn to diet in earnest tomorrow), I sighed. 'Nobody stays home anymore. Or they don't answer their phones, at least.'

'One doesn't have to be at home these days to answer a phone,' he pointed out with that exasperating logic of his. 'We're not at home. Probably Walter and Sue have gone to a play or concert and turned off their mobiles. As they should. Why don't you try Lynn and Tom?'

'You know, just when I've decided you're driving me crazy, you come up with something that makes me decide to keep you after all. Why didn't I think of them?'

He wisely forbore to answer.

I waited to call our best friends in London until we were back at the guest house and ready for bed. Tom and Lynn Anderson are a couple of American expats like me, but there the resemblance ends. Tom recently retired from an extremely lucrative position with one of the multinational oil companies, so they have pots of money. Their house in Belgravia is the last word in elegance, with paintings all over the place, many of them Impressionists, all of them priceless originals. I used to wonder what the expense in insurance might be, and then decided to stop wondering. Whatever it was, they could afford it.

Besides being wealthy, they are also two of the nicest people I've ever met, clever and funny and ready to help a friend at the drop of a hat. And as Alan had remembered, they know a great deal about art.

The call was brief. When I'd finished, I reported to Alan, who had retired to bed with a book. 'They're in the south of France right now. But yet, they know a good conservator, and they'll look up her number and email it to us. It'll be waiting for us when we get home. You're brilliant, my dear.'

'I know. And modest. And extremely lovable.' He dropped his book and quirked his eyebrows at me. I turned out the light.

Friday, September 19

We didn't leave Caernarfon till after ten the next morning. That was when the gallery opened. Our picture was ready, beautifully framed, but Mrs Davies had to show it to us to make sure we were happy with it, and then wrap it elaborately for safe travel, and then there had to be the mutual exchange of courtesies. I had to go outside and walk Watson up and down the street to keep from screaming with impatience. At last, at last, we got started, and I heaved a huge sigh of relief.

'You're as impatient as I was on the way to Wales,' said Alan, smoothly negotiating a complicated double roundabout.

I loosened my death grip on the armrest and nodded. 'I didn't know why we were coming all this way, and I confess I wasn't terribly enthusiastic about it. You were right and I was wrong. Now I have the same feeling of urgency about getting home.'

'Because of Lynn's message about the conservator?'

'No. I mean, yes of course I'm eager to get in touch with the woman, and get her here to find out what Matt's talking about. But it's not that, or not entirely. I just feel we have to get home.'

Some men would have said something moderately annoying about women's intuition. Even Alan might have, once, before he began falling prey to forebodings he couldn't explain. He nodded, and concentrated on driving.

When our hunger and Watson's needs could no longer be ignored, we stopped at a petrol station just off the motorway. I walked Watson so he could anoint every post on the property, while Alan filled the tank and bought us some food. 'Sorry, love,' he said as he handed me a bag. 'All they had.' But I was in such a state of impatience that packaged sandwiches and chocolate bars were adequate provisions. I poured a little bottled water into a bowl for Watson and put it on the floor of the back seat. He'd probably spill most of it, but it might satisfy him till we got home.

I had expected the usual infuriating delays around the big cities, but by some miracle the roads were clear, so we got home by teatime. We hadn't thought to warn Gillian that we were coming back early, and she was probably at the art college still, so the house was dark and chilly. Alan built a fire while I rushed about making tea and rummaging in the cupboards for anything edible to go with it. I found only a rather elderly box of mixed biscuits, a forgotten gift that had gone soft and tasted of nothing in particular. 'Sorry, Alan,' I said when we sat down. 'This is as bad as lunch. I'll come up with something good for dinner.'

'No, you won't. I'll do some shopping now and some cooking in a bit. You go and find that name and number Lynn promised to send you, and get that project started.'

I did as he suggested. There was still a strong feeling, some-where around the back of my neck, that this was not my most urgent chore, but I might as well get it done. I sat down, booted up my computer, and went to my email.

After dealing with all the spam, and wondering what life would be like if there were no email and all this junk had landed in paper form in my real mailbox, I found Lynn's message. I was copying down the name and number (yes, with a pen; I'm still not a techie) when my phone rang.

'Dorothy! Thank God! Are you home?'

'Yes, Gilly, we got home an hour or two ago. What's wrong?'

'There's been another one! Can you and Alan come to the college, right now?'

I didn't waste time telling her Alan wasn't home. I didn't ask 'Another what?' I was afraid I knew. I ran next door, asked if Jane would drive me to the college, and phoned Alan on the way. 'Something terrible has happened. I don't know what, but Gilly just called me from the college, in great distress. Jane's taking me over there. Meet me there just as soon as you can, will you?' I hung up knowing that this, whatever it was, had been the source of my unease all day.

When we got near the Fine Arts building, we saw swarms of police cars. Students were milling about; a gurney was being loaded into an ambulance. Jane let me out and went to find a place to park.

'I'm sorry, madam, you may not come in,' a uniformed officer began, but Gilly ran through the crowd to me, crying. I put my arms around her and stroked her hair. 'All right, sweetheart, it's all right. Do you want to tell me what's happened?'

Alan drove up just then and parked, regardless of the double yellow lines and the police. He came up to the two of us as the same officer approached, looking furious.

Alan pulled out his old warrant card and flourished it. It was plainly stamped 'Retired', but it had its effect. The officer stepped back. 'I would like to speak to DCI Morrison, please, if he's here,' said Alan in his voice of command.

'Yes, sir, I'll find him, sir.'

Gilly was still sobbing on my shoulder. Alan touched her arm gently. 'We need to know what's happened, Gilly.' There was still enough of the chief constable voice left to quiet her sobs.

She pulled out a tissue, blew her nose, and said unsteadily, 'It's Braithwaite. He's been attacked. I don't know if he's still alive. I found him. It was horrible!'

We saw Derek approaching. Alan conferred with him for a moment, and then said, 'Take her home. I've told Derek I'll make sure she's available to question when she's feeling better. Take the car; I'll catch a ride with Jane or someone. I'll be back as soon as I can.' He handed me the keys and hurried off.

I bundled Gilly into the car and turned on the heater. It wasn't really cold, just chilly, but Gilly's teeth were chattering. She was suffering from shock and needed to be kept warm.

When we got home I put the kettle on, first thing. The kitchen was pleasantly warm from the Aga, and Watson, with his sure instinct for a human in need of comfort, came and lay on Gilly's feet. Sam strolled in and jumped on her lap, purring. When the tea was ready I put plenty of sugar in Gilly's cup, and then sat down to keep her company and keep an eye on her.

She finished her tea and poured another cup and then sat back with a shuddering sigh. 'That's much better. You're a good therapist, Dorothy.'

'Nothing like hot tea and warm animals,' I said. 'Did you have any lunch?'

'Yes, but I lost it, back there. I don't think I'm quite ready for food yet.'

'Do you want to talk about it? Don't if it's going to make things worse.'

'No, I think I want to talk. Maybe it'll stop me reliving it every moment.' She shuddered strongly.

'Turn it into a police report,' I suggested. 'Cut and dried, just a record of observations.'

'I'll try.' She took a deep breath. 'Where should I start?'

'How about from the beginning of the day?'

She nodded. 'I went to the college as usual this morning and taught a lecture class first thing. Then I had some papers to mark, and then I went to work in the studio until I started getting hungry and realized it was well past lunchtime. I'd brought sandwiches, so I went and ate them in the staff room. No one else was there, probably because it was so late. I usually eat in the studio, but the work wasn't going so well today and I didn't want to sit and look at it.' She finished her tea and lifted the pot, which was empty.

'I'll make some more,' I said, though I was afloat. The sugar, at least, was helping Gilly. 'Go on.'

She swallowed hard. 'Some of my students were hanging about in the corridor when I came out of the staff room, and they wanted to talk. So we chatted for . . . I don't know how long. Maybe even as long as a half-hour. I know it was almost four when I got back to the studio, because the light was beginning to look late, so I glanced at the clock. I worked for a little while longer, but the head didn't get any better. I looked around for a tool I sometimes use, but I couldn't find it anywhere.'

'What sort of tool?'

'A kind of scraper, for putting texture into clay. It was the African woman I was working on, and I couldn't get the hair right. I thought the tool would help, and when I couldn't find it I was really annoyed. Sometimes the printmakers nick our tools, because they can be useful for making blocks. Not wood, of course, but linocuts. It can ruin the tools, and I was really furious at the idea that someone had taken it. So I went charging upstairs to have it out with the thief.'

She paused and drank some of the fresh tea. We were coming to the bad bit, I thought.

'You already know the walls are too thin in this building. The floors and ceilings conduct sound well, too. There was no one in the print studio. I started to look for my scraper, but then I heard noises over my head.'

'That's the painting studio, isn't it?'

'Yes.' She sipped more tea. 'I could hear shouts and thumps. It sounded like two men having a frightful row.'

'You're sure it was two men?'

'At least two. I couldn't distinguish any words, only voices, but they were angry male voices. And then . . . then I heard a scream, a man's scream. I've never heard anything like it. It was . . . frightening. And then there were more thumps and bumps, and then . . . nothing.'

I reached over and took her hand. She steadied her voice and went on. 'I didn't want to go up and see what had happened. Oh, so very much I did not want to go up! But . . . but I couldn't not go, you know? It was so obvious that something bad had happened, and if I was the only one who had heard, and I did nothing . . . anyway, I went. And found him.'

'Found Braithwaite.'

'Yes. He was lying on the floor, and there was blood every-where, and . . . and that's when I lost my lunch. I made it to the loo, and as soon as I could I phoned the police, and then I phoned you. And that's all.'

TWENTY-FIVE

I t was far from all, I knew. Derek would want a great many
more details. But there was no point in making the poor girl
go over everything with me and then again with them.
Despite the tea and the comforting animals, the warmth and
cosseting, Gillian was still looking pale and strained. And no
wonder!

'Look, I have an idea. Why don't you go up and have a little
nap? Alan will be home soon and has plans to cook us something
good for dinner. I imagine that when you've rested a bit, you'll
be hungry.'

'I'm not at all sure of that. But a nap sounds great.' She put
Sam gently on the floor, nudged Watson away, and climbed the
stairs like someone many, many years older than she. I made a
quick trip to the bathroom (very necessary after all that tea), and
sat down to think.

This latest crime made a hash of all my theories about the
earlier ones. I'd come to be more and more sure that Braithwaite
was at the bottom of all the ugliness. True, not everything fit.
I still couldn't work out why he would have wanted Chandler
dead. And I had no idea how anyone could have done the
deed, with Chandler supposedly in Greece at the time his body
was apparently lying at the bottom of the shaft. But I wanted
it to be Braithwaite, and so many details *did* fit. He was such
a nasty man, for a start. He'd almost certainly been blackmailing Chandler about something. He was just the sort to
send Gilly obscene phone messages. He had trampled quite
deliberately into the print studio mess, making it very hard
for anyone to tell exactly when the inks and so on had got on
his shoes. And Matt had some sort of suspicions about his
paintings.

Oh! I'd done nothing about the paintings! The latest emergency
had put it right out of my head. I looked at the clock over the
stove. After seven. Way too late to call anyone at a business, but

the matter was urgent, I felt. I wondered if Tom and Lynn had a home phone number for their pet expert.

I pulled out my phone and called them.

Tom answered the phone with 'Well, D., you're having an exciting time in your little burg, aren't you?'

'Wait till you hear the latest.'

'Oh, we've heard, unless there's been something more since the "murderous assault on world-famous painter".'

'Oh. The news.'

'BBC at six. Lead story. I guess it's been a slow news day. Does this have something to do with your need for a painting expert?'

'In a way. I'll explain everything when I can, but right now I need to know if you have an evening phone number for said expert. Everything got a trifle hectic around here for a while, and I forgot to call her.'

'Curiouser and curiouser! You two owe us a fancy dinner and full details when things have settled down. Wait a minute, I should have her number right here – yes. She's become a good friend over the years, and she won't mind you calling her at home.'

He gave me the number.

'Yes, the fanciest dinner you want, at the fanciest place you want to choose. *Thank you,* Tom!'

I heard Alan at the door just then, and went to meet him. He was laden with groceries. 'Oh, good, you remembered to get food.' I took one of the bags from him. 'What's the latest? Is Braithwaite alive?'

'Only just. He was stabbed several times; one of the injuries was critical. He lost a good deal of blood.'

'Gilly said there was blood all over the place. Do the police have any idea about who?'

'Not so far. It's early days yet, and of course they need to talk to Gilly. Did she tell you anything?'

'Nearly the whole story, but I wouldn't let her go into detail. She's upstairs asleep. At least I hope she's asleep. I gave her quite a lot of sweet tea, but she wouldn't eat anything. I hope you weren't thinking of roast beef for dinner, or anything like that.'

'Stir-fry, with prawns.'

'Oh, good. That sounds perfect. I'll leave you to it. I have that phone call to make, and then I'll wake Gilly.'

'Phone call?'

'To the conservator. I was just about to call her when Gilly called.'

'Ah.' He started sorting out groceries and I went to the parlour to make my call.

I suppose voicemail is a wonderful thing. It may save endless repeat phone calls. But it's frustrating in the extreme to an impatient person like me. Alan has often chastised me gently for my irritation when the world fails to adjust itself to my needs. I plead guilty as charged.

I identified myself as a friend of the Andersons, left a detailed message requesting a callback at any time of the day or night, and went upstairs.

Gillian was sleeping so soundly I hadn't the heart to wake her. She had fallen on the bed in her clothes, not even bothering to take off her shoes. I gently removed them and spread a light blanket over her before I turned out the light and left the room. She'd had a rough few weeks, poor child. Let her sleep.

Alan and I were exhausted, too. It had been a very long day; the conversation with Matt seemed to have taken place months ago. We had a simple supper of scrambled eggs and toast; it seemed a pity to make something elaborate for just us, and the ingredients Alan had prepared would keep just fine for a day. He said that Derek didn't plan to see Gillian until tomorrow, which was a very good thing. We tidied up the kitchen, had a modest nightcap, and were just about to let Watson out one last time and then go up to bed when my phone rang.

'Ignore it,' said Alan.

'I can't, not with everything that's been going on. It could be something important.' I pulled it out of my pocket and answered.

'Mrs Martin? Kate Winston. You called me about an art question? It's rather late, I know, but you did say any time.'

'Oh, yes, I'm so glad you called! It's not really late at all, and I'm sorry if I sounded irritated. It's just that it's been a long day, and I was headed for an early bed. The thing is, I need your expert opinion about some paintings.'

'If you're thinking of buying, I charge rather a lot for authenticating—'

'No, it's nothing like that. It may be a criminal matter, and it's pretty complicated to explain over the phone. Do you think my husband and I could come and talk to you? We live in Sherebury and could be there any time you like.'

'I don't quite understand. Are you connected with the police?'

'My husband is a retired chief constable, and we're looking, unofficially, into some disturbing events at the Wolfson College of Art and Design.'

'Ah. Wasn't the head killed some time ago in rather peculiar circumstances? Fell down a lift shaft or something?'

'Or something. There are people under threat, Ms Winston.' I thought about Gilly, asleep upstairs. 'It's really quite important that we talk to you.' I heard my voice wobble, to my disgust.

'I see.' I could tell from her voice that she didn't, but she was softening. 'I actually have an appointment near Maidstone tomorrow morning. I could stop and see you sometime in the afternoon, if that would work out for you.'

'That would be perfect. We can meet you anywhere you like.'

'You live in Sherebury?'

'Yes, next to the Cathedral Close.'

'Then let's say the Cathedral. It's one of my favourites, and I've not seen it in some time. I'll phone to let you know when.'

I filled Alan in and we went to bed feeling that some progress was being made at last.

Saturday, September 20

We all felt much better in the morning. Gillian was somewhat subdued, but she made a good breakfast. It was a beautiful day, clear and crisp, with autumn definitely on its way. When she'd had all she wanted to eat, we told her about finding Matt.

'Oh, that makes me feel so much better! But why hasn't he come back?'

I'd worked out an answer to that one. 'He needs some time to himself. I think he's still grieving, and as you would understand, the past few weeks at the college have been . . . distressing.'

Alan chuckled at that. 'And you say we English have the gift of understatement!'

Watson, who had sensed some tension in the air, relaxed and joined in the laughter with several joyous barks. Sam took exception to the commotion and hissed at Emmy, who hissed back and began to chase Sam around the kitchen.

'Let joy be unconfined,' said Alan. 'Oh, I had a call early from Derek. I thought you'd both want to know Braithwaite's holding his own. Not conscious yet, but they think he'll pull through.'

'I don't suppose,' I said, 'they know anything about who attacked him.'

'Not a lot. They found the weapon in the art studio, a painting knife.'

'A palette knife,' I said, ever the pedantic retired teacher.

'No, a painting knife. I didn't know they were different, either. Apparently a palette knife has a fairly long, broad, blunt, flexible blade, while painting knives are of varied shapes, including short and pointed, with more rigid blades.'

'Oh, yes,' said Gilly. 'I remember those from the one painting class I took as an undergraduate. I was hopeless with them, or with a brush, either, come to that. *Not* my medium. But I never quite saw the point of painting with any sort of knife. Those pointed ones – well, not pointed, exactly, more tapered – I kept gouging holes in the canvas with them. I can see how they could do quite a lot of harm to a person, though I'd think it would take a bit of strength. The point isn't at all sharp, nor is the rest of the blade.'

'Well done, Gilly,' said Alan. 'That's exactly what the forensics people are thinking. Snatched up in the heat of the moment, used without real thought, but with plenty of fury behind it. The attacker was almost certainly left-handed, by the way. Which rules out perhaps eighty-five per cent of the population.'

'But not eighty-five per cent of artists,' said Gilly with some authority. 'For some reason heaps of artists are left-handed. Dürer was left-handed. So was Paul Klee. Almost everyone knows Leonardo was a lefty, but not so many know Michelangelo was ambidextrous. And then there's Rembrandt, and . . . oh, so many others.'

Alan sighed. 'One day, something's going to be easy. I don't suppose you'd care to say how many of the students and staff of the college are left-handed?'

'I've no idea,' she said, seriously considering. 'But, for what it's worth, I am.'

He sighed again. 'And I don't imagine for a moment that you attacked William Braithwaite, but I'd just as soon you didn't tell the police about your little peculiarity, at least for now. If you're ready to go, I'll drive you to the studio.'

'It's a lovely day. I can cycle easily enough.'

'My dear girl.' Alan was using his most patient voice. 'I recognize and salute your independent spirit, but I remind you again that a murderer is out there, and almost certainly connected with the college. I'm not your father, and I can't insist. But I'd greatly prefer that you allow me to drive you back and forth, until we've caught the villain.'

She grinned. 'Do you know, I actually keep forgetting? I'll be honoured to have an escort, thank you, sir.'

'And can I, then, persuade you to come home at a reasonable time? Suppose I plan to come and fetch you around six.' He made it a statement, not a question, and she didn't demur. I thought it wouldn't be a surprise if she called to try to negotiate a later time, but that was Alan's problem.

Meanwhile I wanted to take some action, see what I could find out before the conservator showed up. I found the list Alan and I had compiled about the crimes and other frightening incidents at the college, and sat down to study it.

When Alan came home, I met him at the door. 'Alan, we never went to talk to Mrs MacInnes. Remember, we were going to, but then we got worried about Gilly not coming home, and then all kinds of things have happened since, and I forgot. Let's go now.'

'Should we phone first?'

'She doesn't have a phone, not even a mobile. And with David ill, she'll certainly be at home. I wish Dennis were here to show us the way, but I think I can find it.'

'Wait.' Alan disappeared upstairs and came back with two teddy bears, a larger and a smaller one. 'The grandchildren are long past caring about these, and perhaps it's the sort of gift that Mrs MacInnes wouldn't be too proud to accept.'

'Brilliant! It won't put food in their mouths, but it'll make the boys happy, if I'm any judge. Which, come to think of it, I'm really not. Too little experience. But they can't hurt.' I wished I had some baked goods to take along. Even the proudest person can't turn away scones or fresh bread or the like, since it would be a slap in the face of the giver. But I hadn't baked lately, and store-bought goodies were in an entirely different category. Then I had a thought.

'One more minute,' I said, and ran quickly next door.

Jane was home, and had just made bread, from the smell of it. I explained my errand and she thrust one loaf into my hands, still warm. 'Jam,' she said, giving me a jar. 'This year's.'

'You are an angel straight from heaven. I already owe you so many favours there's no point in trying to repay, but I won't forget this.' I took my parcels to the car Alan had taken out of the garage, and we were off.

Predictably, I got lost, but Alan managed to find his way, more or less by feel, when I described the house and the neighbour-hood. I did recognize the house when we came to it.

'Rather grand place once,' said Alan, shaking his head sadly.

'A very long time ago.' We rang the bell at the back and waited.

I was prepared to remind Mrs MacInnes of who I was, but she remembered me. 'You've had measles?' was her first question when I introduced Alan. He nodded,

'Come in, then. I'm afraid David is a bit fretful this morning.'

'I hope this might distract him,' said Alan, holding out the bigger bear. 'It belonged to my grandchildren, but they're far too old for such things now. It's been well-loved.'

'I can see that.' Mrs MacInnes studied the rubbed places, the eye that had been replaced a little off-centre, the half-torn ear. 'I think perhaps it's become Real.'

'Oh! You know *The Velveteen Rabbit*! It's my very favourite children's book, but I didn't know it was popular in England.'

'A Canadian friend sent me the book for the children, and it's nearly fallen to pieces.' Without another word, Amy MacInnes and I had formed a bond, the instant bond of those who love the same book.

'And Alan's brought another bear for Bruce, so he won't feel

left out, and I ventured to make a contribution as well. My
neighbour is the best baker in Sherebury, and when she offered
me the bread and jam I thought I'd like to share them.'

That was stretching the truth only a little, and Amy graciously
accepted the offering. She led us downstairs into the dark,
crowded flat, where David lay on the couch whining a little.
'Darling, look what a friend has brought you.' She handed him
the teddy, putting a hand on his brow at the same time. 'Isn't he
a lovely teddy? What will you name him?'

'Dennis,' said the little boy promptly, and hugged the teddy
to him.

'What a nice name! Now would you like a glass of milk? And
there's bread and jam for our tea!'

'Dennis wants bread and jam, too.'

'He can certainly sit with us while we have ours.'

She helped him off the couch. He was a bit unsteady on his
feet, and when his pyjamas parted a little at the top, I saw a fine
rash on his neck and chest. 'Oh, he'll be feeling a bit better,
then, now that the rash has come out,' I said. 'How's the fever?'

'Much better. He's fractious now from inactivity more than
anything else. And of course the itch. Lotion helps a bit, but . . .'
She shrugged.

'And Bruce?' I asked. He was standing in his crib, bright-eyed,
listening to the conversation and eyeing David's teddy.

'The nurse came and vaccinated him as soon as we knew
what David had. There's still a chance he might get it, but I'm
hoping.'

'Mummy? My teddy?'

'Yes, darling, the nice man's brought one for you, too, see?'

It took a little time to get everyone (including the teddies)
provided with bread and jam and milk, real or imaginary, and
tea for the grown-ups, but Amy managed it calmly. She served us
as graciously as if we were seated round a damask-spread table
drinking out of Royal Doulton cups, instead of being perched
on various items of furniture with chipped mugs and plastic
plates. The kitten got into the act, naturally, wanting some milk,
wanting to explore the plates with bread and jam, wanting to
know about the teddy bears, wanting to be everywhere at once.
It turned into quite a hilarious party, with all of us laughing at

the antics of the tiny, self-important creature. Never mind that it was closer to elevenses than teatime. We all enjoyed it.

When the boys and the kitten had eaten all they wanted, and the loaf was reduced to crumbs, Amy settled them for naps (the kitten stretching out in the crib with Bruce) and then sat down with us. 'I do appreciate the treat, and the toys, and so do the two bairns, but I imagine you didn't come here just for that.'

TWENTY-SIX

There was an awkward little silence. I cleared my throat. 'Well, no. There are some things we wanted to ask you about the college, if you don't mind talking about it.'

'It's easier when the boys are asleep and I don't have to watch my language,' she said with the first trace of bitterness I had heard in her voice. 'It's quite a trick to talk about that place in terms appropriate for the young.'

'I can understand why,' I said warmly. 'Amy – may I call you Amy?'

'Of course.'

'Okay, and we're Dorothy and Alan. And to tell the truth, I'm not very sure what to ask you. We've met quite a few of the staff of the art school, and got a sort of idea of how it functions, but – oh, I guess we just want to get more of a feel for the place. So many awful things have been happening, and we, or at least I, can't seem to get a handle on who's responsible, or why. You know the people, and I imagine Dennis has told you most of what's been going on. What ideas do you have about it all?'

She took her time about replying. 'I'm not an impartial witness, you know,' she finally began.

'Almost no one is,' said Alan. 'My wife didn't tell you, but I used to be a policeman, and I've heard a lot of witnesses. I'm not certain I can remember a single one who was completely impartial.'

'Dennis told me about your position,' she said. 'It's why I'm inclined to trust both of you. One reason,' she amended, glancing at her sons sleeping with their teddy bears. 'You've been very kind. Till now, Dennis is the only one who's bothered with me at all. You wouldn't know, I think, how those one thought were friends run away like the proverbial rats when one's ship is sinking. I don't know if they think ill-fortune is contagious, or they're simply ashamed to be around someone who has nothing.'

'Or maybe they just *are* rats. I've never been reduced to your sort of circumstances, no. But when I lost my first husband to a mid-life heart attack, I was devastated by the number of friends who simply disappeared. I suppose they didn't know what to say, or didn't want to get mired in my grief, or something, but I found it hard to forgive them. I vowed then I'd try never to act like that, and I hope I've kept that vow.'

'You have with me, anyway. So. You want to know what I think about the murder and mayhem at the college. I'm sure you can guess who I'd like the villain to be. I don't think I've ever met anyone as totally and utterly cruel and selfish as William Braithwaite. He has a certain amount of superficial charm, but believe me, it is entirely superficial. Strip away the very thin layer of veneer and you find a man who would do anything to make sure he gets exactly what he wants.'

'And what does he want?'

'In general terms, money and power. Specifically, the headship of the Fine Arts department and eventually the whole college. He'll never get the latter, of course. The design people have a lock on that position, as Design is seen as more economically viable, and Fine Arts as a pretty-pretty frill. But Braithwaite has never let reality stand in the way of his goals.'

'So you think,' said Alan, frowning, 'that he might have killed Chandler in order to take over his position. Not even considering all the technical difficulties that present themselves, that end seems far from a sure thing.'

'Of course, and any sensible person can see that. Braithwaite isn't sensible. I'm not even sure, and this is honesty talking, not mere prejudice, I'm not sure he's entirely sane.'

'"A madman at large in our college". Dennis said that,' I said.

'And I quite agree with him,' said Alan. 'Matters have progressed, or perhaps the word is regressed, from murder for what might be an understandable, though damnable, motive, to threats making little sense, to vicious and apparently senseless destruction. I can easily fit Braithwaite into the villain's role for many, if not all, of these events. I dislike the man myself, and have done from the moment I met him. But I must remind you both that the most recent attack was upon Braithwaite himself, with injuries almost impossible to have been self-inflicted.'

'I haven't heard,' said Amy in a carefully expressionless voice, 'any idea of his prognosis.'

'He's expected to survive.'

'Oh.'

Her voice sounded bleak. I was sure she was thinking what I was, heaven forgive me. I changed the subject. 'Amy, there's one more thing. Those personnel records that went missing. Why do you suppose someone took them, and what might they have done with them? Chucked them in the fire?'

'Really, it's hard to imagine why anyone would want them. All of the data, as I told you before, are computerized. I don't even know why we kept the paper records, really, except perhaps in the case of a computer crash.'

'Even then,' I mused, 'someone knowledgeable can usually get the data back. Well, someone took them for some reason, and maybe I can work out why if I put my mind to it. Now, Amy, would you be terribly offended if I brought you a few groceries? The thing is, I'm more and more certain that you're going to get your job back, sooner rather than later, but meanwhile you and the boys have to eat. Alan and I have more than we need. Won't you let us share?'

'I don't like to take charity.'

'This wouldn't be charity, not in the way you mean. It's a gift from friends. That's different, isn't it?'

'I . . . will you let me pay you back when I can?'

'Of course we will! Oh, I'm so glad you've said yes! Now, do you want to tell me what you need, or just let me use my own judgement? Alan will have to help me when it comes to things for the boys. I never had children, so I'm not sure what they like.'

'And my grandsons are far older than your boys,' said Alan, 'but I remember when I was a lad, what I wanted was a great deal of anything that wasn't good for me. We'll bring you an assortment, Amy, and what you don't want you can pass on to someone else who could use it.'

We left before her stammered thanks became tearful. 'We must do more for her than simply help with food,' said Alan as we got back in the car. 'It's insupportable that she and the children should have to live like that.'

'I know, but what can we do?'

'For a start, get in touch with her landlord. There are laws about decent housing, and he's breaking several of them.' Alan sounded as grim as I've ever heard him.

'But . . . is there any danger that the child protection people might get into the act? I don't know what they're called over here, but there must be agencies that look after children. And in America, sometimes the kids are taken away from mothers when the do-gooders don't think they're being looked after properly.'

'That can happen in this country,' Alan acknowledged with a sigh, 'but there must usually be actual physical abuse, or proof that the parent is mentally ill or using illegal substances. I agree it could be a concern, but I still have some influence in this county if something untoward were to happen. I think we can keep social services and the NSPCC out of it. I'll phone our solicitor the moment we get home.'

I worked out, after a little trouble, that NSPCC must stand for National Society for the Prevention of Cruelty to Children, the human equivalent of the RSPCA. I was a little dubious about Amy's reaction to any kind of interference, but if Alan wanted to take action, let him approach her about it. I had grocery shopping to do.

Bearing in mind Amy's very small refrigerator and limited cooking facilities, I bought a lot of vegetables that would keep well without refrigeration, and would make a good hearty soup with the chunk of beef I threw in. Milk, of course, and good wholemeal bread. Butter. I thought about and rejected orange juice. Oranges were better and would keep longer. Apples, too. Potatoes. A pound of mince would just about fit in the fridge, and would make a cottage pie with the vegetables, or hamburgers if the kids preferred them. Peanut butter, very nutritious and shelf-stable. With a good selection of canned fruits and vegetables and soups, chosen to match what little I knew of childish preferences, that did it. At the last minute I tossed some chocolate biscuits in the cart, a pound of sugar and a large box of tea bags, and checked out. Then I turned around and went back for salt and pepper. Amy probably had some, but I couldn't be sure.

I took my bounty home. Alan could deliver the many bags

more easily than I, and I needed to stick around for the phone call from the conservator. We had a quick sandwich lunch and then he took off with the food and I sat around waiting for a phone call.

Aeons ago when I was in high school, I read an assigned book of which I remember almost nothing. One thing stuck with me, though. The author mused about the nature of time, and its lack of consistency. It flows at different rates, depending upon the circumstances. The approach of something dreaded makes the clock whirl. Awaiting something desired slows time to a near-stop. When one is bored the day passes endlessly, but a week of boring days is gone in the blink of an eye.

That afternoon of waiting for the phone call from Ms Winston was one of the longest I remember. It wasn't so much that I was eager to talk with her, though I was. My real problem was that I was pining for action, and there didn't seem to be anything useful I could do, except talk to this art expert. I didn't even know what to tell her to look for. Blast Matt anyway, for being so cryptic! He had something in mind, but I had no idea what.

I paced. I tried to knit. I tried to read. I picked up a cat at random and plopped it on my lap, but I was too edgy; it jumped down. I could have done with Watson to sleep on my feet, but Alan had taken him with the thought that the boys might enjoy seeing him, though I had my doubts about Watson and the kitten. Worry about that occupied me for a good two minutes.

At last, at last (after perhaps an hour of clock time), the phone rang. 'Mrs Martin? Kate Winston. I'm about to go in to the Cathedral, the south door. Where shall I meet you?'

'The south porch is perfect. I'll be there in less than five minutes. Oh, and I'll be wearing a hat.'

Kate turned out to be a petite, attractive woman of about forty, dressed in a charcoal grey pantsuit. I had crammed a knitted orange hat on my untidy hair, and wore the jeans and pullover I'd had on all day. She looked at me quizzically once we'd introduced ourselves. 'Is there a rule here about hats for women? I thought that had been passé for years.'

'You're quite right. I wear hats because I like them. Also, this time, for identification. When we go on in you'll see I'm wearing absolutely the only one in sight.'

'You don't mind if I take a little time to see the Cathedral? You sounded quite urgent last evening.'

'The matter is urgent, or may be, but something about this place changes one's perspective. I'm happy to wander around with you, or not, as you choose.'

She preferred to sightsee by herself, so I slipped into the prayer chapel for a moment and then sat at the back of the nave soaking up the vast peace. I would, I thought, be quite happy to die in this place, when the time came. One felt so close to the eternal here that the transition would surely be seamless.

Ms Winston was more serene when she rejoined me. 'You're right about the changed perspective,' she said. 'It's been a hectic day, but I feel much more relaxed now, and ready to hear what you need from me.'

I suggested we walk to my house. Discussions of murder and mayhem were inappropriate in the Cathedral.

'The thing is,' I said as we walked through the close, 'that a great many unpleasant things have been happening at the college. The death of Mr Chandler was just the beginning.' I sketched out the sequence of events, leaving out the phone calls to Gilly, but including Matt's disappearance. 'We've been in touch with him, though, and he suggested something rather odd. He wouldn't say why, but he wants an expert like you to study some of William Braithwaite's paintings, older ones and then some more recent.'

She frowned. 'What would I be looking for?'

'I have no idea. He seemed to think you'd find something important.'

'Hmm. It would certainly help if I knew what he had in mind. Perhaps I should talk to him.'

'I don't know where he is.' That was literally true. I didn't know his precise whereabouts at that precise moment. 'And he isn't answering his phone. I know this is an imposition on your time, and Alan and I are willing to pay you whatever you ask. But could you just spend a little time this afternoon at the college looking at his work? There are several on display, both old and new.'

She shrugged. 'I go back to London tomorrow, but I've no obligations for the rest of today. Why not?'

We were at my house by that time, and Alan had returned,

so the three of us packed up in our car and drove to the college. It was a relief to know we wouldn't find Braithwaite lurking around some corner. The atmosphere of the place seemed to be much more pleasant without him, though that was no doubt my imagination.

We found Gilly, who showed us the way to the gallery where the permanent collection rotated. Three of Braithwaite's early paintings were hung there. We waited while Ms Winston looked at them with the naked eye and a magnifying glass she whipped out of her bag. 'Typical of his work,' she said at last. 'I've never cared for his style, but it's certainly popular. I can't imagine what your printmaker expected me to find.'

'He wanted you to look at the more recent work as well,' I said. 'Gilly, there'll be some in the studio, won't there?'

'Of course. He's been working like mad, and I think several are almost ready to be shipped off to the gallery in London. I'll show you.'

Ms Winston brightened when she saw them. 'I'd heard he'd improved lately, and it's true. The palette is more sophisticated, the composition more interesting.' She walked over with her magnifying glass and started studying them closely.

She spent a long time over them, going back and forth from one to another. She took a powerful flashlight out of her bag and shone it, not on the paintings, but across them, and then studied them again with her glass.

At last she looked up. 'Well. I know now what your printmaker wanted me to find. These paintings are not by William Braithwaite. They are excellent imitations of his style, and I'd swear the signature on this one is genuine, but it's quite certain these were painted by someone left-handed. Which Braithwaite is not.'

TWENTY-SEVEN

We invited her to dinner, and she was happy to accept. We all needed to talk over this astonishing development and its ramifications.

Before we'd left the college, Gilly had helped us lock up the faked paintings in a secure closet. Whatever the story turned out to be, we needed to make sure those paintings didn't suddenly disappear. And Alan had insisted that Gilly come home with us, even though it wasn't yet six.

I quickly assembled the prawn stir-fry ready to cook, and while we waited for the rice we sat over drinks in the kitchen and tossed ideas back and forth.

'We now know,' said Kate, 'why the man's paintings have improved so much of late. I'd heard rumours, but it had never occurred to me that someone else was painting them.'

I took a good swig of my bourbon. 'But I don't understand at all. I can see someone painting fake Braithwaites to sell. It's done all the time. The number of Old Masters out there far exceeds what those painters could have done in their lifetimes. But the forgers also fake the signatures. You're convinced that the signature is genuine. Why would Braithwaite sign a painting that isn't his?'

'Before you answer that, let me ask one,' said Alan. 'What makes you so certain the signature is Braithwaite's?'

'I can't answer that without using a cartload of technical terms that would mean little to you. But one obvious bit of evidence is that the signature is quite plainly right-handed. So whoever signed that painting, it wasn't the chap who painted it. And it would take a powerful suspension of disbelief to work a third person into the plot.'

'Why do you say a chap painted them?' asked Gilly, a slight edge to her voice. 'Why couldn't it be a woman?'

'It could. I used the male term partly because the he/she bit is awkward, but also partly because there are physical differences between male and female painters. Not just the obvious ones!' she added in response to our laughter. 'Detectable in their paintings, I mean. Mostly the brushwork. Our arm structures are different from men's, and in heavy oils, like the ones we're discussing, the differences can be spotted. But they're subtle, and it would take more than a cursory look to say for sure. I'm fairly certain, though, that the new Braithwaites were painted by a man, and absolutely certain that they were painted by a lefty.'

'So someone painted imitation Braithwaites, and then Will himself signed at least one of them. Why?'

'Oh, Dorothy, surely it's obvious!' Gilly was getting impatient. 'The great Pooh-Bah's paintings weren't selling anymore. They'd got to be parodies of themselves, dashed out carelessly, and the punters could tell the difference. So he gets someone to paint fakes, signs them, and they sell. His star is once more in the ascendant. I wonder how much the sod paid the real painter.'

'Who,' said Alan pointedly, 'was left-handed.'

I got it first. 'Like the person who attacked him.'

'Exactly.'

'A left-handed painter, then.'

'A *good* left-handed painter,' Kate amended. 'Or at least a first-class forger. One doesn't know whether he could do anything original.'

I personally thought most four-year-olds, given the proper materials, could make reasonable copies of a Braithwaite, but I didn't say so. 'A student? Or would it have to be someone with more experience?'

Both Kate and Gillian chuckled. 'Braithwaite's work isn't very sophisticated,' said Kate. 'He happened to catch on, though I have never understood quite why. The brilliant colours, I suppose, coming at a time, twenty years or so ago, when the world felt drab and wanted brightening. He got a rave review by the art critic of *The Times*, and that did it. He became the man of the hour, the painter to acquire as an investment, or for the snob appeal.'

'Nothing succeeds like success.'

Kate nodded. 'But it doesn't succeed forever, not unless there's real worth behind it. Braithwaite rode that wave for a long time, but the market became saturated, and his painting didn't change, at least not for the better. Collectors are tired of him. He had to do something. He leads, I hear, a wildly extravagant life.'

'Certainly a wild one, so far as women are concerned,' I said acidly. 'Or at least, so I understand. I wonder why his wife puts up with it.'

'Probably the money, my love. Many women consider money to be a sufficient incentive to marriage. I've always been profoundly grateful that you're not one of them.' Alan raised his glass in salute.

'Hmm. So if the money wasn't coming in anymore, she might have started looking for greener pastures. But would he have cared, since he's the compleat philanderer?'

'Of course he would have cared! His wife is one of his possessions. No woman could even think of leaving a marvellous man like him.' Gilly's voice dripped with sarcasm. 'What a frightful blow to his self-esteem. No, he couldn't allow that to happen.'

'So,' I said, thinking out loud. 'Let's say the other painter is a student of Braithwaite's. He sees that the boy – yes, I know, Gilly, but for the sake of the argument – that the boy is talented, and he, Braithwaite, gets an idea. He begins to give private lessons to the boy, and as an exercise, he *says*, sets him to copying one of his own works. An earlier one, because the style was better back then. And the boy does a brilliant job. The copy, Braithwaite can see, is actually better executed than the original.

'Braithwaite is delighted. He tells the boy that his work is so good, he thinks there's a market for it. If he, the student, can do a dozen or so paintings fairly quickly, Braithwaite will send them to a gallery he knows and see what happens. He encourages the boy to use the same style as the copied painting because there's a built-in market for that sort of thing. Ooh, I can just see him, that smarmy smile, the fake modesty, the sort of "you paint like me and one day you'll be pretty good, son" speech. And the kid laps it up and paints like mad and turns them over to Braithwaite, and sure enough! They all sell, for a couple of hundred pounds each.'

'Only Braithwaite has signed them and sold them as his own for thousands of pounds each, and pockets the difference. Very neat.' Alan finished his whisky.

'And so it goes,' I went on. 'Only one day – what? What happens to make the whole thing blow up?'

'The student shows up unexpectedly,' said Kate, fully into the spirit of the thing, 'just when Braithwaite is about to ship off another batch of the kid's paintings. Which would have been fine, except that Braithwaite has already signed one of them, and the kid sees it and gets suspicious. And they have a shindy, and the kid picks up a painting knife—'

'In self-defence,' said Gilly with a frown.

'In self-defence, if you want it that way, and stabs Braithwaite, who falls. The kid is appalled, runs off, Gilly shows up. Tableau.'

The timer went. I dished up, and while we ate, we thought over Kate's scenario. 'The only snag I can see,' I said when we had finished and I was serving a defrosted tiramisu, 'is, why didn't the student come back and take away the painting Braithwaite had signed? That one little detail is what gave the show away.'

'But only to someone like me. Almost anyone could look at those paintings, signed or not, and say without question that they were Braithwaite's. Plainly the gallery that's dealing in them has accepted them as genuine. And oh, what a brouhaha there's going to be when they find out the truth! It's going to shake the art world!'

'And destroy Braithwaite's reputation.' Gilly spoke with pardonable satisfaction.

'All right,' said Alan, pushing his plate away. 'That was superb, dear, by the way.'

'You can thank Mr Sainsbury for the dessert. But thank you. I flatter myself I do defrost well. You were about to say?'

'That we seem to have a tenable theory about the attack on Braithwaite, barring the small detail of finding the student, or whoever's responsible.'

'I hope you don't,' said Gilly.

Alan ignored her. 'But. Unless you ladies can come up with probable cause for the student to have done the other things, that leaves us no closer to solving the main body of our problem. Namely, first, the death of Mr Chandler.'

'I still think it was Braithwaite,' said Gilly, 'but I don't know why, except that he's such a rat.'

We sat in silence for a moment, and then I got up. 'I don't know about the rest of you, but my brain has done all the work it intends to today. I'm going to clean up the kitchen with anyone who wants to help, and then Alan, in the morning I think we need to talk to Derek and see what progress the police have made with any of this. There are so many threads hanging, we could weave a net out of them.'

'A net to catch a killer,' said Alan, and after that the rest of us didn't say much.

Sunday, September 21

I woke in the morning with that feeling of general malaise that means a cold coming on, or worse. My head was stuffed with cotton, my throat felt as if someone had sandpapered it in the night, I was sniffly, and everything ached just a little. I wanted nothing more than to stay in bed, but I wasn't anything like sick enough to justify that, and there were things to be done. Feeling like a martyr, I plodded in my bathrobe down to the kitchen.

Alan had made a pot of coffee, but he looked me up and down and turned on the kettle. 'Toast?'

I shook my head. 'Just tea.' It came out in a rasp, and told Alan all he needed to know about my condition.

He brought my tea when it was ready, along with a carton of yogurt. It slipped easily down my sore throat and, with the tea, made me feel almost human. Watson had come to lie on my feet.

Alan poured himself a cup of coffee and sat down. 'Not feeling quite the thing?'

'Crummy. Nothing definite yet, just that sense that I'm going to feel perfectly awful in a few hours.'

'Need anything from Boots?'

'No, I think I've got all the cold remedies they sell. Nothing helps much anyway. It just has to run its course.' I sniffled and reached for a tissue in my pocket.

'Will you think me a neglectful husband if I leave you for a while? There's church, and then I thought I'd drop in on Derek and see if he knows anything new and exciting, but if you want to be cosseted . . .'

'For heaven's sake, I'm not at death's door! It's just that my head has no brain cells today, only something grey and woolly that's beginning to ache. I'm going back to bed.'

He kissed the top of my head. 'Sleep well, then, and I hope I'll have some news for you when I come home.'

I grunted something, sniffed again, disentangled my feet from Watson, and went upstairs. I rummaged in the medicine cabinet, found a packet of cold tablets, and took two before crawling into bed.

The next thing I knew, Alan was sitting on the edge of the bed, and the room had a late-afternoon feel to it.

I sat up, and then fell back against the pillows as a wave of dizziness swept over me. Alan's look of indulgence changed to one of active concern. 'Are you all right, love?'

'I'm fine,' I croaked. 'Just a little light-headed there for a minute. I think it's those stupid pills.'

'You don't sound "fine". Shall I bring you some tea?'

'No, I'll come down. What time is it, anyway?'

'Half-five, nearly.'

'Good grief! I've slept the day away. Now I'll never get to sleep tonight.'

'More of those pills, and you will. Are you truly feeling better?'

I swallowed experimentally. 'Truly. Throat a little raw, that's all. And I think I'm hungry. And I want to know what you found out while I was doing my Rip Van Winkle act.'

'You shall know all. Soup, or scrambled eggs?'

'I think there's some chicken soup in the freezer. The traditional cure-all.'

'Right. It'll be ready any time you are.'

I tried to convince myself I felt somewhat better once I'd showered and dressed. It was nearly dark by that time; I felt the guilt of someone brought up in the Protestant work ethic. Sleeping all day! But I was in fact still a little rocky, so I supposed I needed it.

The soup was steaming away on the stove when I came down. I couldn't smell it, but when Alan set a generous bowlful in front of me, I found it tasted almost like chicken soup. He'd poured me a glass of white wine, as well.

'Tea might keep you awake,' he explained. 'I suspect what you need more than anything is sleep.'

'It'll need more than wine to send me back to sleep after my disgraceful sloth today. But you were going to tell me what Derek has learned.'

'A few interesting things. For a start, the lab people were able to work out the probable cause of the man's death. It was the trashing of the darkroom that put them on the trail.'

'All those deadly chemicals!'

'Yes, well some of them are certainly deadly. So they decided to try tests for them, one by one. The most likely would have been the potassium cyanide, which is very quick acting, as you would know, given your choice of reading material. But it's also quick to dissipate, in or out of the body. So they tried other things. I hate to think what the bill will be for all that. Fortunately it's not my headache anymore. At any rate, they finally came up with traces of formaldehyde, which led them to . . .' He paused suggestively.

'Antifreeze? That metabolizes to formaldehyde.' I had good cause to remember that, because my cat had almost died once from ingesting antifreeze.

'Close. Methanol. It's used in some developing agents.'

'But I had an idea it killed very slowly, if very surely once the process has begun.'

'Usually, yes. But it kills by damaging the kidneys, and it seems that our Mr Chandler had quite a lot of kidney damage already.'

'But – I don't understand. How could anyone have forced Chandler to drink some of the developer? And even with kidney damage, it wouldn't have killed him on the spot. He would have felt ill, called the doctor or taken himself to the emergency room. He still would have died, but not at the bottom of the shaft!'

'Indeed. And they thought about that, and then did a little more searching. And what they found is going to make you gnash your teeth, I'm afraid.'

I waited. I could feel my temperature rising, and not just from whatever bug had invaded me.

'All the signs point to Chandler having died of a cerebral haemorrhage. A stroke, in other words. Natural causes.'

I refused more wine and went back up to bed.

TWENTY-EIGHT

I slept fitfully that night, having slept too much during the day, but I must have dreamed, because I woke once or twice with the tail of an idea disappearing around a corner.

I had had great hopes that my usual cold treatment of lots of rest and lots of fluids would do the trick. Not this time. I woke Monday morning unable to speak at all and feeling like death warmed over.

Gilly brought me my morning tea. I couldn't taste it, but it was hot, and soothing to my throat, though swallowing was painful.

'I think you need to see a doctor,' she said, hovering over me.

I shook my head. 'Just a bad cold,' I mouthed. 'Don't get too close.'

'I think you should have some antibiotics, or a jab, or something.'

I shook my head again, lacking the energy to argue that antibiotics were of no avail against virus infections, and that I'd already had a flu shot.

'Well, if you're sure. But I'm going to ring Alan at lunchtime to check on you. And he and I agreed, since you're out of the hunt for now, I'm going to nose around a bit at the college, see what I can find out about those missing personnel records.' She saw my look of alarm. 'Don't worry, I'll be careful. But with Horrible Will out of the picture – oops, sorry, didn't hear that coming – with him in hospital, I should be safe enough.'

'We don't know for sure,' I tried to say.

'That he's the one,' she finished for me. 'I know. I'll be careful. I must go; Alan's waiting. I told him I could bike it, but he insisted. Take care of yourself!'

I burrowed back under the covers and into restless sleep again.

This time my dreams were near the surface. They formed the familiar frustration pattern: something, never clearly defined, that I needed to do but couldn't because of hindrances at every turn.

In intervals of near-consciousness I had to search my pockets.
Or someone else's pockets. Pockets. Pita pockets, dry as dust.
Pocket billiards. Air pockets, and I was falling . . .

I clutched the bed frantically to save myself and woke up fully,
my mind still whirring with thoughts of pockets. My mouth was
dry; I'd probably been sleeping with it open, since I was so
stuffed up. I reached for the bottle of water on the bedside table,
but it was empty.

I had to go to the bathroom anyway, so I struggled to get out
of bed. Both cats had somehow managed to get into the room,
and were weighing down the blankets. They made quite a racket
when I tried to dislodge them, especially Sam, whose Siamese
yowls can raise the dead when she really gets going. Watson
came loping up the stairs to see what was going on, followed
closely by Alan.

The cats shut up as soon as I stopped moving, and lay purring,
soft, warm, and innocent. Watson tried to jump on the bed to
join everybody, but Alan caught him in mid-leap and held him
fast.

'What can I get you, love?'

I gestured toward the bathroom. He swept the cats off the bed
with one whip of the blankets and helped me up. I pointed to
the water bottle; he nodded and took it downstairs, herding
animals ahead of him. (Or trying to. Not for nothing is 'herding
cats' a metaphor for frustrating activity.)

I had a drink of tepid water from the bathroom, but when Alan
brought up the chilled bottle, I drank a long draught with great
relief and sank back on the pillows.

'Better?'

'Not much.' It was a croak, but at least it was audible. I cleared
my throat. It still hurt like fury, but there was something I had to
tell Alan, if I could only get the words out.

'Pockets,' I whispered.

'Pockets,' he echoed, whispering himself. 'What about
pockets?'

'I don't know. Important. I dreamed . . .' I stopped. Impossible
to go into the whole story of my dream, and my feeling that
pockets were somehow vital. 'Search.'

'You want us to search someone's pockets?'

People do reply to whispers with whispers. It's a natural reflex. Somehow I was finding it irritating. 'Don't know.' Easy, feverish tears were starting. 'Never mind.'

'I'll work it out,' said Alan. 'Rest.'

I took two more cold tablets, along with another large swig of water, and drifted away in a fog of fever and, later, chills.

I don't remember much of the next few days. I slept, drank tea, took pills, had nightmares I couldn't remember afterward. My throat stopped feeling as if someone had used industrial-grade sandpaper on it and moved on to the chopped-with-a-meat-cleaver stage. They had the doctor in, they told me later. He diagnosed a strep infection and wanted to take me to the hospital, but Alan refused. Gilly moved to the couch in the parlour so Alan could have the spare room bed, but I believe he slept very little in the intervals of nursing me.

All of this went on while I was semi-conscious. I roused only to take pills and drink something. They fed me some horrible liquid that tasted like wallpaper paste, but I was too sick to resist.

One morning I woke to a quiet house. It felt early; what sky I could see from my bed was a pearly pink. I turned to look at the clock. Seven-thirty. Surely someone ought to be stirring by now. What day was it?

I got up to go to the bathroom and realized that, though I felt hollow and was more than a little tottery, I wasn't light-headed with fever. Nor – I swallowed – did my throat feel like raw meat. In fact, I didn't feel awful at all. I realized that my nightgown was damp with sweat, cast it off, and stepped into the shower.

I was dressed and downstairs with a pot of tea in front of me and animals all around me, when Alan came down. He was dressed, but he looked a trifle haggard, as well he might. 'Are you back among the living then, darling?'

I hadn't tried talking yet. I cleared my throat. 'Risen from my bed of pain. And hallelujah, I can talk! What day is it?'

'Sunday. You've been away for a week, love. And there was a day or two . . .' His voice shook a little, and he became very busy making coffee.

'You know, that's exactly the way it feels – as if I've been away. I'm sorry I gave everyone so much trouble. Did the doctor come? I can't quite remember.'

'He did. Are you aware that you had a very bad case of strep?'

'No. I just know I felt like nothing on earth. What have you all been doing, meanwhile?'

'Looking after you, for the most part. Do you remember that Gilly was going to try to track down the missing personnel records at the college?'

'Vaguely. And there was – was there something about pockets? Or did I dream that?'

'You dreamed it, but you said something about searching pockets to me.'

'I don't think it was searching pockets.' I frowned, trying to remember the dream-urgings. 'There was something terribly important in someone's pockets. It was – I think it was meant to point the way to a search. If that makes sense.'

'Not a lot. The only thing I could imagine that you might mean was what we found in Chandler's pockets. There wasn't much.' He pulled a list out of his own pocket and read it. '"Two ten-pound notes, one fiver, three pounds seventy-three in coins; a plain white handkerchief, clean; two flyers for an exhibition of architectural drawings at the Design Museum in London; one small picture of a grey tabby cat." I wouldn't have thought there was anything of great interest there, but that is truly all there was.'

'A picture of a tabby cat. That seems a most unlikely thing for Chandler to be carrying around. A photo?'

'No. A drawing. Or rather, a print of a coloured drawing.'

'A print. Could it have been one of those computer-generated prints? What do they call them? Something French.'

'Giclée. I suppose it could be. What are you thinking?'

'I'm not quite sure. But suppose it was a print. That could lead in the direction of a printmaker. And the chisel in his back points to a sculptor. And he was poisoned with some darkroom chemical. Suppose all these things were planted as clues to his murderer?'

'If so, they rather cancel each other out, don't they?'

'Yes, but they do lead one away from a painter, don't they?'

'Hmm. Not terribly sensible, really.'

'Is good common sense a characteristic one would attribute to William Braithwaite?'

'I take your point. If, of course, Braithwaite is our man. And not forgetting that nobody could have killed Chandler, because he was in Greece. And in fact no one did kill him; he died of a stroke.'

'The fact remains that, unless we're all victims of mass hypnosis, someone did put him in that elevator shaft.'

Alan sighed. 'I'll ask Derek about the cat picture. But right now, would you like something to eat?'

'I would. Something smooth. My throat's still a little scratchy.'

So he scrambled some eggs and poured orange juice, and then made himself a more substantial breakfast, and we ate in companionable silence. Presently he said, 'Were you thinking of going to church? It's nearly time.'

I almost never miss church, but I shook my head. 'I'm still pretty shaky on my pins, and there's a tickle at the back of my throat that tells me I'm about to enter the coughing stage. You go, if you want. I'll be perfectly okay by myself.'

'Not by yourself.' Gilly entered the room, yawning and stretching. 'I have some students coming this afternoon to help me pour a small bronze, but I can stick around for a while. And I have something interesting to tell you.'

'I'm afraid there's no more tea, but I can make some.' I started to get up, but she put out a hand.

'You're still to be pampered. I'll do it. Darjeeling or Earl Grey?'

Earl Grey seemed just the ticket, fragrant and not as assertive as Darjeeling. A good brew for a recovering invalid.

'Well!' Gilly gave me my mug and sat down with hers. 'Do you remember I was going to see what I could do to track down those missing credentials?'

'Vaguely.'

'You were pretty vague about everything for a while there, you know. We were all worried about you.'

'I wasn't really sitting up and taking notice, was I? I don't remember ever feeling quite so awful, except maybe fifty years ago and more, when I had my tonsils out. But go on. The credentials.'

'Yes. Well, the more I thought about it, the more I thought I could pin down the disappearance to one or two people. If

Horrible Will was blackmailing Chandler because of something in his past, and there was some incriminating evidence in those papers, then either Will took them for safe keeping, in case he needed to carry out his threats of exposure, or Chandler took them himself to checkmate Will.'

'Sounds reasonable.' I sipped my tea.

'So I checked Braithwaite's office first, and then his studio. The only interesting thing I found was—' she reached into her pocket –'ta-da!' She pulled out a passport and tossed it on the table.

It was the standard burgundy-coloured booklet with the gold coat of arms, looking well-used. I frowned.

'Open it.'

I opened it, glanced at it, and then took a closer look. 'But . . . but . . .' What was John Chandler's passport doing in Will Braithwaite's possession?

'I thought you'd be interested. It was in Will's studio, under a stack of canvases. Hidden away, I'd say.'

I looked at it more closely. 'You know, if Braithwaite were a little fatter, and had grey hair, he'd look quite a lot like Chandler.'

'Mmm. I suppose so. But though this is interesting, it isn't the most important thing I found. Not in Will's territory, but Chandler's. I suppose I should have left them where I found them, but I brought them home just in case. Too many weird things have been happening at the college.'

'Gilly, I'm not strong enough yet to cope with suspense. What did you find?'

'The missing files. All of them. Tucked away behind old exam papers in Chandler's filing cabinets.'

'But they would just be the paper originals of the data on the central computers, wouldn't they?'

'Not quite. You see, Chandler's were faked.'

'What do you mean, faked? Things were erased, or something?'

'Dorothy, when I was an undergraduate, I worked in the records office for a while. I didn't actually need the money, but I didn't want to sponge off my parents for life's little pleasures. They were paying out so much for my education, you see. So I did filing. As boring as a job could be, basically, but I handled hundreds of transcripts from all over the country. All over the world, for that matter. We had students from everywhere, lots from the United States. I know what a transcript from an American university looks like. Chandler's file had what purported to be a transcript from the University of Dartmouth, taking a Master's degree with high honours in architecture. It was no such thing. It was faked.'

'And you can prove this?'

'Easily. It wasn't even well done. He'd used the right sort of font, and the layout was more or less right, but he'd done it on A4 paper. They don't use A4 in America. And the paper was white, with no background colour, and there was no university seal embossed into the paper – oh, dozens of little things.'

'So that's the hold Braithwaite had over him. He never got the degree he was claiming.'

'Not just that. I don't think anything else in his file was genuine either, the letters of recommendation, any of it.'

'What about that architecture award he was so proud of?'

'That wasn't in his file. The certificate hangs on his office wall, and I have to say it looked real enough. If an expert took it out of the frame, they could probably tell for sure.'

'I think I'd like to have that done. Gilly, have you told Alan all this?'

'Not yet. He was so worried about you. I thought he didn't need anything else to bother about.'

'That was kind of you, but now I think he'd better be told, just as soon as he gets back from church. The police can check the authenticity of Chandler's background a great deal more efficiently than we can, and plainly it needs to be checked. And as soon as Braithwaite can be questioned, he has a few things to talk about.'

When Alan did come home, he brought with him the dean of the Cathedral and his wife. Kenneth and Margaret have been our close friends for years, but they're usually far too busy on a Sunday to visit. Jane was with them too, carrying something that smelled very appetizing.

Kenneth came up and took my hands. 'I'm happy to hear you're feeling better, Dorothy. We haven't time to stay, but I've brought you Holy Communion.'

The others retired to the kitchen to leave us to private worship. When I had received the Sacrament, with gratitude to the dean, he inquired searchingly after my health.

'Really, I'm over the worst of it. Still a little shaky, but I've eaten almost nothing for a week, and had no exercise at all. But I'm almost well, and eager to get into the swim of things again.'

Margaret came into the room. 'Mind you don't dive too far into the deep end, then. You know you have a tendency to get in over your head sometimes. Kenneth, we really must go. Dorothy, I'll pop in tomorrow to see how you're getting along.'

Jane had brought a cottage pie for our lunch; that was the source of the lovely smells from the kitchen. 'Easy on your throat,' she said gruffly, warding off thanks. She'd used hamburger instead of her usual small chunks of beef or lamb, and it did go down smoothly with a small glass of wine. Gilly stayed to eat with us; then she was off with Alan to do her casting, and I went up for a nap. I was on the mend, but I wasn't well yet. With two cats on one side of me and Watson on the other, I drifted into the best sleep I'd had in a week.

And woke with the best idea I'd had in a month.

Getting out of bed was the usual extrication process, the animals being disinclined to move. Suddenly, though, ears pricked up. They heard Alan doing something in the kitchen. They all jumped off the bed to go down and investigate, and I was freed.

'I'm glad you came down,' he said. 'I was just about to go and pick up Gilly, and I didn't want to leave without telling you.'

'What's it like outside?' The sun was low, but the sky was clear and I could see no evidence of wind.

'It's been a lovely day, a real St Luke's summer day. Warm, almost no breeze.'

'Then I'm coming with you. I've had a really terrific idea, I think, and I want to try it out on you.'

'Sure you're up to it?'

'Sure.' I gave him a quick kiss. 'I'll just put on a hat.'

Alan brought the car around and tucked me in as tenderly as if I'd been at death's door. I rather enjoyed the cosseting. Tomorrow I would probably be back to my normal independent, rather bristly self, but for now I could revel in being treated like glass.

'So.' He turned into the High Street. 'What is this splendid idea of yours?'

'I haven't worked it all out yet, but the skeleton's there. Did Gilly show you all she'd found?'

'Yes, before lunch, while you were with the dean. I must say I'm not terribly surprised. I knew there must be something incriminating in those documents, or they wouldn't have gone missing.'

'Yes, of course, and that will all have to be checked, find out what Chandler's real background is. But what about the passport?'

'That, I confess, has me baffled. It's all of a piece, though, with the confusion about Chandler being in Greece at the same time, apparently, that he was being murdered here. I haven't been able to work that out. One of the few things we know for certain is that Chandler did go to Greece just after the end of term.'

'No.' I probably looked like a cat with cream. 'What we know, in fact, is that *someone* flew to Athens on Chandler's ticket. Someone presented Chandler's passport to the Greek authorities.'

TWENTY-NINE

Alan thought about that for the length of the High Street. 'You're saying,' he said finally, 'that it wasn't Chandler. Someone else travelled on his passport.'

'Did you take a good look at his passport picture?'

'No. I checked it for the Greek stamp. Which was there, of course.'

'Yes. It would have to be. The thing is, I did look closely at the picture. For a moment I couldn't think who it reminded me of. You remember, I've never seen Chandler alive. But then I thought, dye the hair back to brown, take off a few pounds, and . . .'

'Braithwaite!' He thumped his hand on the steering wheel. 'By heaven, Braithwaite! He could have done it. Powder in his hair—'

'How about white paint? He'd have easy access to that. His colouring is the same other than the hair; even the eye colour is right. He could stoop a little to add age, wear some of Chandler's clothes – at least, the man lived alone, didn't he?'

'He did.'

'Well, then.' I was about to launch into a narrative when we arrived at the college. Alan pulled up to a double yellow line and got out, leaving the car running. 'Move it if you have to,' he instructed, 'but I should be right back. I want to hear the rest of this story!'

I kept a sharp and nervous eye out for traffic wardens, but Alan and Gilly appeared in a trice (whatever that is). 'Alan tells me you've figured the whole thing out!' she said as she jumped in the back.

'Not the whole thing. But I do believe I've come up with the solution to the big problem of Chandler being in two places, indeed two countries, at the same time. Listen to this and see if I've made some stupid mistake.'

I paused. 'All right. I'm Braithwaite. Chandler is lying dead at my feet.'

'How did he die?' asked Gilly.

'And why was his body—?' That was from Alan.

'I'll get to how in a minute, but I only have a glimmer of why – why everything. Stop interrupting, both of you. He's dead. I'm delighted, of course, but all the same I can see that I suddenly have a big problem on my hands. Here we are, just the two of us, alone in the college. What if he told anyone that he was meeting me? What if someone saw one or both of us arrive? Not that anyone knows I would have any reason to want him out of the way, but all the same . . .

'He was about to leave the country, I think. No one will miss him for ages. If I can get the body out of the way, no one will know until it's far too late to connect me with him in any way at all. Trouble is, a body isn't an easy thing to dispose of. Chandler's about my height, but he weighs more than I do, and I'm out of shape.

'The holidays have begun and the college is deserted. That buys me some time. I think of various ways to get rid of the body, but the only thing that seems feasible is to tip him down the elevator shaft. We're in the photo studio. That's where he found me and did – whatever he did that made me so furious. That's where he had his stroke, and I seized my opportunity. He didn't die at once, so I gave him some highly poisonous developer, and that apparently finished him off. They'll find that poison in his system and trace it to Sam. Good! I've never cared for Sam. But then it occurs to me that I hate the rest of the staff, too. Why not scatter lots of red herrings around? I leave him in the photo studio for the moment and go down first to the print studio, where I pick up a small print to put in his pocket. Oh, I am so clever! Then one more floor down to the sculpture studio, with all those nice sharp tools around. I choose a hefty chisel and a thinner one, take them upstairs, and drive the hefty one into his back.

'Now I'm ready. I've been careful, of course, to touch nothing with my bare hands. I take the thin chisel, force the shaft doors open (first having sent the elevator to the top floor), and push him down. He lands on his face, the chisel showing nicely.

'That's that. No one will find him for ages, so I have time to cover my tracks. I can go to Paris on the next plane. My wife is away. She can't tell the police where I have been or when I left town. And then I come up with my brilliant plan. Chandler was going to Greece. I run all the way down to his office and rummage through his drawers. There is his ticket, or the computer printout that serves to get me on board, and there is his passport. I'm much better looking than he is, of course, but I can look enough like him to pass, especially with Greece in such a muddle and idiots probably manning passport control. He's leaving in a few hours. He's probably already packed.

'I run back upstairs to my studio and artistically streak some white paint through my hair. Watercolour, so I won't have a dreadful time getting it out again. I go to his flat, use the key I found in his pocket to let myself in, and Bob's your uncle. There's his suitcase, all ready to go. I make sure I also have my own passport, go to my own house and put on a couple of clean shirts and an extra pair of underwear under my clothes, to make me look fatter. Then I get myself to Heathrow.

'On the way, I have time to think out what to do next. I've travelled all over Europe, of course, and I know the ropes. The easiest thing will be simply to come back to England, as myself. So I get to Athens, I go through passport control, as Chandler, and then I go to a washroom, get the grey out of my hair, throw away my extra clothes, or buy a small carry-on to put them in, and go back in and hop on a plane to Heathrow, travelling this time as William Braithwaite.'

'No, you don't,' said Alan, who had been following along closely. 'Not if you're as smart as you think you are.' He brought the car to a stop in front of our garage. 'Pour me a drink, you two, and I'll finish your story for you.'

We were more than ready when he came in and sat down. 'Now. In the last instalment, Braithwaite had just left the airport as Chandler. He stops somewhere and turns into Braithwaite again. And then . . . he goes directly to the railway station.'

'The *railway* station?' I said.

'Aha! For once I'm ahead of you. Did you know that it's possible to go by train from Athens to London, all the way? It's a slow and rather tedious journey, much of it through the Balkans.'

'The old *Orient Express!*'

'Over some of the same track, indeed, though probably much

less luxurious. I think that's what Braithwaite would have done. The great advantage, for someone wanting to leave as few tracks as possible, is that train travel is far less regulated than air travel. An airline keeps flight manifests, checks passengers in, pretty well knows who's on every plane. To catch a train, one buys a ticket and climbs aboard. No booking ahead, unless to assure a berth; the journey takes two or three days. And to make things even better for a shy traveller, the route goes through several countries, some of them with fairly unstable governments that are none too friendly with Great Britain. Enquiries can be made, of course, will be made, and we'll check Braithwaite's passport, but there may well be gaps in the sequence.'

'And probably nobody would check his passport to see that he wasn't officially in Greece at all. Alan, I do think that's what happened, don't you? That's how the other boarding pass, the return from Athens to London, ended up back at the college. Braithwaite forgot to throw it away and somehow dropped it in the studio. But why would he go through all that elaborate charade?'

'We won't know that for certain until he's well enough to be questioned.'

'Oh, yes, how's he doing?'

'Greatly improved,' said Alan. I saw Gilly make a face and then quickly suppress it. 'He'll be out of hospital in the next day or two, and we – that is, Derek and co. – will be very eager to talk to him about a good many things. His wife, incidentally, is making life unpleasant for the police, the college authorities, the hospital, in fact anyone she can think of. They've had to bar her from the hospital, she was making such a fuss. Now she's threatened them with a lawsuit.'

'Delightful lady. I suppose she's worried that her meal ticket might be in danger.'

'As it certainly is. Braithwaite's facing a number of charges, and I doubt he'll earn much in prison.'

Days passed. September drifted into October, the lovely weather continuing. Braithwaite made slow progress toward recovery, while I kept on wondering why he had wanted Chandler dead. Perhaps Chandler had refused to pay up any longer. Had he decided to brazen out the claim of falsified credentials, thinking that Braithwaite couldn't prove his allegations without the carefully hidden documents? That was foolish, if so. A few phone calls to the relevant institutions in the States would have confirmed that Chandler never spent time there, or at least was never granted degrees. Even then, Chandler could have trumped him with the Marlowe Award. That was the significant credential, compared to which all the others paled.

Derek phoned Alan the day after Braithwaite was released from the hospital. Alan replied in monosyllables, ended the call, and then asked me, 'How would you like to come with me to the college? Derek is going over to talk to Wicked Will, and I thought you might like to sit in. He says he has a surprise to spring, and it could be interesting. It's not an official interview, or you couldn't come. He agreed, since you've been involved from the start, that you could be there if you stayed in the background.'

I gladly abandoned my book. It was one of my favourite Agatha Christies, but I'd read it so often I knew not only the ending, but virtually every word of dialogue along the way.

Derek picked us up. His driver used an unmarked car, not a panda car, but it could still be parked anywhere without reprisal. Somewhat to my surprise, another car followed, also discreet, but containing uniformed officers. 'Are they expecting trouble, then?' I whispered to Alan, who shrugged. Irritating man!

St Luke's summer had abruptly ended the night before. As November lurked just on the horizon, the weather had turned grey and chill. A treacherous wind blew the last leaves from the beech trees and tugged at my hat. I pulled it down more securely and shivered.

We were dropped off just in front of the Fine Arts building. Students gave us curious glances as we battled the wind and entered, accompanied by a swirl of dead leaves. I peered into the sculpture studio as we made our way to the elevator, but didn't see Gilly.

Braithwaite paid not the slightest attention to us when we walked into the studio. He was standing at an easel, cigarette smouldering in a saucer nearby, applying thick paint in an eye-jarring colour I thought was called cadmium yellow. At least it

jarred me, sitting on the canvas next to the brightest purple I'd
ever seen. As I was there only on sufferance, I retired to an
inconspicuous corner and mentally stretched my ears.

'May we speak to you for a moment, Mr Braithwaite?' asked
Derek with utmost courtesy. 'We did phone to say we were
coming.'

'This is not a good time. I'm extremely busy,' Braithwaite
said, without turning his attention from his painting. He added
a few dots of brilliant magenta. I had to look away. The colours
swam before my eyes, and I was getting a headache.

'We won't keep you for long, sir. Perhaps we could sit down.
And possibly you could put out that cigarette. I believe smoking
is forbidden in this building.'

'That's no business of yours, is it? And I'm very far behind
in my work! This painting was due at my gallery last week, and
as you can see I've barely started it. Can't this wait?'

'I'm afraid not, sir. The sooner we get started, the sooner we
can leave.'

'Oh, very well!' He threw the brush down pettishly. It sprayed
dots of magenta over the floor and, I noticed with regret, on to
Alan's trouser leg.

He perched on his stool, smoking ostentatiously, and turned
to face the two men. Derek pulled two chairs from the side of
the room, taking his time, and he and Alan sat.

'Now, sir, we've come across some interesting information,
and we wonder if you'd like to comment on any of it. For a start,
we've learned that several paintings you've recently sold were
not, in fact, painted by your hand.'

'You're referring, I suppose, to the paintings by the boy Philip
Benson. Of course I didn't paint them. He's rather good at
imitating my style, and I thought he might be able to make a
little money with his work. I feel sorry for him. Starving artist
and all that. He'll never be any good, you know. No originality.
Now if that's all—'

'They were sold with your signature.'

Braithwaite's face turned an ugly colour. 'Now that's going
too far! I allowed him to paint in my style, but forging my
signature—'

'The signatures are genuine.' Derek allowed a little more steel in his voice. 'We had them authenticated. You didn't paint those pictures, but you signed them and sold them as your work. Now why would you do that, sir?'

'Oh, all right! I signed them. I told you, I felt sorry for the boy. They'd obviously fetch a far better price with my name on them. Is that a crime?'

'Probably, though I'm not up on art crimes. It is a crime, though, to keep most of the money. How much of it did you turn over to the real painter?'

'I can't say I care for your tone! Those paintings would never have made a penny for Benson if I hadn't persuaded my gallery to sell them. I'm entitled to a brokerage fee!'

'Of exactly how much, sir? Ninety per cent? Ninety-five?'

'Exactly what are you implying?' Braithwaite stood up and began pacing around the studio.

'I'm implying nothing, simply stating facts. We've looked into those transactions. We know how much of the sale price you turned over to Benson. I was interested to know whether you'd admit it.'

'I want my attorney,' shouted Braithwaite. 'And I want you to leave, this instant!'

'Certainly. You might be interested to learn one thing that we recently discovered, however.'

'Get out!' Braithwaite picked his brush off the floor and threw it at Derek, missing him but catching Alan full in the stomach. That pair of pants, I thought ruefully, would have to be thrown out.

'Now, now, sir,' said Derek calmly. 'I'm sure you don't want to be summonsed for assault. And I think you'll be quite interested in what I have to tell you. You see, we've discovered that your late head, Mr Chandler, had used the same ruse you recently employed, passing a student's work off as his own. That Marlowe Award design was in fact created by one of his students, back in America years ago. *Good* day, sir. We'll talk again.'

But Braithwaite had changed his mind about wanting them to leave. He was beaming. 'Oh, so you finally worked that out, did you? I knew long ago, years ago. He was a spurious architect, a spurious chap all round. He'd no more idea about running an art program than I would about managing the Hotspurs. I'll do a far better job when my appointment becomes permanent. I've had quite a nice little income from him over the years, useful in many ways, especially as my wife doesn't know about it. Nor do the Inland Revenue chaps, hah!'

'I must caution you, sir, that you do not have to say anything . . .'

Braithwaite ignored him. 'The little toad decided to stop paying up, you see. He said he'd deny everything, and I couldn't prove it. Well, that was simply stupid. Of course I could prove it. But he went too far. He said he'd discovered I was doing exactly what he did, defrauding a student. Rubbish! The two cases were entirely different. He'd waltzed off with a major award that should have gone to the real designer. I was merely helping a student up the ladder. But I couldn't have him blabbing all over the shop. We got into a slanging match, and it was too much for him. He passed right out! And that was when I had my brilliant idea!'

We sat around on an evening two days later, a trifle crowded in my parlour, but cosy with a crackling fire. Outside, the rain was pelting down, as it had done so much these past weeks. But our stalwart builder, Mr Pettifer, had found an ingenious way to weatherproof our windows, so the rain was staying where it belonged.

Besides Alan and me and Gilly, we'd invited Jane and Amy and Dennis for dinner and drinks. Matt was still in Wales, and Sam had declined with thanks, saying he'd read all about it as soon as it was in the paper.

'He went right round the twist,' said Gilly, who had walked into the painting studio near the end of Braithwaite's extraordinary performance. 'He was raving about how brilliant he was, and how carefully he'd planned everything, even though he'd had to think it out on the spur of the moment.'

'It seems,' said Alan, 'that they had an appointment to talk about the blackmail. Chandler had wanted to do it a day earlier, probably so he'd have plenty of time to get ready for his holiday, but Braithwaite wanted no one else around. He, Braithwaite, had been careful to make sure no one else knew what he was doing.'

'Except for me,' put in Gilly. 'He wasn't careful enough, that time in Chandler's office.' She shuddered. 'I hate to think what would have happened if he'd caught me listening!'

I hated to think of it, too. I put my hand over Gilly's and gave it a squeeze.

'Why trash the studios?' asked Jane.

'Oh, he explained that quite thoroughly,' I said. 'He was most upset with the police, who were being so stupid about his carefully-strewn red herrings, so he decided to call yet more attention to the other artists on staff. He waxed eloquent over the pains he had taken in the print studio, and was furious with Gilly for interfering as he was about to wreck the photo department.

'Sculpture was next on the list, by the way, Dennis,' I went on, 'but things moved a little too fast for him. His nemesis caught up with him before he had a chance to destroy all the work that was still in clay, all the moulds, everything except the bronze. But he had tried to frighten Gilly off with those phone calls.'

'It was almost funny, in a frightful sort of way,' said Gilly. 'He strutted round the studio like a peacock, banging on and on about how clever he was, and how he'd done only what he had to do to save his career, and how important his art was to the world. And he finished by saying he'd enjoyed the little chat, but now he had to get on with his work.'

'And that's when we left,' I said. 'None of us wanted to see him dragged off in handcuffs. Derek phoned later to say that he fought like a tiger.'

'I wouldn't have minded seeing it,' said Amy. She hadn't spoken all evening. 'I would have cheered.'

That shut us all up for a moment. I took a last long sip of my bourbon.

Dennis stood and raised his glass. 'Dorothy, you may want a bit of a refill, for I have a toast to make.'

I accepted a little more, though I'd already had quite enough.

Dennis cleared his throat. 'It isn't I who ought to propose this toast, but as there's no one else to do it, the job falls to me. I met this afternoon with the head of the Fine Art and Design Faculty. That's the umbrella faculty for the Fine Arts department, Dorothy. The head is a design man. They almost always are. However, that's beside the point. I had resurrected, a few weeks ago, my paperwork requesting a promotion. Chandler had stuffed it away, fortunately, rather than throwing it in the bin. I send it to the Head of Faculty, and he called me in today. So, first of all, to the once and future secretary of the Fine Arts department, Amy MacInnes. And second, a very self-aggrandizing toast to the new Head of Fine Arts at the Wolfson College of Art and Design, Dennis Singleton!'

THIRTY

I t was a lovely spring day. Even in grimy, grey London the sky was a softer blue, the pocket gardens in the little squares were a riot of red tulips and yellow daffodils. Alan and I hurried down Bond Street from the Piccadilly Tube station.

A small crowd spilled out of one of the art galleries. They carried champagne glasses and were chattering brightly. We wormed our way past them and went inside.

Dennis spotted us. 'There you are! Get yourself a glass and sit down. Gilly's about to make a speech.'

She stood at the front of the room, poised, beautifully groomed, her face full of joy. Around her were lovely little bronze heads of men, women and children of different nations and ethnicities. They were exquisite in detail and seemed to shine with a light of their own. Off to one side stood a serene *Summer*, flanked by *Winter* and photos of *Autumn* and *Spring* in clay. *Summer* was clearly marked 'not for sale', while 'sold' stickers adorned several of the other pieces.

She began to speak. I don't remember what she said. I sat and smiled so hard my face hurt afterward. I thought about all that had nearly kept her from this moment of triumph. I thought about Dennis, who had nurtured her talent, and about Derek and Alan, who had brought her tormentor to justice. I thought about Matt, now happily creating his miraculous woodcuts again, and Sam, teaching his students the fine points of film photography. I thought about the power of art to transform the human condition, and the terrible power a twisted artist could wield.

I took Alan's hand, and with my other, reached in my pocket for a tissue to catch the tears trickling down my face.

PRA O51415. 490224 JUNE
ADV.